Wynter's Discontent

A Wynter Thriller

Nigel Draper

Get an Exclusive Wynter Short Story

Enjoy a free, exclusive short story, "**Wynter's Cruise**," by joining my mailing list. You'll get advance notice of new releases, and an occasional newsletter which will reveal more about Wynter's life and the stories behind the books.

Building a relationship with readers is one of the most satisfying things about writing and I look forward to welcoming you into Wynter's world.

Get Wynter's Cruise for free at www.nigeldraper.com

Dedication

For EPD,
who taught me to love books.

Prologue

Wynter reckoned he had twenty-four hours before they came looking for him. That's how long it would take for them to find out there wasn't a report, wasn't a mine and wasn't any silver. That's when the Kontakis brothers would realize their hundred thousand dollars had vanished. That's when they'd start tearing Chicago apart looking for a French Canadian named Bourdin.

They'd never find him.

He didn't exist.

Wynter had disposed of Bourdin's fake passport and driving license in a dumpster headed for the incinerator and had reverted to being an Englishman, a role he much preferred. He was now intent on disappearing. That's why he was travelling by bus across the Mid-West.

Greyhound buses got left behind in the twentieth century's rush for speed. They survived as transport for the poor, and, like the poor, everyone knows they're there yet no one really sees them. For the duration of their journey

1

people that ride buses insulate themselves behind their belongings. Bags, newspapers, headphones, radios and candy wrappers are piled up around them like the walls of a medieval castle. With all these barriers, conversation is difficult and more sleeping than talking gets done on long journeys. Leave on Monday, arrive a thousand miles later on Wednesday, and by the time the bus pulls out fellow travelers won't recollect what you looked like and the driver can't remember your name. For those three days you may as well have disappeared from the face of the earth.

Wynter's grubby white T shirt, jeans and battered leather jacket didn't draw any attention but his accent caused the driver to raise an eyebrow. When he explained he was English, the driver just nodded and carried on chewing gum. Settling into a seat near the back of the bus, Wynter got his head down and tried to get some sleep. When he awoke they had left the sprawling Chicago suburbs and were speeding south through the Illinois countryside.

Wynter closed his eyes again and smiled. He cast his mind back over the last few weeks. He had good reason to be pleased with himself. The set-up had gone smoothly. He had shown just enough disinterest to make it sound intriguing. He'd always believed in backing off once you've hinted at the proposition. Don't try the hard sell. If they're interested they'll follow. If not, you haven't wasted too much time. His smile still lingered when he re-opened his eyes and gazed over the unchanging sea of wheat. Kansas City was getting closer, but more importantly Chicago was a few miles further behind.

No-one could accuse the Kontakis brothers of being pleasant. Mike ran a down-market bar and two strip joints while brother Milo looked after a few arcades of slot machines. When you stepped into the semi-darkness of their strip clubs you left whatever law you thought protected you at the door. Fights were normal and broken bones not unusual. Mike proudly displayed a row of teeth that he'd knocked out of quarrelsome customers behind the bar of one of the strip joints. One of these customers was the reason Wynter had been in Chicago.

It wasn't so much his jaw that Mike Kontakis had broken, though that was painful enough: it was Henry Concannon's pride that Kontakis had hurt. He had sworn revenge every day of the two months his jaw was wired up. When he'd recovered sufficiently, Henry contacted Wynter in the usual way, and three months after he had been thrown out of Mike Kontakis' bar, Henry was sitting in a diner discussing the options over coffee with Wynter. After examining the problem from every angle, and taking into account the psychology of the Kontakis brothers, they had agreed to work the mining scam.

Reading and sleeping seemed the only things worth doing on a bus journey. Wynter had tried watching the countryside but came to the conclusion that the Great Plains had to be where God took a nap between creating the Mississippi and the Rocky Mountains. Wynter pushed his hair back off his face and turned his head to the window. The corn-colored monotony of the landscape spread endlessly out in front of him, and if the bus was making progress it wasn't noticeable. Only when he looked down at the road was he aware that they were moving at a steady sixty miles per hour.

Every time Milo Kontakis asked about the deal, Wynter changed the subject. Same thing with Mike - except Mike wouldn't let it go. Mike Kontakis had taken the bait. It was with a wonderfully measured reluctance that Wynter had slowly laid out the proposition. Wynter had learnt to be careful with descriptions - the investment was in thousands, returns always in millions. Large sums excited and unbalanced people. They also interfered with the normal thought process, causing the target to focus on the money he stood to make rather than the sum he stood to lose.

Wynter yawned, tried to stretch and decided his body wasn't designed to undergo long distance bus travel. Standing just over six feet tall and weighing a hundred and eighty pounds, he was a squeeze-fit in most seats. Rubbing his legs to restore the circulation, Wynter made the decision to find a hotel in Kansas City for the night. Perhaps he had been over-ambitious thinking he could make Omaha in one day. Five hundred miles from Chicago was far enough. The Greyhound Company had served its purpose - the Kontakis brothers would never believe the sophisticated Bourdin had left by bus.

Wynter had explained to Mike Kontakis that the mine hadn't been doing too well for the last four or five years and word was it was thought to be worked out. Old man Stark had secretly commissioned a survey to see if the mine was viable. That report was now in and the contents were mind blowing. A new vein of silver had been located in a part of the mine difficult to reach, and the survey estimated that it was worth a conservative five hundred million dollars, probably much more. Wynter said Stark had kept this to himself and was busy trying to buy out the rest of the stockholders, telling everyone that the mine was worked out … finished.

The bus pulled into bay twelve of the Kansas City Bus Station and the driver turned the engine off. Like most bus stations it looked sad and unloved. The rich didn't know that it existed, and the poorer members of the community wished they didn't either. It hadn't seen a proper paint job in over twenty years, surviving on a lick of paint just when and where it was needed. Wynter stepped off the bus and waited as the driver retrieved his suitcases and parcel from the hold. He found a taxi and asked the Polish driver if he knew a moderately priced hotel. Wynter didn't bother getting out of the car when they pulled up outside what appeared to be a run-down tenement building. The driver turned in his seat and smiled hopefully but Wynter shook his head. Obviously the driver hadn't understood the word moderate; something had got lost in translation. Patiently Wynter explained that he was looking for a clean, comfortable hotel in a quiet, unobtrusive part of town. You know, he joked, the sort of place you'd take your mistress. The driver's face broke into a large grin, and ten minutes later they drew up in a tree lined street opposite a large, well tended hotel and garden.

The driver kept grinning at Wynter as he took the two

suitcases and parcel from the trunk. As he paid him, Wynter couldn't make up his mind whether the driver thought he was meeting a woman here, or this was where the driver had spent passionate nights with *his* mistress. Either way Wynter got the feeling that between the two of them they were definitely a woman short.

Wynter had explained to Mike Kontakis that he knew old man Stark's son, Joshua wanted to unload his fifteen per cent holding in the mine, and knew nothing about the new, rich vein of silver. Joshua and his old man had argued twenty years ago and hadn't spoken since. Joshua now needed a hundred thousand dollars to pay off gambling debts in Vegas. He also needed it in a hurry or he faced the prospect of spending the rest of his life in a wheelchair. Wynter didn't have the hundred thousand or he'd do the deal himself, but if Mike Kontakis could raise the money, Wynter would introduce him to Joshua … for a small fee.

Greed and the thought of all that silver had proved too much for Mike, and he met Wynter early the next morning with a bag full of money. A suitably disguised Henry Concannon, acting the part of Joshua, turned up ten minutes late looking nervous and displaying a morbid fear of wheelchairs. Henry wasted no time in passing the share certificates over to Kontakis, and took the bag. While Henry nervously checked to see that all the money was there, Wynter quietly pocketed an envelope containing fifteen thousand dollars. Satisfied that everything was as it should be, Henry closed the bag, said goodbye and vanished.

Wynter warned Mike that the authorities would look

upon what they had just done as insider trading. It could lead to twenty years in prison. Mike laughed. A dumb French Canadian warning him about the law must have sounded rich. It was a shame, really; the French had once been tough, good in a fight. They used to have an empire for chrissakes!

Henry and Wynter divided the one hundred and fifteen thousand dollars in the gentlemen's washrooms of a nearby hotel, and an hour later Wynter was on the morning bus to Kansas City. He had no desire to wait around to see Mike Kontakis' reaction when he found out that the mine not only didn't contain a newly discovered vein of silver … it didn't exist. In fact, Mike Kontakis was now the owner of two thousand shares in a soft toy company. True, the two companies' names were similar. So similar that all Henry had to do was change three letters with the aid of chemicals and ink. After a night's work, the stock certificates in the toy company were transformed into that of a mining conglomerate. Still, Mike could look forward to receiving a cuddly toy dog for Christmas … the company prided itself on that.

After a good night's sleep and a shower, Wynter transformed himself from the down at heel loser who had ridden the bus into a casually dressed executive. He strolled out of the hotel and had breakfast in the diner down the street. Having serious doubts about his body's ability able to cope with consecutive days of bus travel, Wynter asked the guy working the griddle about used car dealerships. Turned out that Kansas City did a brisk trade in pick-ups; no doubt due to the surrounding farming community.

Finishing his coffee, he took a leisurely walk around to a couple of used car lots. He found what he was looking for in Jim Reavis's 'Kansas City Pick-Up Centre' - a three year old Ford. Wynter paid cash, drove off, and parked the pick-up outside the hotel. Emerging twenty minutes later, he loaded his two suitcases behind the seats and put the parcel into the passenger foot well, then set off towards Omaha on the first leg of his trip to the Cascade Mountains.

Wynter had never been to Oregon. It seemed as good a place as any to disappear.

Chapter 1

Oregon, 1984

Wynter had spent time in worse places, but he couldn't recall any of them being as remote as Alyson. Lost in the Cascades, the town was as far from civilization as you could get before you headed back. At best it was a one dog town. Wynter reckoned the horse had left years ago and even the dog was beginning to look bored.

Searching for something approaching excitement on a Friday night, Wynter found a card game in the room behind the general store. Pushing open the door, a jumble of jars, boxes and packets met his gaze, and a smell of coffee beans mixed with cheese smacked his nose. The middle of the room was taken up by a round wooden table covered by a worn baize cloth, with a single light bulb dangling above it. Six men sat around the faded green cloth, a bottle of whiskey and some glasses keeping them company.

Invited to sit down, Wynter pulled up a chair and glanced around the table. Two of his opponents seemed decent, tie-wearing men whose wives probably insisted they went to church on Sundays. He had run into men like that all round the country, social types playing at being gamblers. The other four were different: they weren't playing at being anything. Rougher and meaner, they were a throwback to frontier days - the type that didn't own a tie or trouble the church much. Dressed by mail order, one had three fingers on his left hand while another had a broken front tooth. Wynter would have bet his pick-up they weren't married, or had ever had their pick of local women ... or any woman costing more than ten dollars.

The first few hands of the evening had played out easily enough. There were a couple of odd house rules, but then every house has its rules. One was that the deal moved to the left after every three hands, which, as far as Wynter could make out, gave everyone an equal opportunity to cheat.

An hour later the whiskey bottle was empty and the stakes had increased. There must have been over three hundred dollars riding on the hand, and Henry was giving off all the signs he shouldn't. Everyone knew he'd been dealt a good hand, and if Wynter hadn't been holding four queens he might have backed the guy to win. Three Fingers folded his hand and Henry gave a nervous smile.

"Louella know you're playing with the house-keeping again, Henry?" grinned Three Fingers.

Henry ignored him. The roughneck with the bushy beard decided a pair of twos wasn't going to make it either and threw in.

"Guess it's down to you and me, Henry," smiled Wynter. "Why don't we just turn over our cards?"

Henry nodded. "Full house. Nines and a pair of threes," he said, fanning out his cards with a flourish worthy of an old riverboat gambler. Wynter looked down at his queens.

"Beats me," sighed Wynter, doing his best to look dejected. Turning in his hand to make sure no-one saw his winning cards, he watched Henry's nervous smile break into a broad grin as he scooped up his winnings.

Wynter wanted to keep the game friendly. He was a stranger in town and just looking for a social night out - a few hands of cards, a drink and some conversation to wind up the week. Losing a little suited Wynter; it suited him real fine.

Losing a little may have suited Wynter, but it didn't sit well with the four roughnecks. Over the past few hands they had increased the stakes, and it had become obvious they intended to clean him out. He wasn't about to let that happen.

Wynter picked up the cards, shuffled and dealt what was to become the last hand of the night. The pile of bills in the middle of the table grew as the numbers on the notes became bigger. Tens were edged out by twenties, and fifties were replaced by hundreds. As the game went on and it became clear that they were trying to break him in one hand. The two tie-wearing players folded early, and the roughnecks dropped out one by one until the game came down to Three Fingers and Wynter. Three Fingers gave a smile, swallowed what whiskey was left in his glass, and turned over his cards on the baize. His three friends sat and grinned, like coyotes waiting on a mountain lion.

"Four kings, Mister Wynter," said Three Fingers, with the knowing smirk of a winner.

The tie-wearing duo sat staring at the pile of money, nigh on six thousand dollars waiting on Wynter to show his hand. Henry loosened his tie and broke the silence with a nervous cough, while his companion ran his handkerchief around the back of his neck.

Wynter's gaze moved around the grinning faces. Odds of four to one weren't to his liking, but it was too late now. He sighed and turned over a straight diamond flush, queen high.

Three Finger's jaw tightened, and then dropped. A look of disbelief had replaced the smirk. Wynter reached out his hand and began picking up the pile of money.

"You leave that right there," said Three Fingers, finding his voice. "How did you get those cards?"

Wynter shrugged and carried on picking up the notes. "Straight flush beats a four of a kind."

"Not here it don't - not tonight."

"Rules of poker say it does."

"Rules? You want to talk rules after your crooked dealing?"

Wynter stopped and looked straight at Three Fingers. "What are you implying?"

"I'm telling you to put that money back."

Four pairs of stone-cold eyes told Wynter that reasoning wasn't an option. Six thousand dollars was a lot of money in a small town, and being a stranger and an Englishman, automatically put Wynter on the wrong side of honest.

Wynter turned to the other two. "What do you

gentlemen think?" Not that he expected their support, but it bought him some time.

"They stopped thinking some time ago," interrupted Three Fingers, "right after they saw you dealing off the bottom."

Henry closed his eyes, hoping to find himself at home when he opened them.

"I dealt the cards right off the top," said Wynter quietly.

"Six people say you didn't."

"Then they're wrong." Wynter picked up the last few banknotes.

"You got some balls, Englishman, I'll give you that. Now, you going to put that money back, or are you going to make us take it back?"

They had left him little or no room to back down gracefully, but it went against Wynter's deepest held principles to return money.

"I didn't cheat."

Three Fingers looked at his companions, "Guess we got our answer." He leaned back in his chair, took the lid from a cardboard drum of chicken feed, reached down inside and pulled out an old Colt revolver. Wynter got the feeling he wasn't the first stranger to have been accused of cheating.

"Put the money down," said Three Fingers as he stood up.

"Look, I …" said Wynter, staring down the barrel of the Colt.

Three Fingers cocked the hammer. "Time for looking's gone."

Wynter slowly put the money on the table. The silence

was broken by Henry's frightened voice.

"Time I was home," he squeaked, "Louella'll be worrying where I am." He got up, grabbed his coat and scuttled out of the door, quickly followed by his tie-wearing friend.

"Louella gave up worrying 'bout him twenty years ago," grinned Three Fingers as he picked up the wad of notes. "He just ain't noticed." He stuffed the money into his pocket, his eyes fixed on Wynter. "Now, stand up."

Wynter got to his feet nice and slow, keeping his hands where they could see them - six thousand dollars wasn't worth dying for. "Couldn't we talk about this?"

Three Fingers shook his head, "No."

"You've got the money."

"We'd have got the money anyhow," said Three Fingers, with a smirk.

Wynter realized it had been a mugging all along, dressed up as a game of poker.

"So … now you've got the money, I'll call it quits."

"You call it what you like, Mister Wynter," said Three Fingers. "We've moved on to retribution."

Psychologists will tell you that violence is usually verbal, but then most psychologists don't play poker on Friday nights with psychopaths. As Wynter watched one of the men pull a length of rope out from behind the bags of dog food, he got the distinct feeling they were going to do more than shout at him.

"Like the Good Book says," continued Three Fingers, "*It is only just to repay with affliction, those who afflict you…*"

The man with a broken front tooth reached up to a shelf

above the fridges and took down an old frayed bull whip.

"*...For the righteous will rejoice when they see vengeance.*"

"*Amen,*" said the man with the whip, his grin exposing his jagged tooth.

"Time we introduced Mister Wynter to the old whipping post," said Three Fingers.

The temperature had dropped below comfortable when they stepped out of the store's back door. The meagre light thrown by the few streetlamps was aided by the moon, but there were more shadows than light. Wynter's sweat-soaked shirt was sticking to his back and he began to feel sick. He'd read stories at school of how the Royal Navy had maintained discipline by flogging. How men had been 'flogged around the Fleet'; how some were sentenced to receive a thousand lashes ... how some didn't survive. Surely these people didn't intend that? Not for six thousand dollars. Wynter took a deep breath.

What was worse, a cat o'nine tails or a bullwhip? He didn't suppose it really mattered: they'd both take the skin off your back; both could kill you. He saw movements in the houses they passed as they moved up the main street. Curtains flicked and shadows moved back from darkened windows, but no-one opened their doors or came out to ask what was going on. The town was not going to interfere. No-one was going to stop this. Wynter looked into the darkness ahead. With odds of four to one the best he could hope for was they didn't mean to kill him.

He took another deep breath, trying desperately to keep his rising nausea at bay. His mind raced with possible ways out. If he offered them more money would they…? Probably not. Three Fingers looked as if he had a sadistic streak too wide to be bought off. Wynter could try running… but where? It didn't look as if anyone would take him in, and out in the open he wouldn't stand much of a chance. Not against four. Not against the Colt. He could end up in a worse…

"Time I cut that old whipping post down."

Wynter almost stumbled into the guy in front as the small procession came to an abrupt halt. He looked around but couldn't see anyone, wasn't even sure where the words had come from. It wasn't quite a shout, but it was loud enough to be heard and the voice carried authority. Three Fingers had swung around to his right and was peering towards a darkened building.

"You're pointing a weapon at a sworn law officer, Travis. I could shoot you dead for that."

Three Fingers immediately let his arm drop to his side, the revolver pointing towards the ground. A tall, wiry figure with a walrus moustache stepped out of the shadows. From his zipper jacket and badge, Wynter guessed this was the County Sheriff: a man confident enough of his authority to keep his gun in its holster.

"It ain't loaded, Rufus, you know that," said Three Fingers.

"So why you waving it around like it was? And don't tell me self-defence again."

"We was only going to rough him up a little."

"Why?"

"Caught him cheating."

The sheriff raised an eyebrow, "Better than you?"

Three Fingers shoved the Colt into his belt. "I play a straight game, you know that."

The sheriff gave a short derisive snort, "Yeah … 'bout as straight as a rattlesnake in a barrel."

Wynter attempted to explain, "I wasn't cheating, I…"

"I'd keep quiet if I were you," cut in the sheriff, keeping his eyes on Three Fingers, "you're surrounded by a pack of trouble as it is, don't make it any worse. I'm guessing the Englishman won the money, that right Travis?"

Three Fingers nodded. "He was dealing off the bottom; we all saw him."

"Sure," nodded the sheriff, "how much?"

"He was dealing …"

"How much?" insisted the sheriff.

"About six thousand," said Three Fingers.

The sheriff raised his eyebrows and sighed. "I ought to lock you up."

"Better lock him up," snarled Three Fingers, nodding towards Wynter.

"That a threat?" asked the sheriff.

Three Fingers gave the sheriff a long hard stare. The law officer moved his right hand and rested it on the handle of his revolver. Three Fingers looked away. Now wasn't the time to challenge the sheriff.

"Good," said the sheriff. "Now all of you get over to my office and we'll settle this." He looked at Wynter. "You too."

As he walked towards the building, Wynter sensed the

sheriff sizing him up, guessing how much trouble he could be.

The office hadn't changed much since the days Butch and the Kid roamed the West. Pretty much everything was wood, from the floor, the walls and the ceiling, to the desk and chairs. A wooden gun rack was on the wall next to the desk, while an old iron stove standing on a stone base in one corner, with a flue running out through the wall, kept the place cosy. A metal coffee pot was warming on the top. Through an open door Wynter glimpsed the cell in the back. It had floor to ceiling bars, just like in the movies. Photographs of what Wynter took to be the town and its inhabitants, going back over the last century, hung on the walls of the office. Behind the desk were three very similar portraits of men, each with a walrus moustache. The post of sheriff was obviously hereditary.

"Put the money on the desk," said the sheriff.

Nobody made a move.

"You know the rules, Travis, money on the desk."

Three Fingers reluctantly put his hand in his pocket, pulled out the wad of greenbacks and placed them on the dull scratched surface. The sheriff peeled off ten one hundred dollar bills.

"That's too much, Rufus," protested Three Fingers. "That's plain greedy."

"That includes the fine for pointing a deadly weapon," said the sheriff, handing the rest of the money back to Three Fingers.

"But it weren't loaded!"

Ignoring him, the law officer turned to the broken toothed man with the bull whip. "You can leave that here too." The man hesitated, looking at Three Fingers for help. "Being in possession of an offensive weapon with intent could get a man five years in the State Penitentiary," continued the sheriff.

Three Fingers shrugged and Broken Tooth reluctantly laid the whip on the desk.

"You goin' to let us keep the rope, or you worried I might hang myself?" said Three Fingers.

"Doubt I'd get that lucky," said the sheriff. "You've got your money, now go." He turned to the other three. "You too."

Three Fingers gave a dismissive snort. The sheriff rested his hand on his revolver. "Go on, get out."

Wiping the back of his hand over his mouth, Three Fingers shoved the wad of money into his pocket and strode through the door. The other three followed.

"That's my money you just gave away," said Wynter.

"Guess it must have been," said the sheriff.

"What do I get?"

The sheriff turned to Wynter.

"You get to keep the skin on your back."

***

Wynter sat back in his chair and tried to relax. The huge adrenaline rush had receded, and deep breathing had helped restore his heart rate to something near normal. His shirt was wet with sweat and he was still a little shaky, but at least the wobble had left his legs. It had been a close call. Too close. Taking another deep breath, he pushed back the hair that had flopped over his right eye.

Sheriff Rufus Richards tipped the metal pot and poured coffee into the two enamel mugs on the desk. Wynter would rather have had a glass of whiskey, but it didn't look as if there was any on offer. Caffeine might not be the best thing to pour down his throat at the moment, but it looked to be the only thing available and he needed to drink something.

The sheriff put the coffee pot back on the top of the stove and hung the rag he'd used to hold the pot-handle back on its nail in the wall. Making his way around the large desk, he sat down in the creaky swivel chair. Something of the early pioneer hung about the sheriff; his lean face betrayed a lifetime of extremes: harsh summer sun followed by vicious winter snows. He pushed one of the two enamel mugs towards Wynter.

"Never had an Englishmen up here before; not one that I can remember, anyways. Don't get much of anyone up here… not unless they got good reason."

The sheriff took a sip of coffee, and stared hard at Wynter.

"You got a good reason, Mister Wynter?"

"Just passing through," replied Wynter. He wasn't, but it would have to do.

"No-one just passes through Alyson," said the sheriff, keeping his eyes fixed on Wynter. "Ain't nowhere to pass through to."

The sheriff put the mug down and leaned back with his

head lined up just below the photographs of previous sheriffs, like he was auditioning for his spot in the next row.

"One road brings you in, and that same road takes you back out. Only things that pass through are elk, coyotes and the occasional grizzly."

Wynter couldn't argue with the sheriff there. Alyson was remote, and the sort of place he'd been looking for when he left Chicago and the Kontakis brothers, but he hadn't counted on the resistance to strangers in small towns.

"Now," continued the sheriff, "why don't you tell me why you really came."

"Curious, I guess. I wanted to see what was at the end of the road."

The sheriff stared intently at him for a while, trying to gauge whether he was telling the truth. Eventually he sighed and shook his head.

"Curious ain't convincing me, Mister Wynter."

"That's the trouble with the truth, people don't often believe it."

The sheriff had followed enough investigations to know that there are some questions that are best left to simmer. He nodded slightly and picked up his mug, took another mouthful of coffee, and tried another approach.

"How come you ended up in the poker game?

"Trying to be sociable and meet the locals."

"Most folks settle for an hour or two in the hotel bar."

"That's where I heard about the game."

"And you thought you'd take a look, maybe win a little from those country hicks."

"No," said Wynter, shaking his head. "I just wanted a game of cards. It wasn't me who kept pushing the stakes up."

"Sure?"

Wynter nodded. "And I didn't cheat. I didn't have to; the cards ran my way."

"Why should I believe you?"

Wynter shrugged. "Because it's the truth?"

The sheriff gave Wynter another long, hard stare, trying to balance what he knew to be fact, against what he was being told. Either way, there was precious little to go on. Main thing that made him lean in Wynter's favour was the fact that he knew how Three Fingered Travis and his friends played poker. He took another gulp of coffee.

"I'd still like to know why you ended up here. You sure as hell didn't come up here looking for a job - not dressed like that, anyhow. And you ain't tried to sell me anything yet."

Wynter said nothing. Never volunteer information you don't have to give; he'd learnt that the hard way over the years. Reaching out, he picked up his mug and took a sip of coffee. Strong and bitter, it swished around his mouth, attacking his tongue and the enamel on his teeth. Wynter pulled a face.

"Bit of an acquired taste," said the sheriff, almost breaking into a smile. "Nothing like two-day old coffee to keep a man on his toes. Mug of three-day will keep him up all night."

The sheriff mellowed a little and leaned back, still trying to figure out why anyone would want to head into the middle of nowhere.

"So, what's an Englishman doing up here ... in *my* county?"

Wynter shrugged. "Getting lost."

"Why?" asked the sheriff. "Who wants to find you?"

Wynter smiled. He could think of at least a dozen people who'd pay good money to find him, in addition to the Kontakis brothers, but right now the sheriff didn't need to know that. "I took a wrong turn and just kept going. Nothing sinister - I promise"

"That turn's a good fifty miles back ... long way for a mistake."

"We all make mistakes, Sheriff."

"You sure made one tonight, Mister Wynter. Travis and the boys are pretty mad at you."

"I don't suppose they're too pleased with you either."

"I'll live with it," shrugged the sheriff. "Good thing for you I stopped them; nearest doctor's seventy miles away. First hospital's over a hundred."

"I'm grateful."

"I tend to keep an eye on Travis when there's someone new in town. Things can get a little out of hand."

"That how people settle things here?"

The sheriff shrugged. "It's a little rural up here in Alyson. Not much changed from the old days."

Wynter nodded. "So I noticed."

"You had to look after yourself back then, Mister Wynter ... no-one else would."

Wynter tried the coffee again. It was worse.

"You should have stayed away from that poker game."

"Good advice always comes too late to take it," said

Wynter, making a mental note to stay away from the coffee.

The sheriff relaxed into his chair again. Until he knew why Wynter had landed in his town, he wasn't inclined to let him go anywhere. "At least you could have let those boys win some."

"They were cheating."

"Course they was cheating!" laughed the sheriff. "They couldn't win a pig's squeal in a straight game. Oh, it don't matter too much when it's just them: what goes around, comes around. But they don't like to see money leaving the valley …" the sheriff leaned forward "… and neither do I."

He paused to let his words sink in, then relaxed back into his chair.

"Best you stay in the back for a day or two; 'til things cool down."

The sheriff nodded over his shoulder towards the open door behind him. Wynter looked through the door and saw the bars of the cell.

"You're locking me up?"

The sheriff nodded. "To prevent a breach of the peace."

"What about my Miranda rights?" asked Wynter.

"I haven't arrested you."

"But you're going to?"

The sheriff shook his head. "No."

"But you're still going to lock me up."

"Look on it as protective custody."

"What if I don't want protection?"

The sheriff shrugged. "Then you take your chance with Travis and the boys. Last time I looked, one of them was sitting in the back of your pick-up."

Wynter balanced his options: face four angry men out there, or get locked up in here.

"Probably one over at the hotel, too," continued the sheriff.

Wynter could feel his sweat-soaked shirt getting colder.

"It *would* be voluntary?"

"Yep," nodded the sheriff. "Voluntary."

"Okay," said Wynter. Better locked up than half dead, he reasoned. "But it's just temporary, understood?"

"Sure," said the sheriff as he broke into a smile, opened a drawer in the desk and took out a large rusty ring with three ancient keys. "You play chess?"

Wynter nodded. "Yes," he said, relieved to have left the subject of poker.

"Good, we'll play some." The sheriff stood up and nodded towards the cell. "Can't deal off the bottom in chess."

Chapter 2

State Senator Hogan Reece eased the hired Lincoln Continental along the floor of the canyon. The car hadn't been designed for this terrain, and it wallowed its way on the soft suspension along a barely discernible track. Although the light was beginning to fade, Reece could see the van, and a car parked alongside it, about half a mile up ahead.

Van Buren's phone call had been unexpected. Reece initially protested that he couldn't possibly make the trip: he had State business to attend, but Van Buren wouldn't listen. In fact, he had been insistent that Reece travel to Vegas and out into the desert. He was to deliver a message, was what he had said. What sort of a message Reece was at a loss to comprehend, but he knew that it would be fruitless to argue. He would fly to Vegas then hire a car and drive out into the desert as he had been told. Truth was he was too scared of Van Buren to say no.

Reece could make out a small group of men next to the van, with what appeared to be a child. As he drew closer it became clear that the child was in fact a man on his knees, and that two men were taking it in turns to beat him with baseball bats while two more looked on. Reece took a deep breath; he could feel the nausea begin to rise in his throat. He stopped the car next to the van and waited. One of the men turned from watching the beating and walked over. Reece recognized him as Jago, Van Buren's enforcer. Reece pressed a chrome button and his window silently slid down.

"Senator," said Jago, removing his dark glasses. "Mister Van Buren mentioned you might drop by." He smiled. "Just in time to watch the entertainment."

Reece felt a shiver run through his body as he looked at Jago. The enforcer betrayed no emotion apart from a twisted smile. His ice blue eyes were those of a psychopath, thought Reece. There wasn't an ounce of humanity behind them that the senator could discern. The beating had stopped and the man had slumped forward, groaning on the ground. One of the men had gone to the car and exchanged his baseball bat for an iron bar.

"Let's just say that you and I differ in what we find entertaining," said Reece.

"There's entertainment to be had in everything, Senator; just got to find it," smiled Jago.

Reece wondered what entertainment could be found in giving a man a beating. A scream rang through the canyon. Before he could stop himself, Reece looked over at the man writhing on the ground. A figure stood over him holding the iron bar. The senator quickly looked away, the horror and discomfort showing in his face. When he opened his eyes again he saw an empty forty-five gallon oil drum being rolled towards the moaning figure.

"I guess you'll be heading for the Fountain Casino when this is over," said Jago, as he leaned against Reece's car. "More your kind of entertainment." He watched the iron bar come down hard, breaking the man's other arm this time.

Reece winced as another scream filled the air. What the hell had this man done?

"I wasn't thinking of going anywhere," said Reece, feeling sick.

"A man's got to be somewhere, Senator," said Jago. He nodded towards the man on the ground. "Mister Petersen is finding that out the hard way."

The oil drum was set upright on the harder ground of the desert track. Small holes had been made in its lower half.

"I think you should call by the Fountain Casino," continued Jago. "Mister Van Buren especially mentioned that to me."

The iron bar once again described a curved arc, and came down on Petersen's right leg. Semi-conscious now and more dead than alive, Petersen's scream tailed off into a low groan.

"Why? What does Mister Van Buren think I'll find there?" said Reece, while he gazed intently at the side of the white van.

"Who," said Jago, "not what."

The three men who had been beating Petersen stopped and looked over at Jago, waiting for his signal. After a few seconds Jago nodded his head. The men picked up Petersen's broken body. They carried him the few yards accompanied by his muted screams and groans, then squashed him into the oil drum.

"Who does Mister Van Buren think I'll meet at the Fountain?"

"An old friend," said Jago.

Reece heard the sound of a large can of liquid being emptied.

"Politicians don't have friends, Jago."

Jago smiled, "True enough, Senator. Then let me put it another way. You'll see Ms Delaney in the hotel foyer. Just pass on a warning."

Reece detected the smell of gasoline.

"Tell her to be careful she doesn't get burnt."

With his last ounces of strength, Petersen began to scream. Reece closed his eyes as he heard the crackle of the flames.

***

The hotel foyer was busy with the constant buzz and churn of people. Couples returning from dinner threaded their way through groups heading out to see late shows while new arrivals dragged suitcases across the marble floor. There was a huddle of people around the reception desk which contrasted with the constant flow of hopeful gamblers into the hotel's casino, where an avenue of starving slot machines gave the eternal promise of a big win.

Between the hotel reception and the casino entrance, a large semi-circular alcove with half a dozen low tables and white leather club chairs served both as an overflow from the coffee shop and a meeting place for the hotel's guests. Most of the tables were occupied: a tanned man in a white suit sipped his whisky with his head buried in the Wall Street Journal's stock prices. An elderly couple stared trance-like at the beckoning slot machines as they drank coffee and took a break from making the casino even richer, while a middle-aged oil executive gave another anxious look at his watch, hoping his neighbour's wife had finally managed to get away for the weekend.

With a view of reception, the casino and the hotel entrance, the alcove was the ideal place to keep an eye on the people passing through the foyer. That's why Meredith Delaney, head of the West Coast section of the Secret Service, was sitting there drinking coffee.

Dressed in a pair of black trousers, a white blouse and a cotton jumper to keep out the chill of the desert evening, Meredith blended in with the other tourists. A few passing men looked twice; she had the looks that were well worth a second glance, but most were too intent on checking in at reception or heading into the casino to pay her too much attention. Hotel lobbies were anonymous places; Meredith knew that well enough. Come the morning few, if any, of the guests would remember she'd even been there, and none would be able to give an accurate description.

She glanced down at her watch: it was getting late. She took a sip of coffee and looked over at her companion, Shapiro. Normally her assistant, Lance Holland, would be with her, but he was watching the service area at the rear of the hotel.

"Perhaps they stopped to get something to eat." Shapiro

shrugged, trying to sound convincing.

"Would you stop with what they're carrying?"

Shapiro slowly shook his head. "Probably not."

"Neither would I," said Meredith.

Shapiro was a good man but his speciality was forensic accounting, not field work. Without columns of figures to comfort him he got nervous; talking was his way of getting rid of tension. Meredith took another sip of coffee and reminded herself that the main reason he was there at all was to persuade the hotel's management she wasn't a hooker.

"They could have parked up someplace," said Shapiro.

She shook her head. "Not these guys."

Shapiro was doing his best to avoid the increasingly obvious conclusion that something had gone wrong. She didn't blame him; she had felt the same way for the last hour. Meredith took a deep breath and tried to relax. She'd been working this case for over a year and really needed to produce something in the way of a result. She had enemies. Questions were being asked in Washington.

"Safest thing for them would be to use the service area or the basement," she said.

"Lance and his team are watching the service area; two men are covering the front and another two down in the basement car park," said Shapiro, happy to quote facts. He was good on facts - planning and speculation he left to people who had their own office. "Nothing's going to happen without us knowing."

What if nothing happened? Meredith bit her lip - nothing was something she didn't want to think about.

Putting the empty cup back on the saucer, she wondered if she should order another coffee. Would these guys even turn up?

They'd left San Francisco, she knew that, but maintaining radio silence meant that she knew precious little else. Her father had warned her that waiting was the worst part of the job. Waiting was bad; waiting without knowing was worse; but waiting with the feeling something had gone badly wrong was almost unbearable.

"Probably got held up in traffic somewhere," said Shapiro. "They're bound to hit some heavy traffic in six hundred miles."

"Yeah ..." Meredith stretched her right leg and drew little circles with her foot. Sitting for long periods of time wasn't good for the circulation. "They must have got held up."

"I'll go check again to make sure."

Meredith nodded. "Be discreet."

Shapiro disappeared through the hotel entrance and Meredith concentrated on flexing her toes and watching the constant traffic of people flowing into the casino. Big smiles going in mixed with tired faces coming out. Meredith had never understood the attraction of losing money. That, and the fact that casinos are designed to disorientate - no clocks, very few windows, and games played at speed to keep the gamblers off balance - made it difficult for her to buy into the excitement of chasing a fortune.

State Gaming Boards assume players are sensible and play logically: half an hour at the tables and most gamblers are neither. Playing logically and sensibly wasn't actually encouraged by the casino management. When a Pit Boss spots someone he thinks is playing the odds too well he'll throw them out. He doesn't mind some guy on vacation winning big because he knows he'll get it all back - but professional gamblers are a different matter. They play the odds and quit when they're ahead. That wasn't how the casino wanted their games played.

Meredith knew that Nevada's Gaming Board checked this place out three months previously. She knew the roulette wheels ran true, the craps dice weren't loaded, and the slot machines paid out 91.26%. Everything was in order except for two smaller roulette tables which favoured one particular quarter. The wheels were slightly out of balance, which the management seemed in no hurry to rectify. Most customers usually worked this out and won a few hundred dollars before the tables closed down for an hour. Both had low stake limits, and the Board had reckoned that the casino was using them as a loss leader to tempt punters in to use the big chip games.

Meredith had reason to think differently.

She'd sent a random selection of people in to play Blackjack and the same thing had happened. Dealers lost hands that would have had them pulled off the floor in any other casino. It wasn't blatantly obvious, but it was being done. She estimated that four or five of the twenty five tables were losing or breaking even at best. It had to be intentional. Between the two roulette wheels and the sloppy dealing, the management had cut down its natural edge, and knew it. It made no sense. Why would a casino want to lose money?

Meredith reckoned the answer was driving along the road somewhere between San Francisco and Las Vegas.

She scanned the reception area then shifted her gaze to the hotel entrance just in time to see a familiar figure enter. Her stomach twisted and she caught her breath. What the hell was he doing out here? This wasn't good. The man stopped and looked around, as if searching for someone. The thought that she should move flashed through her mind but it was too late, he had seen her. The man's face broke into a crooked grin. He had known that she would be here.

Straight out of a Ralph Lauren window in a light blue jacket, stone slacks and tan loafers, Senator Hogan Reece was a nominal Democrat who trimmed his allegiance to suit whichever political wind happened to be blowing hardest. Meredith was surprised to see him; known to be tight-fisted, she imagined he would be averse to risking any of his own money in a casino.

"Meredith ... Meredith Delaney," said a smiling Reece, holding out his hand as he walked over.

"Senator," said an ice cool Meredith, ignoring his outstretched hand.

"A recreational visit to Vegas, or is this official?" smirked Reece, taking back his hand.

"I could ask you the same question. You're a long way out of Sacramento."

The frost glinted in her words.

"I've always had a deep and abiding love of the desert, Meredith. Such an unpredictable place. Your father understood that." He smiled and made a move towards Shapiro's chair. "Mind if I sit down?"

"Yes, I do," said Meredith, who had the distinct feeling he was laughing at her. "If you sit down, I leave. The less time I spend in your company the better I feel."

Reece stopped with his hand resting on the back of the chair. For a second his thin lips twisted in hate then relaxed back to their usual scornful smile.

"Inherited none of your father's goodwill, I see." He leaned forward, putting his head closer to hers, and dropped his voice, "Well just remember, gambling can be a hazardous pastime, Miss Delaney. Don't get burnt."

Senator Reece gave a warped smile, then turned and oiled his way across the floor into the casino, leaving Meredith with a nasty taste and a strong sense of foreboding. Something bad had happened.

Five minutes after Reece had disappeared Detective Wilson of the Las Vegas Metropolitan Police Department pushed his way through the hotel's front doors. Glancing over towards the alcove, he spotted Meredith and made his way over.

"Evening ma'am," said Wilson as he arrived, then his voice dropped almost to a whisper. "I'm sorry but that consignment you're waiting on isn't going to arrive. Not tonight anyhow."

"Why, what happened?" asked Meredith, as she stood up.

"An accident … in the desert."

"What kind of accident?"

Wilson took a breath. "The terminal kind."

Meredith closed her eyes and took a deep breath.

"Sheriff Krueger suggested there's not much point in you sticking around here any longer," continued the detective.

Meredith nodded. "I'll pull my team out."

Wilson nodded and looked down at his feet. "I'm sorry, ma'am."

"So am I."

There was a pause as Meredith took another deep breath, her mind whirring with events. Wilson shuffled his feet.

"If that's …" he was waiting to be dismissed. Wilson was old school: he reckoned you didn't just turn your back on a Secret Service boss.

"Yes," said Meredith. "Yes … thanks."

"No trouble, ma'am." Wilson had half turned away when Meredith's voice stopped him.

"What exactly happened in the desert, Detective?"

"I'm not sure … I haven't been out there," said Wilson, twisting back to face her. "Stop by the Sheriff's office; they'll fill in the details."

Meredith nodded. Wilson knew, but didn't want to talk about it.

"Have a safe trip back, ma'am," said the detective, and strode off.

Meredith watched him disappear through the hotel's large front entrance and wondered if she should wait for Shapiro to return, or go and stand people down herself.

She decided to go herself.

***

Clark County and the Las Vegas Police Departments had merged to become the Las Vegas Metropolitan Police Department ten years previously. Headed up by the sheriff of Clark County, its headquarters were in the city, a mile from the hotel. While Shapiro drove, Meredith tried to piece together the night's events. The delivery had definitely been scheduled for that night. Her source had a one hundred per cent record and she trusted him. The small truck had left San Francisco; she knew that. It had been seen outside Fresno and tracked through Bakersfield. At Barstow it had taken the Interstate 15 towards Las Vegas. Somewhere between Barstow and Las Vegas it had disappeared. The need for radio silence had made it impossible to know where - until reports of the accident came through.

Without knowing details, everything was just speculation, but Meredith had that twisting feeling in her gut telling her that her plan had gone wrong - badly wrong. Someone was dead. Detective Wilson's reluctance to discuss it had told her that much, and she didn't need to guess who it was. The biggest investigation the West Coast Division had undertaken in twenty years, and now she had the feeling that all that hard work was threatened.

Shapiro parked the car behind headquarters and walked through the staff entrance. He flashed his Service badge at the desk sergeant and introduced Meredith. The effect was electric and they were immediately escorted up to the next floor by a lieutenant who knocked on a panelled door marked Deputy Sheriff Krueger.

"Andy Krueger, pleased to meet you, ma'am, if pleased is

the right word in these circumstances," said Krueger as he shook Meredith's hand.

"It isn't, but I appreciate your sentiment," said Meredith. "So, what happened?"

"Well, it wasn't an accident."

"I'd kind of guessed that."

"We're still piecing it together…"

Krueger seemed reluctant to continue; he hadn't expected the Secret Service boss to be a woman.

"But …" prompted Meredith.

"Yeah, well," said Krueger, taking a breath, "it happened off the Sandy Valley Road, past Goodsprings. There are a lot of tracks up there heading off into the desert; you could lose a fleet of trucks up there. That's where we found him … in a canyon off one of the tracks."

"When did it happen?"

"Took us about forty minutes to get out there, so I guess it must have been just after dark, about eight thirty."

"Yeah,' said Meredith nodding. 'That when you got the phone call?"

"How did you know we got a call?"

"How else would you know where to find him? You said yourself you could hide a fleet of trucks in those canyons."

"Yeah … we got a call."

Meredith nodded. "What did they do to him?" She hoped it had been quick. Krueger hesitated and the look in his eyes told her it hadn't been.

"We don't know, *exactly* …"

"But you can make a guess."

Krueger took a deep breath.

"Looks like they broke his arms and legs, tipped him into an empty oil drum, poured gasoline over him, and ..."

"Jesus Christ," said Shapiro, visibly shaken. He turned and looked at Meredith. "You said it was an accident."

"Nothing accidental about gasoline," said Krueger.

"That's for sure," said Shapiro, feeling sick.

"Difficult to make a positive ID," said Krueger. "What's left of him is in the morgue waiting for the pathologist, I'll let you know as soon as I hear anything."

"Any sign of the truck?" said Meredith.

"We found tracks, but no truck. Tracks of other vehicles too."

Shapiro spent the next ten minutes fighting his desire to throw up while he tried to rid his mind of oil drums and cans of gasoline, as Meredith and Krueger went over the details about timings, the telephone call and any subsequent sightings of the truck. Eventually Meredith was satisfied they'd covered everything.

"My guess is that the victim's name was Raul Petersen," she said. "Run his name through your systems to see if it comes up. If I hear anything at my end I'll let you know."

"I'd be grateful, ma'am."

"Thanks for your help, Sheriff," said Meredith, smiling and shaking Krueger's hand, "and I appreciate Detective Wilson updating me on the situation."

Krueger nodded. "Ma'am."

Meredith walked out of the office followed by Shapiro. As she descended the stairs, Senator Reece's words came back to her:

'Gambling can be a hazardous pastime, Miss Delaney; don't get burnt.'

It had been a warning.

Chapter 3

Next morning found Wynter studying the chessboard as he worked out his strategy. It was going to have to look good - as if he had really tried. Sheriff Richards wasn't a good chess player, just as those poker players the previous night hadn't been particularly good: some hadn't even been competent. There again, competence could pass for genius up here; the competition wasn't likely to be hot. Stretching his hand through the bars, he picked up his knight and moved it across the checkered surface. As he did so, the sheriff appeared through the office door followed by a grizzled old Labrador.

"Made your move?"

Wynter nodded. "Queen's knight."

The sheriff sat down in the high backed chair and studied the board.

"You sure about that?"

"I'm sure," Wynter nodded. Right now, the sheriff was the closest thing to a friend Wynter had; he needed to keep him on side.

The sheriff picked up Wynter's knight and replaced it

with his bishop and leaned back in the chair.

"You're going to have to try harder."

"Guess I didn't see that coming," said Wynter.

"That's your trouble, see. You're concentrating so much on what *you're* doing, that you forget to look at what *I'm* doing. Want me to tell you what you're next move's going to be?"

"How would you know that?"

"Intuition," said the sheriff.

"Yeah?" said Wynter.

The sheriff nodded. "Yep, that's why I'm on this side of the bars ... and you're not."

"How do I get to be your side of the bars?"

"You lead a good life, Mister Wynter. Go to church; avoid strong liquor; don't mess with loose women ... and leave cards alone."

"Good advice," nodded Wynter, who failed on all counts. "But how does that tell you my next move?"

"Watching people is a big part of my job. Watch them long enough and you get to know how their mind works. When you know that, you can make a pretty good guess as to what they'll do. And I reckon your next move will be your bishop to put my king in check ... right?"

Wynter stared down at the board, 'It was going through my mind.'

"Do that and you'll lose another twenty dollars."

"How?"

"Play it out and see."

Wynter looked up at the sheriff and hesitated; then he

moved his bishop. Ten minutes later he was opening his wallet and handing over a crisp, twenty dollar bill to a satisfied sheriff.

"You got a good job, Mister Wynter?"

"Why?"

"Losing can get to be an expensive business."

Wynter smiled. Losing twenty dollars was small change compared to the money he'd taken off the Kontakis brothers.

"How's that three fingered guy? Has he cooled down yet?"

The sheriff shook his head. "He'll brood for a week or so."

Wynter closed his eyes. Now might be as good a time as any to leave town. The sheriff could let him out of the cell and five minutes later he would be on the road.

"Look, there's nothing I need at the hotel - some clothes, that's all; might even fit you - so, if you let me out of here, I could be out of town in a few minutes. Just give me the keys to my pick-up."

"Wouldn't do you much good if I did," said the sheriff as he re-set the chess pieces ready for another game.

"Why not?"

"Cody slashed your tires last night. Guess he got fed up of waiting, then when it started to rain …" the sheriff shrugged. "Pretty smart for Cody: he ain't known much for his thinking."

"Since when has criminal damage been pretty smart?" asked Wynter calmly.

"It sure stopped you from going anywhere: didn't think Cody would figure that."

"He could just have let the air out."

"I told you, he's not known for thinking."

"Are you going to arrest him?"

The sheriff shook his head. "No."

"What about my tires?"

"What about them?"

"But …"

"But what? No-one saw him do it and without a witness I got no case," shrugged the sheriff. "Cody was the only one there at the time and he ain't likely to turn himself in."

"But …"

"But what?" said the sheriff again, staring at Wynter. "How far do you think you're going to get in this town?"

They both knew that no-one in Alyson was going to speak up for a stranger.

Wynter took a deep breath and turned back to the chessboard.

***

Mopping the sweat from the back of his neck with his blue spotted handkerchief, Wynter looked through the bars, along the corridor and through the open door. The view, dominated by the mountains, inspired both awe and wonder. You had to admire those early settlers. He couldn't even begin to imagine what had been going through their minds when they battled through those peaks and valleys. To set off over a thousand miles, with everything you owned, through a country you didn't know, to face hazards you could only guess, and believing that God would protect you, was the height of bravery - or insanity. Wynter guessed they must have been leaving less than nothing and praying they were going to find more than enough - or why do it at all?

The door to the office opened and the sheriff appeared, followed slowly by the old dog. The sight of Wynter mopping his face with a handkerchief seemed to amuse him.

"Hits over a hundred in August."

"Really?" said Wynter, who had no intention of being there in August.

"Hundred and seven's the record. Ever get that hot in England?"

"Not that I can remember," replied Wynter, running the handkerchief over his forehead.

"Bet you wish you were back in England with all that rain."

"It would be pleasant," nodded Wynter.

"*Pleasant*," repeated the sheriff with a broad grin. "I love the way you English put things, Mister Wynter. I guess it would be *pleasant*."

He moved to the high backed chair while the dog pushed its nose through the bars and began to wag its tail. Wynter stretched out a hand and stroked its head. The sheriff moved to the high backed chair and sat down.

"Well, you'll be pleased to know that Maine ain't got nothing on you, and neither does Maryland," said the sheriff. "New England don't want old England by the looks of things."

Wynter was puzzled. "What d'you mean, nothing on me?"

"I've been doing some checking, seeing if you got any outstanding warrants."

"Warrants? Why?" Wynter was concerned. "I'm here for my own protection, according to you."

"Yeah, but I like to know who I've got in my jail. Besides, someone may have put a reward out on you."

The Kontakis brothers may have put a contract out on me by now, thought Wynter. He was also certain the sheriff wouldn't find any outstanding warrants for him - not under the name of Wynter at any rate. And as he hadn't taken any fingerprints he had no way of checking any other names that Wynter may have used, however temporarily.

Wynter shrugged. "The town doesn't seem big enough for much real crime."

"A couple of the boys get drunk now and then. Just keep them for thirty-six hours. Long enough for them to sober up; long enough for them to know they been locked up. Don't let them out 'til the cell's clean, neither. They get a bucket and mop and get to clean up whatever they thought they'd leave."

"Is it true what they told me at the poker game?"

"About what?"

"The Sundance Kid?"

"That old story," said the sheriff with a dismissive smile. "You've seen this town. Now tell me, why would Sundance want to come here?"

There was a pause then Wynter spoke. "Money, I guess."

"Then he'd have been disappointed. Did you see a bank out there?"

"Don't think I did,' said Wynter, shaking his head.

"No, you didn't. Nearest bank is in Gresham … always was." The sheriff flung out his arm and pointed through the open door. "Railroad's a hundred and twenty miles that way. No bank … no trains. Only thing that gets held up round here is clothes lines. Sundance may have had interests other than robbing banks, Mister Wynter, but I never heard tell washing clothes was one of them."

Wynter smiled. "Perhaps he heard about the poker game."

"And who'd have told him? For the first forty years we was here we didn't see another living soul, and not another living soul saw us. Not even a mountain man. What does that tell you?"

Wynter looked blank and slowly shook his head.

"It tells you that if Hole in the Wall was hard to find, this place was damn near impossible! It's a good story, Mister Wynter," continued the sheriff, "but that's all it is. Sundance was Wyoming and Utah; he never set foot in Oregon."

As the sheriff finished speaking, the sound of breaking glass was heard through the open door to the office. Instantly on his feet, the sheriff peered through the partially open door. His right hand automatically drew his revolver from its holster and Wynter heard him cock the hammer as he pushed the door open to see more clearly. With all senses on edge, the lawman moved cautiously into the office. The old dog had realized something was wrong and had levered itself to its feet, and was growling and looking around.

Wynter was left looking nervously at the open side door. Create a distraction at the front, and while that was being investigated, slip around to the side – it was a trick as old as the mountains that surrounded them. Wynter realized that the only thing between him and any intended harm was the flimsy fly screen. He stood up and moved back from the bars. The phrase *sitting duck* bounced around his brain. By now the dog was barking and looking around at Wynter for encouragement. He gave a frozen smile at the dog, which continued barking and now began wagging its tail.

At that moment the sheriff re-appeared through the office door carrying a stone the size of a clenched fist.

"Didn't see no-one out front," he said. "See anyone through there?" He nodded towards the open side door. Wynter shook his head. The sheriff sighed, "Guess we both know who it was."

Wynter was shaken but was determined not to let it show. "How long does he usually brood on something?"

The sheriff shrugged and looked at Wynter. "You'd better come and sleep in the hotel, where I can keep an eye on you."

"But you didn't think the hotel's safe, you said one of …"

"I don't mean the public part. I'll speak to Harriet. There's a room, off of hers, you can have."

Wynter considered this proposition for a few seconds then frowned. "Won't that be dangerous – I mean for her?"

"Not when I'm in there with her it won't."

"Ahh," Wynter slowly nodded, as he understood the full

implication of the sheriff's statement.

The sheriff turned and threw the stone out of the door. The dog, now the excitement was over, was lying down by the bars of the cell. It lifted its head when the stone hit the ground and rolled off into the dirt, watched it until it came to rest, gave a subdued bark, then lowered its head onto its paws with a drawn out sigh.

The sheriff sat back down at the chessboard with a smile, "Your turn to open. Twenty dollars still OK? Or d'you want to make it thirty?"

"Thirty's OK by me," said Wynter and moved his Queen's pawn. As he did so the telephone in the office began to ring.

"Damn," said the sheriff between gritted teeth. "That'll be someone telling me I got a broken window." Shaking his head as he got up from the chair, he disappeared into the office.

Wynter stroked the old dog's head as the sheriff's voice drifted through from the office.

"Yes Harriet, I'm okay… she called to tell you … yes, I know, got glass all over the floor …"

The Englishman sighed and looked through the bars and out of the open door at the end of the corridor. He watched as the shadow of a cloud passed over the highest peak. It was a long way from the grey, flat landscape of Eastern England where he had grown up. A greater contrast would have been difficult to find, but there was a connection. Many of the early American settlers had come from that part of England. Some of the people on the Mayflower had been born and had grown up in East Anglia. Wynter wondered if they had been driven to emigrate by the weather, not that he would have blamed them if they had. His memories of English summers were mostly dreary, damp and dismal. A good, hot summer usually happened every twenty years or so - three in a lifetime … four if you were lucky.

Wynter didn't regret coming to the States; there would never have been the same opportunities in England. Starting in a small way, he had worked his way down the East Coast, from Boston to Miami. People found his English accent comforting, reassuring even, and very, very believable. He was soon returning a very good profit - free of all State and Federal taxes. He began to enjoy himself, and grew to like and admire his adopted home. Admittedly there were places it would be foolish to return to, but then in his line of business it was prudent not to look back. He didn't feel the need to. Ahead of him stretched an almost inexhaustible supply of ambitious people. People he felt sure would fall over themselves to open their wallets.

"No, make up the bed in the box room … yes, the room off of yours … yes, that's the one …" Wynter heard the sheriff giving Harriet instructions.

There was another great attraction about America - it was big. With getting on for three thousand miles from New York to Los Angeles, there was an ocean of space in which he could drown any inconvenient past and re-invent himself. America suited Wynter - it suited him very well. All he needed was to get out of this town in one piece, and America would suit him perfectly.

He heard a tinkle of the bell as the receiver was replaced, and the sheriff ambled back and sat down. The old dog raised its head and wagged its tail but otherwise didn't move. Wynter reached down again and stroked the dog's head.

"Used to be a pretty good gun dog when he was young," said the sheriff, "they do much hunting in England, Mister Wynter?"

"You mean shooting?"

"That's right."

"We don't have any bears, only birds, I'm afraid - grouse and pheasants mainly," said Wynter.

"What about you," said the sheriff, "you shoot?"

"Never had the chance."

The sheriff looked quizzical.

"We had to sell up," continued Wynter.

"Sell up?"

Wynter looked modestly down at the chess board and gave what he hoped looked like an embarrassed smile, "Our estate."

"You owned an estate?" asked the sheriff, impressed.

"Almost six thousand acres," said Wynter.

"Six thousand acres?" said the sheriff with a look of disappointment. "That wouldn't amount to a backyard on some of them prairie ranches."

"Not much by American standards, I know."

The sheriff gave a quizzical look. "You had a big house, like that Brideshead Castle on TV?"

"Oh no, nowhere near as grand as that," Wynter shook his head. "He was a Marquess." Wynter began to have a warm glow. The kind of glow he got when he scented an opportunity.

"*A Mar-kiss*. What are you?"

"We're just Baronets."

"What's the difference?"

"Well, strictly speaking, we aren't noble. Not even aristocratic."

"Not as rich?"

Wynter shook his head. "Not as rich."

The look of disappointment returned to the sheriff's face. "Baronets," he said, turning it over in his mind. Then he perked up and gave a little laugh, "Well, well … I just locked me up a real English lord."

"Oh no, no, baronets are just *Sirs*."

"A Sir! *Sir* Wynter. Wait 'til I tell Harriet."

Wynter gave a satisfied smile. Experience had taught him that although the Founding Fathers had forbidden the creation of their own aristocracy, the American people had maintained a profound fascination with the nobility of others, the richer amongst them going so far as to arrange marriages for their daughters to impoverished Dukes, Earls and Barons. Many previously freezing English country houses had American money to thank for modern plumbing and central heating. American hostesses prized members of the aristocracy at their dinner table, feeling that an ancient title elevated the gathering above the pursuit of money and the grime of finance. Wynter reckoned the news that the sheriff had an English baronet in his jail wouldn't take long to circulate even this remote Oregon valley.

It wasn't the first time that he'd wrapped himself in the Wynter family history, and the more he wore it, the more comfortable it became. The beauty being that he could invent or discard members as required. So much more convenient than the tedious relations with whom he'd been born. The title was just enough to set him apart from the crowd, but not so grand as to be off-putting, nor very easily checked. Coupled with Wynter's easy-going demeanor and good manners, it instilled confidence in his audience, especially if it was introduced as an afterthought, rather than a boast. By the time they found out that the baronetcy was fictitious, *'Sir Wynter'* had disappeared.

"So," said the sheriff, sitting forward in his chair, "you were telling me about your estate and having to sell it."

"That was years ago."

"But why sell it? No-one round here would sell so much as a square foot."

"There was no other way we could pay."

"Pay? Pay what?"

Wynter looked embarrassed.

"Debts?" asked the sheriff. Wynter nodded and the sheriff sighed and shook his head. "It's a narrow path, and I've seen many good men slip off. They fall in with people it's best not to know. What was it? Drink? Gambling? Women? Gambling always did attract the wrong sort of woman."

"I could understand if it had been, sheriff, but no, it wasn't," said Wynter, wondering who the sheriff thought was the right sort of woman. "It was the First World War."

"The war?"

"Yes," said Wynter, "the war. You ever heard of death duties?"

The sheriff shook his head.

"Worst tax anyone invented. The government charges you money when you die. My great-grandfather, the General, was killed on the Somme, and my grandfather got blown to pieces three days before the war ended. Both died doing what their country had asked them to do - fight. How did the country repay their widows? It taxed them! We had to sell two thirds of the estate to pay the bill! The final straw came was when my father was blown up in his tank at Tobruk during the Second World War - the government took sixty per cent of everything that was left. By that stage there wasn't much, but they grabbed virtually all of it. Fighting for their country cost the Wynter family everything."

During Wynter's explanation, the sheriff became visibly shaken, then angry.

"Well, if that don't beat all. Is England a communist country? Sure sounds communist. That's just the sort of thing those pinko bastards would pull. And I thought California was left wing. Hell, that's no way to treat anyone, least of all soldiers!"

"At least with women and gambling we could have enjoyed ourselves, sheriff, even if they were the wrong sort of women."

Before the sheriff could continue his rant about communism or what constituted the right sort of women, the telephone rang again. He got up and stomped off through the door, muttering about commies and his hatred of governments.

Wynter guessed the phone call was from the Harriet over at the hotel. Another twenty minutes and Harriet would be circulating the Wynter family history around the valley - that, and the fact that England had turned communist. He smiled and looked through the door at the mountains. He stroked the dog's head while its tail swept an arc on the floor.

Chapter 4

It was a going to be a difficult meeting. Meredith sensed the knives being sharpened.

Alex Tobin, the Treasury's chief investigator, had flown in from Washington. Tobin had a reputation for being unforgiving when it came to failure. His languid manner concealed a sharp Harvard mind, and his assistant, Felix Boles, was referred to as the Treasury attack dog. Boles didn't like flying, and for him to get on a plane meant that Tobin was coming loaded for bear.

There had been friction, occasionally degenerating into open warfare, between the Treasury and the Secret Service for as long as Meredith could remember. Nominally in charge of the Service, the Treasury tried to exert financial control, which the operational Service did its best to ignore. It might be a war the Treasury would win in the long run, but that didn't mean it should win every battle. Meredith had spent the flight from Las Vegas considering every angle from which Tobin could approach the meeting, and how far he would be prepared to push it.

Meredith's ace in the hole was Bill Bradshaw, the

Director of the Service. After reaching the sanctuary of her hotel room in Vegas the night before, she had put a call through to him in Washington. They had a long conversation ranging over the events of the day: the murder of Peterson; the probability of a mole in the operation; the coming meeting, and her future with the Service. A contemporary and great friend of her father, Bill had followed her career, offering advice and guidance while not hesitating to push her when he thought she needed it. He had believed in her enough to have appointed her Section Chief of the West Coast Region, and he made it plain that he wasn't about to desert her now. When Meredith ended the call half an hour later, she lay back and relaxed on the bed. Taking slow, deep breaths, she felt the tension melt away from her body. The telephone call had reassured her. As long as she had Bill's backing, she was safe.

***

Meredith put her coffee down on the long conference table and sat down. She would normally take the head but Byron Grey was chairing the meeting and Meredith had taken the seat on his left. Looked upon as a safe pair of hands, Byron had risen to be Assistant Director of the Secret Service by making life a little easier for those inside the Beltway. He was also six months from retirement, leaving Meredith wondering how far he would go in her defense.

"Unfortunate that your informant was murdered," said Tobin, sitting down opposite Meredith.

Betrayed would have been a better word, thought

Meredith. "Yes," she said in a measured tone.

"We still have no evidence that there was anything in the truck," said Boles, who sat next to Tobin. "Just your word."

Why don't you call me a liar, thought Meredith as she smiled at Boles. "They would hardly have driven Petersen six hundred miles just to show him the sunset in the desert."

Boles smiled back; he didn't like smart-ass answers. "So you think the drop was still made?" said Boles.

Meredith nodded. "They just changed their plan."

"They used somewhere else for the transfer?" asked Boles.

"It looks that way," said Meredith. She was wary behind her smile. Boles might appear stupid, but he had a string of successful cases behind him that spoke to the contrary. True to form, Tobin had briefed his deputy to make the running, preferring to stay in the background himself.

"So they killed this guy then gave us the finger," said Boles, trying to provoke her.

Meredith felt Tobin's gaze home in on her, probing for a reaction or any sign of weakness.

"Too much to think of it as a co-incidence?" said Grey, after a pause.

"What do you think?" asked Meredith, keeping her eyes on Tobin.

The Assistant Director of the Service may have been sitting at the head of the table, but it was the Treasury that would call the shots on this case.

"They knew we were watching them," said Boles, "yet still went through with it."

"And what does that say?" asked Tobin.

"It means that they were confident we couldn't touch them," said Meredith.

"And why should they think that?"

"They were told."

There was a silence as the implications of Meredith's statement sank in. Finally Tobin's soft voice broke the silence. "By whom?"

"You tell me," said Meredith.

"How do we know you didn't tell them?" asked Boles.

Meredith paused and looked at Boles, then Tobin, and finally at Grey, scanning each of their faces for a clue to their thoughts. She found nothing.

"You don't," she said, breaking the silence. "But it could just as easily have been anyone in this room. We all knew the schedule."

"And outside this room?" said Tobin.

Meredith shuffled the papers in front of her and pulled out two typewritten sheets. One she pushed towards Tobin, the other towards Byron.

"Knowing the day and time of the delivery is one thing," said Meredith. "Knowing that the informant was aboard the van is another. The names on the left are the people who knew of the delivery. Those on the right are the people who knew the name of the informant."

Tobin and Grey studied the lists. Boles gave a sideways glance at Tobin, trying to get a look at the piece of paper.

"You knew the delivery time, and the name of the informant," said Byron, looking up at Meredith, who nodded slowly.

"Yours is the only name which appears on both lists," said Tobin. "It's also the only name amongst the people in this room who knew the informant's name." He put the piece of paper flat on the table and looked over at Meredith. She nodded. It was no good trying to deny an inescapable fact. Boles gave a sly grin.

"The date of the delivery was operational knowledge, but only four people knew the name of the informant," said Meredith.

"Best to keep the two separate ... Service policy," said Byron.

"What's Service policy on murdering informants?" snarled Boles.

"Are you serious?" asked Byron.

"I don't think Mister Boles meant to say that," said Tobin. "I'm sure he'll apologize."

Meredith didn't believe them. Tobin wanted the accusation out there. He wanted her to feel the pressure.

"I'm sorry," said Boles through a disingenuous smile.

It was a well rehearsed ploy, thought Meredith. Byron might be able to ignore what they were doing, but she couldn't. She began to feel the pressure on her mount.

"How did they find out the name?" Byron chimed in.

All eyes turned to Meredith.

"I'd say they've got someone inside our operation," she said. However much she hated to admit it, it must be true. The Service was being betrayed from the inside. She looked over at Tobin. Apart from a small tightening around the mouth, he showed no emotion.

"That narrows it down to four," said Tobin.

She nodded, "On the face of it."

"Of which you are one," said Tobin.

There was no getting away from it: he had her down as chief suspect.

***

Meredith was back in her office: it had been a bruising interview. She sat back in her chair and tried to relax, her eyes closed. Tobin and Boles had gone over and over the operation. Who knew what? How much did they know? When did they know it? She sighed. Circles within circles, and they were still none the wiser. There was a knock and her assistant, Lance Holland, put his head around the door.

"I've got the pathologist's preliminary report from Vegas."

Meredith waved him into her office. She slipped her feet back into her shoes under her desk and sat forward in her chair.

"Let me see," she said, as she held out her hand.

"It's pretty much what the sheriff described," said Lance as he handed her a thin file. "Both arms and legs were broken and the burns are in keeping with what he'd expect to see from an intense gasoline fire." He lowered himself into one of the two comfortable chairs opposite the desk.

Meredith scanned the two written pages. The fact that there wasn't a lot to read reflected the fact that there wasn't much of Raul Petersen left to write about. She moved to the photographs which had been included. The man that she had spoken to last week was a charred shape laid out on a mortuary slab. The intense heat of the fire had contorted his muscles and flesh until his face had become a grotesque screaming ball, as if it had come from the depths of a papal nightmare by Francis Bacon. It was human in the sense that it possessed two arms, two legs and a head, but it was clear they were going to have to rely on dental records for a true identification. Meredith studied the images. What she had initially thought was a trick of the light turned out to be exposed bones poking through the seared flesh. She had seen photographs from crime scenes over the years, but these were in a class of their own. She closed her eyes and sighed. When she eventually spoke it was in a quiet, subdued tone.

"He didn't deserve that. No-one does." She put the photographs on top of the two sheets of paper and closed the file.

"Someone must have tipped them off," said Lance.

Meredith nodded.

"Who?" continued Lance.

"That's what Tobin and Boles want to find out, and guess who's top of their list of suspects?"

Lance frowned then it slowly dawned on him that she was referring to herself. He shook his head. "No … I don't believe it, not you."

Meredith nodded and gave him an ironic smile. "I could do with a drink," she said, standing up. "Want to join me?"

***

The bar was slowly filling up with customers stopping off on their way back home from work. Meredith and Lance sat at a table at the back where it was relatively quiet.

"Do you think the leak is coming from within our office?" asked Lance, nursing a bottle of Budweiser.

Meredith shook her head. "I don't know." She cast an uncomfortable glance at Lance.

"Remind me about the Vegas police," said Lance.

"I only told the police chief in Vegas, and that was out of courtesy, no details. That was about an hour before the shipment was due. Enough time for him to tell someone, but not enough time for them to do anything."

"Yeah … rather rules them out."

Meredith nodded.

Lance shrugged. "Then who?"

Meredith took a breath. "My guess is there's a political connection."

There was a pause as Lance waited for Meredith to explain.

"I met Hogan Reece in the hotel foyer. He *knew*."

Lance frowned. "Reece? … How?"

"He knew. Warned me that gambling was a hazardous pastime and I should be careful I didn't get burnt."

"But …"

"He *knew*. I don't know how, but I'll swear he knew."

"Did you tell Byron Grey or Tobin about meeting Reece?"

Meredith shook her head. "It's the one thing I've got that they haven't." She took another mouthful of beer.

"Tobin's got you down for the mole," said Lance.

"Tobin doesn't like me - doesn't agree with women being in authority. That's why I didn't tell him about Reece."

Lance nodded and took a thoughtful swig of beer. "Where do you think we should be looking for the leak?"

Meredith shrugged. "The District Attorney's office; our office ... the Treasury?"

"You think that ..."

"I think that far too many people seem to have got involved in this investigation."

Lance nodded.

"If we're right," continued Meredith, "and Van Buren is the man behind the counterfeiting operation, then I think he's bought Reece."

"It makes sense of Reece's comment, and Reece never did have a conscience" said Lance.

"Which means that Van Buren has got political protection."

"Reece doesn't have national influence; he's a State Senator," said Lance, shaking his head.

"There will be others, and I think Van Buren trusts Reece as much as I do, so let's keep an eye on the Senator. Find out where he goes, who he meets, and who he talks to ... he didn't show up in Vegas by accident." Meredith took a thoughtful gulp of beer. "For an operation this size, Van Buren will need to pull a lot of heat, and that means Washington."

"So what do we do? Two of us can't take on Washington."

"No, not head on," sighed Meredith. "We'll have to find another way."

Chapter 5

Harriet cleared the chess pieces and chessboard from the table and replaced them with a plate of roast beef, potatoes and vegetables. She was about to disappear into the office when she stopped at the door. She hesitated, then turned back to Wynter and asked a question that had obviously been on her mind. "You know the Queen, Sir Wynter?"

"Know her?" repeated Wynter, picking up the knife and fork. "No, I can't say I *know* her." He saw the look of disappointment on Harriet's face. "I've met her, of course … at Ascot. She's a great one for horse racing."

"Ascot … really?" squeaked Harriet, her face lit up again.

"I was presented," nodded Wynter, "in the Enclosure."

"Presented." Harriet was impressed, but Wynter could see that she was grappling with the details. "What's the enclosure?"

"The Royal Enclosure?"

"Yeah, what's that? Some sort of corral?"

Wynter tried his best to suppress a smile as his mind raced, imagining a large paddock into which members the Royal Family were herded each night, only to be released in the morning.

"It's a special paddock area at the race track, fenced off for the Queen, her friends and guests … got a grandstand and everything."

"Just for her and her friends" nodded Harriet, carefully memorizing every detail.

"Well, you *can* apply for tickets."

"They sell tickets? So anyone can go in there, I …"

"No, not really" said Wynter quickly, before her next question. "You have to be approved, vetted, by the Queen's Representative."

"Oh," Harriet's excitement evaporated. "Security, I guess?"

"That, and to keep out undesirables," said Wynter. Yes, he thought, undesirables like himself.

"You got in there, but then I guess you would, being a baronet and that."

Before he could do more than smile a reply, the sheriff bustled through the office door with a plate of apple pie and cream.

"Harriet makes the best apple pie west of the Missouri, he said.

"Oh, go on with you, Rufus Richards," said Harriet in mock protest. "My Ma made them better."

"No she didn't, and I tasted them both."

For a couple of seconds Harriet's face lit up in a radiant smile and her eyes sparkled. Wynter could see what had captivated the sheriff all those years ago.

"Well, I can't stand here talking all day, got things to do. I'll get your dishes on the way out, Rufus. Now, leave Sir

Wynter to finish his lunch." Harriet pushed the office door open. Sensing the sheriff hadn't moved, she turned around. "Come on now, let him eat in peace."

"I'll only be a couple of minutes, Harriet …"

"Rufus!"

"It's official business."

She looked him in the eye, smiled, then moved into the office, leaving the door ajar.

"Fine woman" said Wynter, looking up from his plate.

"She always was," said the sheriff softly, his mind drifting back almost forty years. Sighing, he returned to the present. "It's not been easy for her these last few years, let alone all her past troubles with her husband, God rest his soul. I try to help, but she's a proud woman; takes after her Ma."

The faint clatter of dishes drifted through the slightly open door.

"Not much call for an hotel up here, I wouldn't have thought. Don't suppose too many people come sightseeing," said Wynter.

They both heard the tinkle of a bell as Harriet lifted the telephone receiver on the sheriff's desk and both politely ignored it.

"A few find their way up here, mostly geologists - got some staying at the moment. There are some pretty fancy rock formations around here," said the sheriff. "Then there are the Vietnam Vets. A bunch of those guys turn up two, three times a year for a get-together. Fill Harriet's place right up. They say they like it up here. It's clean, the air's good … and we leave them in peace. Guess they've been through enough, without people asking damn fool questions and raking it over."

They heard the murmurings of one side of a conversation from the office. Harriet was busy winding up the County grapevine real tight. "No, he's met her … yes, really …" Wynter smiled and took another mouthful of beef. "… Presented … the enclosure … I know, that's what I said, sounds like a corral …"

The sheriff looked embarrassed. "You know what women are like. Just have to tell someone."

Wynter smiled, nodded, and slipped the dog a piece of beef.

"Spoke to Jeb Swayne about your tires," said the sheriff, changing the subject. "He's going down to Prineville tomorrow morning, says he'll pick some up."

"Thanks," said Wynter, genuinely relieved. The telephone bell tinkled again as Harriet replaced the receiver, then they heard the front close as she left. The sheriff visibly relaxed.

"Some of the boys and I have been talking about what you said … about that death tax. We just can't figure out how the government tells men they got to go off and fight, then takes all of what they got when they gets killed. That ain't right. I mean, I thought the whole point of fighting was to protect your family and your property."

"And democracy."

The sheriff gave Wynter a dismissive look. "Democracy may be *the* big thing for politicians, but it spreads pretty thin outside election-time."

"I agree ... but, as Winston Churchill said, it's the best of a bad job."

"Democracy?" said the sheriff, leaning forward in his chair. "You know about the Civil War, Sir Wynter?"

"A little"

"A little," said the sheriff. "Well, let me tell you a *little* more. The Southern States voted, quite democratically, to leave the Union in 1860, as the Constitution said they had the right to do. Except that wasn't the right sort of democracy ... not according to the North, anyways. Over a quarter of a million men from the South died fighting, Sir Wynter; *a quarter of a million.* They voted, perfectly legally, to secede ... not get themselves killed." The sheriff paused and sat back in the chair. "What kind of democracy you get depends on who's holding the gun. My Grandma came from the South ... from Georgia. You ever heard tell of Sherman's March?"

"From Atlanta to the sea," nodded Wynter softly.

"Yeah - Atlanta to the sea, just like the song. Well, there wasn't much left of Georgia when Sherman's boys done marching. My Grandma may only have been a child but she saw what they did, and she never forgot," said the sheriff. "Sherman destroyed everything in his way: cities; towns; railroads; animals; crops. What cattle he couldn't drive off, he killed. What horses he didn't need, he shot. If it moved, he killed it - if it didn't, he burned it down. Men, women and children starved to death, Sir Wynter ... starved!" The sheriff stopped and spat through the open door at the end of the corridor. "That's what democracy got the South."

Quite how a woman from Georgia had ended up in a forgotten valley in one of the remotest parts of Oregon was not a question that Wynter felt able to ask at this point, however much he'd have liked to know the answer. His mind turned to all the reading he'd done recently about America: its geography; its economy; its politics; its history. From one of his mind's deeper recesses, he managed to dredge some half-forgotten facts.

"Britain was always sympathetic to the Southern cause," said Wynter. "I believe we came very close to recognizing the Confederacy as a separate country."

"Shame you didn't; might've saved an awful lot of lives."

"At least the Confederacy didn't charge soldiers' families for getting them killed. Not like the British Government charging mine."

"I can't get over that," said the sheriff, sitting back. "You don't expect that sort of thing from your own side. Hell, what's the point of fighting at all?"

"We didn't get over it. Not financially."

"Must have been a shock, having to sell your land an' all."

"It had been in our family for over six hundred years."

The sheriff gave a low whistle. "Six hundred years!"

"Six hundred years that counted for nothing. The new politicians wanted to destroy the aristocracy ... and they did."

"Just like Sherman and the South" nodded the sheriff. "So what did you do? You qualified for anything?"

Wynter gave a quiet smile and shook his head. "No, not

qualified, I just kicked around for a few years."

"That when you learned to play cards? From what I gather you know all the moves." Wynter smiled to himself as the sheriff continued, "Must have been quite a player who taught you."

Wynter smiled again. It was time to cast the line.

"My Uncle Andrew," said Wynter.

"Another English gentleman?"

The sheriff's question hit a sore point. "I know what you must be thinking, Sheriff: gentlemen don't cheat at cards. I can assure you, I wasn't cheating."

"No?"

Wynter shook his head. "Didn't have to. The three fingered guy and his friends were cheating more than enough for everyone, except they weren't very good at it. There must have been at least three kings of clubs circulating the table at one time. I just played a straight game and had the run of the cards. I got lucky. It happens."

The sheriff smiled. "I'm inclined to give you the benefit of the doubt, Sir Wynter. Not necessarily 'cause I believe *you*, but mainly because I know Travis and his friends too well and the way *they* play cards. They would have been concentrating on their own cheating and wouldn't have noticed what you were doing anyway. Even if you was cheating."

"I promise I wasn't cheating," said Wynter, relieved that the sheriff agreed about the standard of card playing in Alyson.

"So, your Uncle Andrew? What was he?"

"A magician."

"Ahh," nodded the sheriff, "and he taught you card tricks?"

"He sure did."

Wynter had told the story a few times before, and now had almost come to believe that he actually had an uncle called Andrew.

In reality, Uncle Andrew was a book, *The Expert at the Card Table*. Written by S.W. Erdnase, it was the bible of all card mechanics and magicians. Erdnase was the pseudonym of Milton Andrews, a professional card sharp. Published in 1902, it had never been out of print since: such is the general fascination for tricks and deception. Wynter had not so much read the book as consumed it. He had practiced its deceits in front of a mirror until *even he* didn't know whether he was cheating or not. It covered everything from dealing off the bottom, to dealing yourself a winning hand, to shuffling a pack of cards into sequence, running from ace to king in their own suits. Of course, the sleights of hand it detailed could also be used for legitimate card tricks, some of which were covered in the second half of the book.

"It all started one Christmas. I was only a kid. Uncle Andrew showed me a couple of tricks. Then, as long as I promised not to tell anyone else, he showed me how they were done. Of course, I made a mess of them to start with, but slowly I got better. I did exactly as he told me, and practiced and practiced."

"So you were going to be a magician, like him?"

"Oh, he didn't make a living out of it. He was a chemist.

Magic was just a hobby. To him, chemistry was the real magic. It fascinated him."

"Sure didn't fascinate me when I was at school."

"Me neither, but then, we weren't working on the sort of projects that Uncle Andrew worked on during the war."

The sheriff relaxed back into his chair. "Yeah?"

Wynter smiled to himself. It was time to concentrate on retrieving his six thousand dollars. He made the first cast to gauge interest.

"You ever hear of Operation Bernhard, Sheriff?" The sheriff looked blank and shook his head. "Not many people have," continued Wynter. "It was a Nazi plan to flood Britain with counterfeit money during the Second World War. Hitler thought that the fakes would lead to the collapse of the economy."

"And would it?"

"Sure, if there was enough of it. All economists know Gresham's Law, *'Bad money drives out good.'*"

"Was there enough?"

"Enough was printed. The problem for the Nazis was getting it into England. There was a plan for the Luftwaffe to drop the notes from the air, but Goering said he didn't have enough aircraft."

"Hell! How much did they print?"

"Almost nine million notes, in denominations of five, ten, twenty and fifty pounds. Face value of over £134 million altogether, worth billions in today's values. They *could* have dropped it by air, but I get the impression that Goering wasn't particularly interested. Guess he couldn't see the advantages of economic warfare."

"So, how did they get them into England?"

"They didn't. British intelligence got wind of the plot, and managed to capture all the Nazi agents before they'd spent much of the money. It gave the government a scare, though. Some of the notes continued in circulation after the war, and forced the Treasury to withdraw all notes over the value of five pounds. Made them design a new five pound note too. It wasn't until a few years ago, in the 1970s, that they even issued a twenty pound note again."

"So, where does your Uncle Andrew fit in?" asked the sheriff with a laugh. "Wasn't a Nazi, was he?"

"No" smiled Wynter. "Not a Nazi. He was in British Intelligence. The Nazis had forced Jewish engravers and printers in Sachsenhausen Concentration Camp to carry out the counterfeiting. Uncle Andrew said the notes were perfect, absolutely indistinguishable from the real thing. That's why the government was so worried. They sent him to hunt down the plates and the presses; they couldn't afford to let them fall into the wrong hands. He finally recovered the plates and the majority of the money from the bottom of Lake Toplitz, where the Nazis had dumped them as they retreated."

By now the sheriff was spellbound. He was listening to his favorite topic being discussed ... money. "What happened to them?" he asked in reverential tones. "The money and the plates?"

"I think the government kept a few notes, for their museum. A few of the people who recovered it no doubt kept a few souvenirs. But the rest of the money was destroyed. Plates were melted down, too."

The sheriff closed his eyes and sighed as he imagined the flames of the furnace licking around all those banknotes.

"What about Uncle Andrew? He keep any?"

"He kept a fifty pound note. But I've no idea where it is today; lost probably. Well, it was over forty years ago."

"Only fifty pounds? He could have revived the family fortunes, right there and then. No-one would have noticed if a few hundred thousand went missing. How could they? As you said, they were perfect notes."

"Oh, he got something more valuable."

"What?" asked the sheriff, wondering what could possibly be more valuable than millions of perfect banknotes?

"After the plates and money were destroyed, he tracked down two of the Jews that had been forced to do the counterfeiting."

"They were still alive? I thought you said they were in a concentration camp?"

"They were, and the Nazis had ordered that they should be killed. But, in the confusion of the Nazi retreat, they escaped. Uncle Andrew traced them. It seems that they'd been working on a number of ways of counterfeiting. It just wasn't British money the Nazis wanted to copy, but Russian Roubles, Swiss Francs, Argentinean Pesos - and the American Dollar."

"The Dollar!?"

"They wanted to destabilize all other currencies while the war was going on."

"Did they make plates for all those other currencies?" asked the sheriff.

Wynter shook his head. "No, they didn't have the time," smiled Wynter. "One of the Jews did tell him, however, that they'd been working on something so secret that only the Camp's Commandant was allowed into the hut they used as a laboratory."

"What?" whispered the sheriff, who was by now hanging on Wynter's every word.

"They didn't have the time to engrave plates for all of the currencies, so they hit on another way of doing it."

Wynter hesitated. The first cast had got the sheriff interested. Now he gathered himself for the second cast.

"They were working on a chemical process to duplicate money. Any money - any note - any denomination."

The sheriff's mouth dropped open. The Holy Grail! Then slowly a frown began to form. "How come we never heard about all this after the war? Plenty of Americans was over there. How come none of them came back and said any of this?"

"Sachsenhausen camp was north of Berlin, in an area over-run by Russian troops as the Nazis collapsed. Your boys got no-where near it, and there was a security clampdown. British Intelligence made sure that very few people got to hear about it and only a handful knew the facts."

The sheriff nodded slowly. "Right."

"As I said, Uncle Andrew managed to trace the two Jews who had been working on this machine and talk to them. They drew him the plans for the machine and gave him details of the chemical process."

"Why didn't the two Jews make one of these machines after the war?"

"Sadly they disappeared after my Uncle spoke to them. The Russians had occupied eastern Germany. Tens of thousands, perhaps millions of people just disappeared at the end of the war." Wynter slowly shook his head. "No-one ever heard of them again."

The sheriff nodded as he pondered what he'd just heard. "That's one hell of a story"

"It was one hell of a time."

"I guess it was ... so what did your Uncle do after the war?"

"Came back to England, left the Intelligence Service, bought a cottage in the country and equipped a small chemical laboratory."

"To do what?"

Wynter smiled. "Well, he did have the plans and the chemical formulas."

The sheriff looked mystified, until the gist of what Wynter was saying began to dawn on him.

"You mean ... you mean he made one of these machines?" Wynter said nothing; just kept smiling. "You're telling me he built a machine that makes money?" continued the sheriff in disbelief, tinged with hope.

Wynter's smile grew wider as he nodded.

The sheriff frowned. "You're kidding me, right?"

Wynter stopped nodding and slowly shook his head.

The sheriff's face creased into a large grin then he began

to laugh. "I just love your British sense of humor, Sir Wynter, it plain cracks me up. Operation Bernhard ... a machine that makes money ... you almost had me going there."

By now, both Wynter and the sheriff were laughing. Even the old dog joined in with a few barks. Wynter stroked the animal's head and congratulated himself for making what he reckoned was a perfect cast.

He didn't expect the sheriff to believe it.

Nobody ever did.

Not to begin with.

Chapter 6

Byron Grey had flown back to Washington, leaving the Treasury team of Tobin and Boles trying to find answers to their outstanding questions. It was late in the afternoon and they were in Meredith's office. As Tobin looked out of the window and Boles draped himself rather indecorously against a filing cabinet, Meredith began to feel uneasy.

"We got lucky with Petersen," said Meredith, in answer to Boles' question.

"Shame *his* luck didn't last. Coming into contact with you proved fatal."

The smile on Boles' face froze and he stared unblinking at Meredith. The hint of an accusation was raised again. Meredith took refuge in the fact that there wasn't one piece of solid evidence against her.

"He came into contact with at least six other people who could identify him," she said.

"But you knew his *name*."

"True, but so did the LAPD. And others might not have known his name but they knew what he looked like," shrugged Meredith.

"That doesn't alter the facts," chimed in Tobin from the window.

What facts, thought Meredith? You've only got one: I knew his name. So what? So did his mother.

"Names are easily changed; it's harder to change your looks." Meredith hoped that her voice sounded calm and without the rising anger she felt. The circumstantial evidence pointed to half a dozen people; she just happened to be one of them. Boles lowered his head a little so that he could look at her over his spectacles, like a school master regarding an errant pupil.

"What happened at the casino?" asked Boles.

"Nothing, they'd been tipped off."

"You sure you didn't see anything out of the ordinary?"

"Not spending my evenings in casinos, I wouldn't know what's ordinary and what isn't."

"You didn't notice anyone watching you?" asked Tobin, still looking out of the window.

"Cameras watch everyone in casinos."

"I meant people," said Tobin, turning from the window.

"While we watched them watching us?" Meredith shook her head. "No."

"Anyone say anything to you?"

His manner suggested that he thought someone had. Did Tobin know about Senator Reece being at the casino that night? Meredith decided to deflect the conversation away from the senator.

"Apart from the guy who tried to pick me up you mean?"

Tobin half smiled, "Apart from that."

"Not that I recall. I spent that evening watching gamblers come and go while we waited."

"We?"

"I was with Jerry Shapiro; you should ask him."

"We will," chimed in Boles.

"Oh, there was someone who came up and spoke to me."

"Yes?" said Tobin, his eyes betrayed a sudden interest.

"Detective Wilson of the Las Vegas Police Department. He came to tell me about the …" Meredith hesitated as she searched for the right word "… *problem* in the desert."

They looked at each other in silence. Tobin had the impression that she was holding something back, and Meredith got the feeling that Tobin knew more than he let on.

"No-one came up and thanked me for pointing the finger at Petersen, if that's what you want to know," said Meredith.

"No-one says you did," said Tobin.

"That's not what it feels like from where I'm sitting."

"It isn't my intention to make you feel uncomfortable. I just want to get to the truth."

You've all but accused me of giving the tip-off about Petersen and lying about who I spoke to in the casino, thought Meredith. You began with a twisted version of the truth, and it looks like you aim to prove it. Meredith sighed. Once you start a hare running down the wrong road it takes a lot to call it back.

"We both want the truth," she said.

"Good to know we agree on that," said Tobin, with a conciliatory hint of sarcasm.

Meredith gave a slight nod in response. But whose truth would that be, she thought? Surely not the one-sided story that you've been following. She took a deep breath and felt proud that she had managed to contain her rising anger.

A few years ago Tobin's probing questions would have met with a salvo of denials, peppered with a few expletives for good measure. She reflected that her boss, Bill Bradshaw, had been right when he told her that management was about effective control, namely self control. Managing to keep her anger hidden was all very well, she thought, but it didn't stop her feeling that she was being set up.

Had someone dripped this poisonous story into Tobin's ear?

Was someone in Washington looking to tie her into the counterfeiting scam?

***

Steve Hellman turned into the Civic Center Plaza, looked across the square at the dome of City Hall and scowled, before walking through the doors of the main City Library.

Hellman wasn't big on books. He wasn't big on anything that didn't have an appreciating financial value. To him, books were simply part of a room's decoration, like wallpaper or paint. Necessary to complete an impression, but that was all. A large building in a prime location, used solely to house thousands of books, was beyond his comprehension. This site could generate tens of thousands a month in rent - fines for overdue library books didn't even keep the windows clean.

He paused, took a breath and straightened his tie before he entered the reception.

The Head of San Francisco's Planning Department, Phil Kaufman, saw Hellman enter the large room and flinched. That was all he needed. Kaufman had overseen the city's development for the past seven years, and in that time he'd dealt with Hellman on a couple of his previous projects. Kaufman realized the construction industry was no place for kid gloves, but Hellman had overstepped the mark on a number of occasions. When he had complained, Hellman had laughed and told him to look the other way.

Hellman finally caught sight of Kaufman and, slowing only to take a glass of wine from a waiter, pushed his ample frame through the crowd. He cornered the Head of Planning and lost no time in getting to the point.

"Your man Joey Battista was going to call me."

"Joey said you'd spoken to him," said Kauffman.

"Yeah, and I've not heard back." Hellman rotated the stem of his glass in his fingers.

"You only rang yesterday; give him a break."

Hellman shrugged. "He's gotta know what sites are coming up, and what sites aren't. It's a pretty simple question."

"Hellman," Kauffman shook his head, "nothing's simple in City Hall."

"Okay, so when do I get a reply?"

Kauffman took a sip of mineral water. "From what Joey told me, you're looking for something pretty big."

"A man should move up in the world."

"And you're on the move?"

"To the top."

"Perhaps," said Kauffman. "You realize it would be easier to go out of town for your site … cheaper too."

Hellman shook his head. "Out of town doesn't suit. It needs to be somewhere people can see; somewhere on the Bay."

"Are you serious?"

"Very," said Hellman, with thinly veiled menace.

"Anyone who owns a bay site isn't going to sell."

"They could be *persuaded*."

Kauffman sighed. It was like talking to an overgrown child. "All the large sites are owned by corporations, pension funds. You can't persuade *them*."

"The City has to own some prime Bay sites."

"Nothing the size you're looking for."

"What about the place next to my office, Victoria Park?"

"Christ, Hellman!" Kauffman shook his head. "You're way out of line."

"I wouldn't want all of it."

"Have you any idea the storm that would stir up with the environmental lobby?"

"I've dealt with them before … remember?"

Kauffman sighed again. "You haven't got the finance for a deal that big."

"The finance is sorted," said Hellman.

"Even for the amounts of money you'll need?"

"My client doesn't have problems with money. He could produce ten million tomorrow, in cash. You just worry about finding the site," said Hellman. "And tell Joey to give me a call."

This was the first time Kauffman had heard of a client. There had to be one, he'd reasoned. This project was way out of Hellman's league; industrial units and small apartment blocks were more his style. Commercial sites on the Bay started at three million, and went as high as you wanted to pay. Kauffman estimated it would cost Hellman anything up to twenty million for the site his client wanted. That was one hell of a client to have. Kauffman's first thought was that it had to be a corporation. His second was that he couldn't think of any corporation that would employ Hellman.

Kauffman closed his eyes in resignation. It had been a long, hard day and he could do without an argument.

"Okay, I'll tell Joey," sighed Kauffman.

***

The restaurant was half-full with people eating dinner. Meredith and Lance sat at a small table towards the back, where there was less noise. Neither of them wanted their conversation to be overheard.

"What about the District Attorney?" asked Lance.

"What about him?" said Meredith, putting a forkful of pasta into her mouth.

"He's a straight guy."

"Mmm," nodded Meredith, savoring the pasta.

"If we went to him … he's clean."

"What about his staff?"

Lance shrugged. "There's no need for him to tell them."

Meredith swallowed. This was really great pasta. Twirling her fork round the plate, she looked up at him. "Doesn't work like that, Lance; you know it doesn't. Have you heard of *anything* staying a secret in the DA's office? Anyway, he's coming up for re-election and might be tempted to say something he shouldn't. How's your steak?"

"Good, thanks," said Lance as he cut into it. "So … it's a problem of jurisdiction. Just when it gets interesting, the police have got to stop at the County line; you aren't keen to let the Feds in on the operation since the Becker fiasco; and you don't trust the DA to keep his mouth shut." Lance skewered a piece of steak with his fork. "With the Treasury breathing down your neck, it kind of cuts your options down."

"I get the feeling Tobin wants to cut me down."

"Then we'll have to tread carefully."

***

Supper was finished, plates washed up, and Harriet was sitting at the kitchen table nursing a mug of hot milk. She watched as the sheriff sat down at the other end of the table and eased the top off a bottle of beer. A man's a jumble of flaws, that's what her ma had always told her; it's how he manages those flaws that makes him what he is. And God, did Rufus Richards have flaws. He was opinionated; self-centered, with a tendency to arrogance; and stubborn as a mule. If he hadn't been so stubborn all those years ago … well, perhaps things might have worked out differently.

Harriet gave a quiet sigh; no point in going down that road again.

"You think he's making it up?" said the sheriff.

"Come on, a machine that makes money?" said a skeptical Harriet.

"It was a machine made every dollar bill in your purse," said the sheriff.

"But that was a government machine, Rufus."

"A machine's a machine. Way I see it, the government only wants *their* machines to make dollar bills," said the sheriff, and he took a swig of beer.

"Yeah, well. It's just ... the way you told it, it didn't sound quite right. That's all I'm saying."

"You ever heard anyone describe a giraffe? They don't sound right either; not unless you've seen one," said the sheriff. "Elephants sound pretty far-fetched too."

"You believe him?"

The sheriff shrugged. "Sounds like he told it how it happened."

"Well Uncle Isaac can't remember it, and he was over there fighting."

"Uncle Isaac can't remember who Aunt Sarah is most of the time. I wouldn't pay too much mind to what he says."

There was a pause during which Harriet lifted the mug of warm milk to her lips and took a sip. She could see that she was losing the argument; she usually did when she discussed money with Rufus. She liked Sir Wynter, he was a gentleman, and that was rare in this part of Oregon. But there was a limit to liking, especially when it involved the truth, and a box that made money just sounded unbelievable.

"Well, I don't remember being taught anything about it at school."

"Far as I recall, we weren't taught much about anything, except it was in the Bible."

"So you really think he could be telling the truth? His uncle really made one of these machines?" said Harriet, not wanting to call Sir Wynter a liar.

"I don't know," shrugged the sheriff, as he took another swig of beer … "could be."

She pursed her lips. "Well, I never heard anything about Operation Bernhard."

"I never heard anything about it either, but …"

"They could fill the Grand Canyon with what you ain't heard about, Rufus Richards," said an exasperated Harriet.

"I was down there last year."

The voice came from the open door and interrupted them. Rufus and Harriet turned to see one of the geologists.

"The Grand Canyon, looking at sedimentation and stratification," continued the geologist. "You've got to see it to believe how *big* it is."

"I've heard that," nodded a startled Rufus, wondering how much of their conversation had been overheard.

The geologist turned to Harriet. "Just wondered if we could order some sandwiches for Thursday, ma'am, and a couple of flasks of coffee? We're aiming to be out all day."

"Of course," Harriet nodded, "I've got some ham, chicken and eggs. That okay for you?"

"Sounds good to me."

"I'll put in some bottles of water. You'll need them up there."

"That's very thoughtful, ma'am. Thank you. Well, got an early start in the morning so I'll say goodnight."

"Goodnight," smiled Harriet, as the geologist turned to go.

"Hold on a minute," said Rufus, "you're a man who might know."

"Might know what?" asked the geologist.

"About Operation Bernhard," said Rufus.

Harriet shot him a worried glance.

"What's that?" asked the geologist.

"It was during the war."

"Sorry, don't know anything about Vietnam. Too young, thank God."

"No, not Vietnam; it was Europe, during the Second World War."

"Oh, history. Sorry, not my subject."

Rufus sagged a little, "Shame."

Sensing his disappointment, the geologist smiled. "A friend of mine might know."

"Yeah?" said Rufus.

"I could call him tomorrow evening, when we get back, if you want?"

"I'd be grateful if you could." He turned to Harriet. "Put that call on my tab."

"Okay," said the geologist. "Obliged for the sandwiches, ma'am. Well, we've got an early start tomorrow, so I'll say goodnight."

Harriet and Rufus both said goodnight and the geologist disappeared. When he was safely out of hearing, Rufus turned to Harriet.

"D'you think he heard?"

"Heard what?"

"You *know* what, Harriet. About Sir Wynter's uncle and …"

Harriet shook her head "Shouldn't think so."

After a little thought, Rufus said, "Who do you expect he'll call?"

"How should I know? One of his friends at the university I guess."

"A professor?"

"Could be," shrugged Harriet.

"Some-one who would know?"

"Better than we do, that's for sure."

"Best not say anything about Sir Wynter's uncle Andrew, or the …"

"I wasn't about to."

"Good. No point in spreading it around. Might not be anything to it."

***

By now it was getting late, and Meredith and Lance were amongst the restaurant's last remaining customers. The serving staff were doing their best to appear as if they weren't bored, fiddling with tablecloths and folding napkins, as they waited for the diners to leave.

"Look," said Meredith, "we can split the counterfeiters into two groups, the printers, and the people who pass the junk notes. From what we know, the printers are beyond our reach down in Central America. That leaves the people who pass the junk - the paperhangers."

Lance took a mouthful of beer and nodded.

"Who are the best paperhangers?" asked Meredith.

"Con-men," said Lance without hesitation.

"Junk money seems to attract them," she nodded in agreement. "I've been thinking of the possibles: the real artists; the crème de la crème."

"So far, everything points to casinos being the distribution points."

"I've got a feeling that the casinos will be going quiet for a few months. The counterfeiters may be looking for other methods of passing the junk notes."

"Introduce a new cog into their machine?" Lance took a thoughtful swig of beer. 'You think that's wise? I mean …'

"Can you come up with something better?" asked Meredith.

"No," he admitted, "but it's risky."

Meredith nodded. "That's why we need someone with a proven track record in the business. Someone who could be relied upon to shift large amounts, quickly … and quietly."

"Who do you have in mind?" said Lance, still not convinced by Meredith's idea.

"Dan Collins is top of the list, but he's just started a ten year stretch in the Ohio State Penitentiary."

Lance smiled. "I doubt they'll let him out to help us."

"Julius Rothstein, otherwise known as …"

"War Bonds Julius," interrupted Lance, with a grin.

"War Bonds Julius," agreed Meredith. "Unfortunately Julius isn't doing too well. He picked the wrong guy for his bond scam and he ended up in hospital down in Louisiana."

"You'll be feeling sorry for him next," said Lance. "Who else?"

There was a pause while Meredith finished her wine, then she looked across the table at Lance.

"The Englishman."

Chapter 7

Hellman replaced the telephone receiver and gazed out of the window. His mind went back to his first collaboration with Van Buren. It had been an Oakland industrial complex. There had been problems at the outset, but then all construction projects have problems. A few members of the City Planning Committee thought that it was too close to a residential area, and it used up one of the area's last pieces of green space. Voices were raised to save it. Their self-appointed leader, an ecologist, spoke on a local radio talk show, trying to rally support to halt the development. A small bunch of people gathered in the appropriately named Preservation Park, and then marched on Oakland's City Hall, where they had made a lot of fuss and noise.

Eventually Van Buren had had to send Jago to explain the advantages of the project to the chairman of the Planning Committee and the ecologist … and the very personal disadvantages inherent in opposing it.

Three weeks later, the chairman had overruled the objections and the ecologist had moved to Florida. With Hellman's enthusiasm and Van Buren's influence, the complex was finished faster than scheduled, and they had both come out with a healthy profit. That had been four years and two further ventures ago. Now, Van Buren's latest project was beginning to worry Hellman.

It was to be a big statement: a sort of memorial building, sited on San Francisco Bay or close to it. Hellman had been skeptical about it from the start, but was too scared to say anything. He reckoned that Fort Mason Centre and the Park around it offered the best chance of realizing Van Buren's project. Technically it was a city park, but if Van Buren offered to make a gift of a new state-of-the-art theatre complex with restaurants, a visitor centre and free space for community use, he thought the Planning Department might be open to a deal, or would at least talk to them. Especially if the planners' got favorite architect got to design the complex. It all came down to how much Van Buren was prepared to offer to get what he wanted.

Hellman sighed and his mind returned to the telephone call.

Joey Battista hadn't been helpful. The city's Planning Department wasn't forthcoming at the best of times, but he had gained the impression that Battista was trying to shunt him off on a track to nowhere. Despite the city's difficult financial position, Joey had said that the mayor and the council didn't think selling property assets was an answer. No sites were for sale, and none were scheduled to come onto the market.

Hellman knew this wasn't true. Municipal property was perpetually changing hands; he knew of three deals being negotiated as they were speaking. The city was always exchanging, selling, or buying property; they were one of the biggest players in the marketplace. It may have been open to question whether they had a site big enough for Van Buren's project, but to say outright that they weren't selling anything was a downright lie. Even Joey had the decency to stumble over the words as he said them.

Hellman knew a lot about lying - he'd done enough of it himself in his career. Lying was the only way to survive in some areas of the real estate business. In his experience, the lie comes just before you do what you said you wouldn't: and the bigger the lie, the bigger the turnaround.

What game was Joey playing? Hellman considered that he had always got on well with him. On reflection, perhaps that wasn't quite the right phrase, but they had a reasonable working relationship.

So: why this? Why now?

Had Phil Kauffman spoken to him following the reception? Was Kauffman putting the brakes on? If so: why? The more he thought about it, the more Hellman began to feel that he was being left out of the loop. He began to speculate that something was about to come onto the market - something that the city planners didn't want him anywhere near.

***

Wynter sat on the bed in the cell gazing through the bars at the chess board. Protective custody had its drawbacks, even if the sheriff did leave the cell door open. He wondered if

Three Fingers and his friends had calmed down. He could see no reason why they shouldn't; after all, they'd got his money. All they had lost out on was the thrill of a violent whipping.

The sound of the sheriff's laughter filtered through the door. Wynter wondered if he'd still be laughing in a day or two. How things turned out would depend on whether the sheriff was curious enough to find out more about Operation Bernhard; whether he wanted to learn more about how Wynter made a living. If he wasn't curious, then the game was over there and then. If he was, then Wynter could see his poker winnings coming back threefold. But it was up to the sheriff to make the first move; Wynter had to adopt an air of complete indifference.

The ping of the telephone as the receiver was replaced jerked Wynter back into the present. He slid his sole remaining bishop across the board as the sheriff appeared in the doorway with a big grin on his face.

"Well, Texas ain't got nothing on you, and Chicago don't want you either."

Wynter wondered how long it would take before the sheriff gave up on the idea of a reward.

"Sounds like the police in Chicago might have a gang war on their hands," said the sheriff as he chuckled again. "Word on the street is that one gang was ripped off for a quarter of a million dollars by the other gang. My cousin Wilbur's boy is a detective up there; gave me the whole story. By the way, Jeb Swayne said he's got your tires and he'll fit them tomorrow."

The sheriff sat down in his chair and studied the chess board. The news from Chicago worried Wynter. It was just as well that his pick-up would soon be ready.

"Tell Mister Swayne I'm very grateful to him. If he'd like to stop by I'll pay his bill."

The sheriff nodded and put his hand out to move his knight.

"All over some worthless mine, my nephew tells me. The two Greeks who got took are ready to kill half Chicago. Time was there used to be honor amongst thieves," grinned the sheriff. "Seems you can't trust no-one these days."

"Yeah?" said Wynter, his mouth going dry.

"Police think it's a rival gang that set it up, revenge or something … Your move, Sir Wynter."

Wynter moved one of his pawns and tried to swallow. The Chicago PD could think anything they want, as long as they didn't think of him. He was surprised that the Kontakis brothers had admitted to the shake-down. He shook his head; there must be more to it.

"Hardly worth going to war over."

"Folks have been murdered for fifty cents before now; and a quarter of a million's a lot of money where most people come from. Anyway, it ain't just the money with gangsters; it's the message it sends." The sheriff moved his remaining knight.

Wynter nodded in agreement; the Kontakis brothers had been hit for less than half what was being claimed. Wynter had walked away with fifty grand, while Henry had taken the rest as his share and compensation for being beaten up.

How had it mushroomed to a quarter of a million? Did the police want a bigger crime for their stats, or were the Kontakis brothers embarrassed at not losing enough? Hell, if they'd said he'd have been happy to take more off them.

"Having trouble with your next move?" asked the sheriff.

"Just trying to think ahead, weighing up my options."

How much time had he got? The police hadn't made any connections, as yet. Could the Kontakis boys trace him here? Alyson was no place to be caught; a dead end town, complete with graveyard. If he ran, the mountains would give him no help. The only people that had ever survived up there, the mountain men, had died out over a hundred years ago. The sheriff had been born and raised here; if anyone knew the country he did ... but even he wouldn't go up there alone. Wynter would have no hope, and he knew it. The only way out of Alyson was the road. He turned his head and looked at the fading evening light through the open door at the end of the corridor. Two questions were on his mind: would the Kontakis brothers ever head along that road; and if they did ... when?

"Take as much time as you like," said the sheriff. "Ain't as if we're going anywhere."

Wynter forced a smile. Jeb Swayne would have new tires on the pick-up tomorrow. He quickly turned things over in his mind and came to a decision: he'd give it forty eight hours. If the sheriff hadn't shown any interest in Uncle Andrew's box by then, he probably wasn't going to. After that, Wynter thought it would be prudent to wave Alyson goodbye and head off down the road. Much as it hurt him to leave poker winnings, he would just have to write that five thousand dollars off. Staying ahead of the game meant staying alive.

***

Hellman eased the Jaguar into the last empty parking space in front of the Civic Centre. On the sidewalks tourists jostled with the city's workforce heading back to their offices after lunch. It was a good time to make an unannounced visit to the City's Head of Planning, as Security would be preoccupied checking staff passes. Hellman strode towards the wide service entrance ramp leading down to the basement car park. He reckoned that people only got stopped if they looked nervous, but he was still thankful when there were no signs of security this side of the elevator. America believed it was invulnerable. Terrorism only happened in other countries.

The elevator's amber light counted off the floors as Hellman ascended to the fourth, where Phil Kauffman had his office. The doors opened and Hellman stepped out into a wide, carpeted corridor. Assuming that anyone on the fourth floor had been cleared by the screening process down at the entrance, security guards were notable only by their absence.

Hellman didn't bother to knock. As he pushed open the paneled oak door marked Head of City Planning, Jenny Bryan, Kauffman's PA, was running a brush through her hair, having returned from lunch a few minutes before.

"Hi Jenny, is he in?" said Hellman, as he marched

towards the door at the end of the office.

"Mister Hellman, you can't …" Jenny put down her brush and started from behind the desk, attempting to halt his progress. "He's not …" but she was too late. Hellman grasped the door handle and pushed. Seeing Kauffman, he turned back to Jenny and smiled.

"Oh yes he is."

"I'm sorry, Mister Kauffman," said Jenny as she stood at the open door, "but …"

"It's OK Jenny. Mister Hellman has a pushy personality," said Phil Kauffman, looking down at his desk with an inward sigh. Giving a quick scowl in Hellman's direction, Jenny closed the door and went back to brushing her hair.

Hellman didn't sit down, but strolled over to the window and looked out over the Plaza.

"You've got a problem."

"I work for the City, Hellman, I don't have problems."

"You've got a problem, Kauffman, because I've got a problem."

"Still looking for your bay site?"

Hellman nodded. "I need that site."

"And I've told you we don't have one. Not the size you want."

Hellman kept staring out of the window. "You still aren't listening. I *need* that site."

"You *need* some manners."

"Four acres on the Bay, Kauffman, that's what I want. And you're going to find it for me."

"Sure, I'll speak to God; see if he can rustle it up. What would you prefer; an island or a peninsula?"

Hellman turned from the window and faced Kauffman. "I don't think you realize who you're dealing with."

"And I'm beginning to think you don't understand English. There. Are. No. Sites."

Hellman gave Kauffman a long, hard stare. "I'm pretty certain my client will react badly if I tell him that."

"Well, I guessed there had to be someone," said Kauffman as he gave a shrug of indifference. "You haven't got the sort of money for a bay site, even if there was one … which there isn't!"

"Then it's time you found one, or started putting one together."

"Yeah?"

"I *mean* it."

Kauffman settled back in his chair, fiddled with a pencil, and gave a little smile. "Your client scares you, doesn't he?"

"He'd scare you too, if you had any sense."

"So, who is he? And don't talk to me about any of the neighborhood gangs; they're just mindless thugs with drugs: wouldn't know what to do with a site like that, even if they owned it." He shook his head. "There's no-one left in the city with that kind of muscle and the political pull to make it work. Believe me, I'd know. We aren't that corrupt … not anymore."

"He's not in the city; he's up in Marin County."

Kauffman frowned, "Marin County?"

Hellman nodded, leaned over the desk and whispered

101

Van Buren's name. Kauffman froze and stared back in silence. He hadn't heard that name spoken in almost ten years.

"I thought he was dead."

Hellman slowly shook his head. "Very much alive."

***

The evening found the sheriff standing on the boardwalk outside of his office, deep in thought. He really didn't want to upset Harriet, but he didn't want to miss out on an opportunity either. It was a difficult situation. He was, after all, the County Sheriff, and what Sir Wynter had admitted to was illegal, no doubt about that. The Federal authorities didn't take kindly to people making their own money, even if it was of a high quality.

On the other hand, Sir Wynter could just be spinning everyone's wheels. He hadn't mentioned it again, and they'd had a good laugh about it at the time; even the dog had joined in. It could all be a big joke: part of that famous English sense of humor. But there had been something in the Englishman's manner that made the sheriff doubt that. Sir Wynter had never pressed the point; never protested it had been true; never insisted about anything. He had just told the story and let it lie there, like a rattlesnake on a rock in the morning sun. And like a rattlesnake you had to take notice of it. The fact it was there gnawed away at you, until you had to go back and check on it.

Question was … what to do about it? He didn't want Sir Wynter to get the idea that he was being pushed: a little finesse was called for. After all, Sir Wynter had met the Queen.

***

In the hotel, Harriet sat at the long kitchen table listening to the young geologist. His long, sandy colored hair made him look like a fugitive from an Irish heavy metal band. Not that Harriet knew any Irish heavy metal bands. He also had a habit of running his fingers through his hair, clasping his hands behind his head, and leaning back after saying something which he thought was important.

"Operation Bernhard was all to do with counterfeit money," said the geologist.

"Your friend knows this for sure?"

The geologist nodded. "He's going to check a couple of small details with Professor Grant, but take it from me, Tom is never wrong on something like this. It's his area."

Harriet nodded her head, satisfied by the explanation. She listened intently as the Nazi plot to flood England with fake currency was retold; much the same way as Rufus had told it to her; the way that Wynter had told it to him. She got up from the table and walked over to where the percolator sat on the worktop.

"I'm going to put some fresh coffee on. I'd be real obliged if you'd stay while I ring the Sheriff so he can come and listen to what you've just told me."

"Sure," said the geologist, smiling. "Cost you a raid on the cookie jar."

Harriet picked up the cookie jar and smiled as she put it

on the table in front of him.

"Help yourself," she said, as she walked over to the telephone, picked up the receiver and dialed. It was a while before the call was answered. She had grown used to waiting for Rufus.

"I'm just going to make some fresh coffee, and the cookie jar is open. Oh, we've got an answer to your question … I think you should come over."

Chapter 8

The early morning sun was shining through the kitchen window and Harriet was sitting at the table drinking her second cup of coffee when the sheriff appeared in the doorway.

"You were up early."

"Place don't run itself, Rufus. Anyway, you were twisting and turning like a raccoon in a cage."

"Didn't wake you, did I?"

"Couldn't rightly say you did, seeing as I never really got to sleep in the first place."

"You should have woken me," said the Sheriff, scratching himself.

"I gave up trying." She refilled her mug. "You want coffee?"

"Yeah," said the Sheriff. He sat down at the long table, yawned and watched as she poured coffee into his mug. Rufus considered whether he should sympathize over her sleepless night, but thought better of it. If he was the cause then least said the better; best not antagonize her.

Harriet picked up the two mugs, walked over to the table and sat down. They both took a sip of coffee and looked at each other in silence. Just as the heat was building outside, tension was rising between them. They both knew they were going to have to talk about it sooner or later, and Harriet wondered if she should get in first. Not that it would make any difference in the long run; but she might just feel better for having her say.

"I won't visit you," she said, taking another sip of coffee. "You know that, don't you."

Rufus frowned, "Visit me?"

"In the State Penitentiary."

"Hell, Harriet, you won't have to. If what Sir Wynter says is true, no-one will know the difference."

She gave a little disbelieving grunt. "What if he don't want to sell it?"

"I think he will."

"Why?"

"Because he'll want to get out of jail."

***

Lance was writing a report, and struggling to remember if parallel had a double 'l', when the door opened and Meredith walked in.

"Ah, you'll know ... parallel: how many 'l's?"

"Three," said Meredith. Lance frowned. "Double 'l' and a single one at the end," she explained.

"Thanks."

"I think we've got a lead on the Englishman."

"Yeah ...?" said Lance, looking up.

"Chicago. Very recently someone sounding very much

like him sold stock in a silver mine to a couple of strip club owners."

"Really? A mine … in Chicago?"

"The mine isn't in Chicago, Lance; not even in Illinois. In fact it doesn't exist. Only thing that *did* exist was the two hundred and fifty thousand dollars that Mike Kontakis parted with for the stock."

Lance gave a low whistle. "That's serious money."

"I told you the Englishman was good. Apparently Mike Kontakis and his brother Milo don't like being made fools of the month, and they're turning Chicago inside out looking for him."

"Yeah," said Lance, nodding, "they would."

"This in turn upset the Chicago PD. They don't like competition - if anyone's going to turn Chicago upside down it should be them. So they picked up one of Mike's strippers, and gently enquired what was going on."

"I'll bet they did," said Lance with a grin.

"It turned out that a French Canadian named Bourdin and an accomplice pulled the sting, then both of them disappeared, leaving Mike Kontakis screaming blue murder."

"The police are looking for this guy Bourdin?"

Meredith shook her head. "Kontakis hasn't made a complaint - guess he's too embarrassed - so officially the police don't know about it."

"Bourdin's a French name. How do you know it's the Englishman?"

"He's used the name once before, five years ago in

Cincinnati; guess he thought it was safe to use it again. I spoke to the Cincinnati PD and they sent a photo fit picture of Bourdin. It's a close match to the description given by the stripper. I think it's him."

"So where is he now? asked Lance.

"I'm following up on it, but I think it's safe to say he's left Chicago."

***

A shaft of morning sunlight darted through the door at the end of the corridor, throwing the chess pieces into relief against the shadows of the board. Chess, however, had lost its interest for the sheriff as he stood waiting for a reply.

"I'm not sure it's what Uncle Andrew would have wanted," said Wynter.

"I'd just want to look."

"Well," Wynter sighed, "I don't know. I promised Uncle Andrew …"

"Meaning no disrespect, Sir Wynter; but your Uncle Andrew is dead. He ain't wanting anything no-more."

"True enough, but …"

"Just looking can't do no harm, can it?"

The Englishman took a deep breath and closed his eyes as he savored the moment. The sheriff had swallowed the bait. All that was left was to reel him in and take the money. Wynter opened his eyes and sighed. "I guess not. Not now I've told you about it."

The sheriff did his best to suppress a broad grin. "I knew you'd see it my way, Sir Wynter. Now, how long would it take to get Uncle Andrew's box here if you sent for it now?"

"Not long."

"A couple of days … a week?" said the sheriff, looking like a hopeful dog.

Wynter shook his head. "About five minutes."

The sheriff's jaw dropped. "You got it here?"

"You don't think I'd leave it lying around, do you?"

"Well no, but …"

"It's in my pick-up."

The sheriff shook his head in disbelief. "I thought it would at least be in a bank - for safekeeping."

Wynter smiled. The irony of keeping a counterfeiting machine in a bank vault amused him. "No, nothing so complicated. Besides, I never know when I might need it."

"Reckon that's true enough," said the sheriff.

There was a silence, then Wynter gave a long sigh, and, he hoped, the impression of fighting his non-existent conscience. "Well … I suppose we could go and get it."

Leading the way out of the jail, the sheriff crossed the square to the dusty, red pick-up. Handing the keys to Wynter, the sheriff stood back as Wynter opened the truck door. He then slid the driver's seat as far forward as it would go, picked up a screwdriver from the door pocket, and undid the four self-tapping screws that secured a piece of the floor. Removing the metal plate revealed a small compartment just over a foot square and almost as deep. Wynter removed a cloth covered package, screwed the metal plate back in place, and moved the seat back to its original position. Re-locking the door, they returned to the jail with Wynter carrying the package.

The sheriff lowered the blinds of the office, then turned and watched as Wynter put the package on the desk and started to remove the cloth wrapping. Made of polished mahogany, the box was almost a foot square and about nine inches deep. The craftsman who made it had had enough pride in his work to cut a decorative moulding round the top, and to add a similar one to the simple plinth. There were four different sized dials, with varying marks and numbers around their circumference, taking up most of one side. A brass-edged slot, wide enough to take currency bills, was positioned towards the bottom of the adjacent side. Two spring clips held a six inch brass and mahogany handle on the top of the box, and in one corner was a brass cap which unscrewed to allow chemicals to be poured inside. Finally, on the side opposite the dials, a brass-rimmed hole awaited the insertion of the handle.

The sheriff stood and gazed at it in reverential silence. A machine that made money - the Holy Grail. He sighed and nodded his head in appreciation as he ran his fingertips over the polished mahogany and brass of Uncle Andrew's box.

"Sure is a fancy piece of work. Craftsman-made too, I'd guess."

"Uncle Andrew commissioned it especially," nodded Wynter. "Solomon and Carter - best cabinet makers in London."

"London," said the sheriff, and let out a low whistle. He slipped his fingers under the moulding running around the top and gently lifted the box. He was surprised at the weight. "Good and solid too."

"Oh, it's solid, I promise you. No plastic or chrome for Uncle Andrew."

"Impressive, Sir Wynter, impressive. Not really what I had in mind, but …"

In truth, he hadn't really known what to expect; something more like a printing press for sure. But then, he'd never seen a machine that reproduced money. It was certainly smaller than he'd imagined, with none of the switches, wires and lights he'd felt it would need. But then, the Germans were a practical race; they didn't go in for all the razzle-dazzle that attracted the American eye. As he gazed at it, the sheriff reckoned the combination of German reliability and fine old English craftsmanship was just about as good as you were going to get. It was a piece of art: very subtle; very English; very old school. It reflected Sir Wynter to perfection.

"You were expecting something a little more modern, perhaps? Something in a garish plastic, or imitation leather?" said Wynter. "Why bother with an understated Rolls Royce, when you can have a flashy Cadillac?"

Wynter enjoyed prodding the American feeling of inferiority when it came to class and the nobility of the Old World. It had to be subtle, just enough to unbalance. He was well aware that however much the sheriff might admire the suave confidence of the English aristocrat, he would play second fiddle to no-one.

"Ain't nothing wrong with a Caddy, Sir Wynter," said the sheriff. "I daresay plenty of folks in England would like one. And all you've done so far is show me a fancy box".

"A box that's made me a rich man."

"So you say. For all I know, you could be showing me a skunk and calling it a mountain lion," said the sheriff, aiming to antagonize Wynter into giving him a demonstration of the box.

"Believe me, sheriff, it's a mountain lion."

The sheriff looked him straight in the eye and shook his head. One final push and he was there. "Telling ain't enough."

Wynter smiled. The last thrash on the end of the line, the last bit of fight - they all did it. That's when he knew he'd won.

"Will a demonstration convince you?"

It was the sheriff's turn to smile. He thought that he'd played his hand well. Not only had he made Sir Wynter show him the box, he had forced him into giving a demonstration. All that was left was to persuade him to sell it.

***

In his office on the fourth floor of City Hall, Phil Kauffman spoke, but didn't look up as he heard the door open.

"I know, Jenny, I'm going to be late for the meeting …"

"Jenny already knows …"

Kauffman looked up and was surprised to see Hellman walking towards him.

"… She's ringing through to say you're going to be even later" continued Hellman, "on account of having an important visitor."

Kauffman gave a weary sigh. "That won't make the mayor any happier."

Hellman smiled. "Perhaps this might cheer him up. I think I've got the answer to your little problem."

Kauffman took a deep breath. "It's your problem, not mine."

"Fort Mason, on the north shore … up by the Marina."

"I know where it is."

"Then you'll know there are a lot of old buildings up there. And space - lots of grass and trees."

"It's a park," said Kauffman, nodding. "It's also a National Landmark - part of the country's history."

"The buildings are looking a little run-down, I was just up there. They need repair and a lot of maintenance."

Kauffman shook his head. "You haven't a hope."

"The city's got other, more important things it should spend its money on, like police, and schools. I can help you there, Kauffman. I could get a maintenance team up to Fort Mason next week. Co-operate, and we can build you a brand new state-of-the-art theatre, and a restaurant; perhaps even an art gallery … a new cultural complex to replace some of the crap that's up there now. A city development you could be proud of. Get your architect to draw up some ideas, tell him to make it memorable. A design that doesn't look too much like a converted warehouse - there are enough of those up there already."

"And …?"

"And?" shrugged Hellman.

"And what would you want in return?"

"We'd just want three acres of the park ... for our project."

"Hellman, you aren't listening are you? It's a *National* Landmark. The President himself couldn't get permission to build there."

Hellman gazed at Kauffman in silence. His neck muscles began to tighten.

"Since when has the city been so rich it can afford to turn down offers from well-meaning benefactors?" He leaned forward on the desk and looked Kauffman straight in the eye. "Since when have you been so sure of your job that you can lay down the law?"

"Are you threatening me?" The vein in Kauffman's temple began to throb. It hadn't been a good day and the last thing he needed was Hellman attempting to play tough.

"Take it as you like," said Hellman.

"I don't like," said Kauffman, standing up. By now he was visibly angry. "You're being bank-rolled by a psychopath. How long do you think *you're* going to last?"

Hellman straightened up. "Think about what I said. Tell the mayor. He might have a different take on the idea ... especially if we offer to name it after him."

"You could name it after the Governor, and it still wouldn't help. Now get this through your thick head, Hellman - there is no site, and will be no site."

Hellman gave one last stare across the desk, then turned and walked towards the door. He turned back before opening it.

"Mister Van Buren won't take this well, Kauffman.

Especially when I tell him that you're personally holding up his scheme."

Hellman slammed the door behind him, leaving Kauffman grinding his teeth.

***

Meredith hurried down the corridor hoping that she'd find Lance still in his office. Opening his door, she breathed a sigh of relief to see her assistant still behind his desk. She closed the door behind her before she spoke.

"Whatever you were doing tonight, cancel it. In fact, you can forget anything for the next few days."

"Why?" asked Lance.

"We're taking a trip."

"To Chicago," smiled Lance.

Meredith shook her head. "A few days ago a County Sheriff from a remote part of Oregon put out a general enquiry. Were there any warrants outstanding or, more particularly, rewards offered for an Englishman called Wynter?"

They looked at each other for a couple of seconds in silence.

"How do you know it's him?" said Lance.

"The description fits the photo fit of Bourdin."

"Might not be him: a lot of Englishmen on the West Coast."

"It's him, Lance, I know it." She leaned over the desk. "The Sheriff also described him as an English aristocrat … and a card sharp. It's got to be him."

"What's he doing up in Oregon?"

Meredith shrugged. "How should I know? ... Getting a good distance from Chicago? Upsetting a County Sheriff?"

"Is he still there?"

Meredith nodded. "I just rang the Sheriff and said I was a Deputy from the San Francisco PD. Pretended that I was looking for a George Winter from Australia. The Sheriff wasn't too impressed that I had miss-spelt Wynter's name - I used an *i* instead of a *y* - that, and the fact that my geography was way off. I got the impression he's got issues with women being in the Police Department."

"But he's still holding Wynter?"

"Yes," nodded Meredith, glancing up at the clock on the wall. "I want you to go home, pack an overnight bag, and I'll pick you up in an hour. We're going to collect him."

"What about Tobin and Boles?"

"Tobin is taking the evening flight to Washington; he'll be there three or four days. Boles won't make a move without Tobin. It's too good an opportunity to miss."

Lance gave a little smile and slowly nodded his head

"Good," said Meredith as she moved to the door. "And don't tell *anyone* where you're going."

Meredith closed the door after her, leaving a puzzled Lance. How could he tell anyone when he didn't know where he was going himself?

Chapter 9

Wynter pulled out his wallet and selected a crisp, new hundred dollar bill. He moved one of the dials three clicks to the right and pushed the flat note into the brass slot in the end of the box. As he did so, he turned the handle and cranked the note inside, the Sheriff watching his every move like a red-tailed hawk. After the note was safely inside, Wynter pushed a small button on the side of the box and the plinth on the end opposite the slot sprang open revealing a secret drawer.

"Well, I'll …" said the sheriff.

"It's where I keep the paper," smiled Wynter as he took a piece of perfectly sized blank paper from the drawer. "Success lies in using the right materials. The paper has to be high rag content or it just doesn't feel right."

"Where d'you get it?" asked the sheriff, prompting Wynter to look up. "Just as a matter of interest," he added, softening his tone.

"From the U.S. Treasury."

The sheriff frowned then his face burst into a grin. "You're joking, right?"

"No," said Wynter shaking his head. "No joke."

"I don't believe it. The Treasury ain't going to send you their special paper so you can print your own bank notes."

"Not only do they supply me, they'll supply you, too."

The sheriff's grin grew wider. "Now I know you're lying."

Wynter said nothing but took out his wallet, opened it and selected four different denomination bank notes. He laid them on the table. "See any similarities?"

The sheriff studied the bills thinking it was a trick question then turned to Wynter. "No."

"Look again."

The sheriff looked again, unsure of what he was looking for.

"OK," said Wynter after a pause. "What have they got in common?"

The baffled sheriff stared at the portraits of Washington, Jackson, Grant and Franklin. Eventually he looked up and shook his head. Wynter picked up the fifty dollar bill and placed it on the hundred dollar bill. He then put the twenty dollar bill on the fifty dollar bill, and rounded it off by placing the dollar bill on the top of the pile. He looked at the puzzled sheriff.

"Size. All US Treasury bills are the same size." The sheriff still missed the significance of this statement until Wynter explained. "Bleach the ink from a one dollar bill, and this machine will turn it into a hundred dollar bill. Even the head of the Treasury wouldn't be able to tell the difference."

"Well I'll be …"

The sheriff stood there and watched spellbound as Wynter carefully adjusted the dials then fed the blank paper into the machine.

"Do you have a little water? I need it to start the chemical reaction."

The sheriff nodded, picked up his mug and rinsed it out with water from the jug on the side. Half filling the mug, he brought it back to Wynter.

"This do you?"

"Fine," said Wynter, taking the mug and pouring a few drops into the hole on top of the box.

"That's all it needs?"

Wynter nodded. "All it has to do is activate the chemicals already in there."

Screwing the cap back on, he then made great play of moving the dials and lining up markers. Finally satisfied, he flicked one of the switches between two of the dials up, and the other switch down.

"OK … now we wait."

"For how long?"

Wynter looked at his watch. "Takes a few hours for the process to work, so eight o'clock should do it."

Despite what people think, time is elastic. The more you're enjoying yourself, the faster time slips away. The more you want something, the longer it takes to arrive. In all his fifty-odd years, if the sheriff had spent a longer few hours he couldn't remember them. Sitting in his office, he divided his time between staring at the polished box on his desk and glancing at the clock on the wall.

Occasionally he would get up and go for a walk around the church, calling in to see Harriet on the way. Mostly he just sat and watched - his mind a whirr of mathematics. He had calculated and re-calculated a hundred times: a hundred dollars every four hours. Allowing time for sleep, that was five hundred dollars a day. That was over three thousand dollars a week: about fourteen thousand a month; more than one hundred and fifty thousand a year. Almost ten times his annual salary.

If this box worked … he wanted it … he wanted it real bad.

***

After setting the box to its work, Wynter had retired to the cell and lay on the bed. The old dog was flopped on the wooden floor. It was hot, and a fan blew cooling air over both of them. Wynter looked up at the heavy beamed roof with a smile on his face, confident that he'd won.

At eight o'clock, the box would produce two identical notes. What the sheriff didn't know was that they were part of a thousand dollar withdrawal that Wynter had made at a bank in Chicago a month previously. The cashier had indulged his request for new and consecutive notes. Later, Wynter had taken two of these notes, one whose number ended in three while the other note ended in eight. Working skillfully, he inked the three to make an eight. To all intents and purposes, he now had two identical notes. One of these he secreted in Uncle Andrew's box; the other he kept in his wallet.

It was time to hit upon a price that he thought seemed reasonable, and one that the sheriff would pay, bearing in mind that being a County Sheriff in the back of beyond wasn't the highest paid job in Oregon. He didn't want to frighten him by asking too much, but then again, he didn't want to appear too cheap. After all, he was offering a lifetime of financial security. He also wanted his poker winnings back. All things considered, he thought twenty thousand dollars sounded about right - with a little leeway for bargaining. Given the sheriff's admitted habit of taking a skim off the top of fines and pocketing what he called *'County expenses'*, he reckoned that he'd be able to find that sort of money without looking too hard.

The old dog sneezed. Wynter stretched down a hand and stroked its head, setting off a train of rhythmic bumps as a tail wagged against the wooden floor. Should he leave tonight if the sheriff bought the box? It would give him a better start and get him a day further away from the Kontakis brothers. On the other hand, it would mean travelling through the night, and the day's heat had already drained him of energy. He'd feel even worse later, and these mountain roads weren't a place to fall asleep. No, he decided it was best to leave it until the morning. Besides, the sheriff might want to have a Bank check the notes over. In fact, it would be worth suggesting that to him.

***

Patience wasn't a virtue. It could be extremely trying, as the sheriff was finding out. He watched as the minute hand dawdled its way around the dial until it was vertical, checked his watch, then strode to the window to check the church tower. It was eight o'clock. Time was up. Give it one more minute to make sure. Did Sir Wynter know that time was up? Was he going to come in, or was he expecting to be collected? The sheriff didn't want to appear too eager. He pulled his handkerchief from his pocket: his skin was damp with sweat. The extra minute was up - no sign of Sir Wynter. The church clock struck the hour. He must have heard that; must know the time was up. No sound from the cell. Sir Wynter might have the patience of a saint, but the sheriff didn't.

He pushed open the bars of the cell door.

"Think your machine's finished working yet, Sir Wynter?"

Wynter opened his eyes and looked at his watch. "Sheriff, is that really the time? I had no idea." He rubbed his eyes, yawned and swung his legs off the bed. "Shall we go and have a look?" Wynter stood up and held out a hand to indicate that the sheriff should lead the way. The old dog followed them both.

Wynter bent over the machine and looked closely at the dials then nodded his head in satisfaction. He flicked the two switches and stood back.

"Well, Sheriff, this is an historic moment. You are about to witness what very few people have ever been privileged to see: a machine duplicating money." He looked over at the sheriff, who, by now had beads of nervous perspiration standing on his forehead. "You alright?" asked Wynter "you look a little overheated there".

"I'm fine, Sir Wynter, really I am," rasped the sheriff hoarsely as he mopped his brow.

Wynter grasped the handle and wound it slowly backwards. As he did so, two, wet hundred dollar bills snaked their way out of the brass slot in the end of the box. The sheriff couldn't help but give a little whistle. Wynter separated them and held one in each hand for examination.

"As the good Book says, Sheriff, *'Go forth and multiply'*."

Trying to control his excitement, the sheriff took his time and gave both notes a thorough examination. After putting them between two sheets of blotting paper to remove most of the moisture, he turned them over, felt the paper, held them up to the light and, using a magnifying glass he'd taken from his desk drawer, scrutinized the detail. As far as he could see, everything had been transferred, even down to the fine little lines and letters. They both seemed perfect. The sheriff gave a little smile. The box worked, just like Sir Wynter said it would: it duplicated money. Trying to conceal his mounting euphoria, he looked up.

"They sure both look good. Which is the genuine one?"

"They both are," said Wynter, smiling. "Keep one ... as a memento."

"And if I pick the wrong one, and get arrested for counterfeiting?"

"You won't, but if you're that worried, why not take them to a bank and get them verified? I'm sure any bank would be happy to oblige."

"I might just do that."

"Better make that different banks, or you could get arrested."

"Eh?"

"The serial number's the same on both notes."

The sheriff checked the numbers. "Right … that'll be a trip to Prineville then; nearest place with two banks. Closed now anyway," said the sheriff, glancing up at the church clock. "Have to wait 'til morning."

"Okay," said Wynter. "You better hang on to the notes 'til then."

"Is this the only machine your uncle made?"

Wynter nodded. "He thought that one of these machines was all the world could take." A wave of disappointment passed over the sheriff's face. "Of course, he left me all the plans and specifications."

"So, you could make another?"

"I suppose I could, but would that be wise? Two machines?" said Wynter. "They could draw unwelcome attention."

"Only thing that draws unwelcome attention up here is a grizzly bear," said the sheriff. "What if you were to sell me that box, and make yourself another?"

"Oh, I don't know about that," said Wynter, shaking his head. "You could show it to people; word might get out; the authorities might get interested. I don't think that's a good idea."

"I ain't about to show it to no-one, so nobody would talk about it. Anyway, who'd they tell up here?"

"Well …"

"Not many people know this place, and even fewer find

it. Take a look around - see anything you'd want to spend money on?" Wynter had to admit the sheriff had a point. "You know I'm a careful man, Sir Wynter; I'm not a braggart and I don't shout my mouth off. I'd make sure I went to Portland or Vancouver to spend any money I made. I truly wouldn't draw any attention to myself."

The sheriff paused, waiting for the Englishman to say something, but Wynter didn't oblige.

"God knows it would sure help Harriet, too," continued the sheriff. "This place is real hard on her." He paused, sighed and then looked Wynter straight in the eye. "Now, what d'you say?"

This was the point in every successful con that Wynter savored, the point where the target was begging to be conned: just begging to give away his money. Wynter wished he could capture it and put it in a jar so he could enjoy it at leisure.

"I'd never thought about making another box until now," said Wynter. "It's not something that's crossed my mind."

"I can understand that."

"I've never shown this box to anyone else, you know that."

"I feel privileged, Sir Wynter, real privileged."

"I suppose I *could* make another one."

The sheriff nodded. "You said you got all the plans for it."

"But ... Uncle Andrew ..."

"I don't think he would have made one in the first place

if he didn't want to see them in the world."

"I hadn't looked at it that way, Sheriff," conceded Wynter. "And Harriet: running a hotel up here has to be tough."

"It surely is."

Wynter took a deep breath, and hoped that he gave the impression of an inward struggle with his conscience. After twenty seconds of some mild facial contortions and thoughtful head movements, he started nodding his head. "If I said twenty thousand dollars, how would that sound?"

"Well …"

"I don't suppose it really matters, does it? You'll be able to make it back quickly enough."

The expression on his face told Wynter that the sheriff was happy enough, but was struggling to keep his feelings hidden in the hope of negotiating a better price.

"Would fifteen be enough? It's all I can lay my hands right now."

Bearing in mind the uncomfortable proximity of Three Fingers and his friends, plus the Kontakis brothers were likely scouring the region for him, and the fact that no-one else was offering him anything at all, made Wynter decide that fifteen thousand dollars in exchange for one hundred and fifty dollars worth of mahogany and brass was an offer he couldn't refuse. But to make his mental struggle look authentic he pulled a few more faces and sucked in his breath a couple of times. Then, finally, he relented.

"Alright, fifteen thousand - in cash."

The sheriff let out an audible sigh of relief. "As long as

the bank passes these two notes, I'll give you fifteen thousand in cash tomorrow."

"And let me leave town," added Wynter.

"And let you leave town. Now, why don't you show me how to set those dials."

Chapter 10

Wynter lay on the bed with his hands behind his head gazing up at the ceiling. There was little else he could do. The sheriff had marched him over from the hotel after breakfast at gun-point and said that he'd have to lock him in the cell while he was away checking on the bank notes. His brother would sit out front while he was away to discourage Three Fingers from starting anything. Just look on it as an extension of protective custody, the sheriff had said.

It was plausible enough; the sheriff was leaving town and didn't feel inclined to leave Wynter wandering around town while he was away. The Englishman might get the idea that he didn't want to wait for the sheriff's return, take the box, and decide to take off. Wynter had to admit that had crossed his mind, but the more he thought about it, the more he realized it would be a mistake. He wouldn't have enough of a head start, and the sheriff could quite legitimately put out an APB to have him arrested for breaking out of custody. That APB would follow him around the country until it caught up with him. No; best let it ride and stay where he was. Besides, the sheriff was coming back to give him fifteen thousand dollars.

His thoughts were interrupted by the sound of the door to the sheriff's office being opened and Harriet appeared carrying a mug of coffee. Wynter got up off the bed and stood up as she offered him the coffee through the bars.

"I ain't got the keys, so it'll do you no good to grab me."

"I wasn't going to," said Wynter.

"Rufus swears by that old coffee pot and just adding water and re-heating it. I thought you'd like some fresh."

"Very thoughtful of you, Harriet … thanks."

She stepped back from the bars.

"Is your conscience troubling you, Sir Wynter?"

It was not a question he was expecting and he took a sip of coffee to cover his confusion.

"I don't think so. Should it?" Wynter said, as he studied Harriet's face, trying to work out her intentions.

"Well, mine's troubling me."

Harriet looked at Wynter intently, searching his eyes for any clue as to whether he was lying.

"You see, I can believe you're a 'Sir'; I can believe your family lost their land; I can even believe that the Nazi printed all that money during the war." Harriet stared more intently. "But I just don't believe you've got a box that makes money."

Wynter shrugged his shoulders, "Well, it's up to you. The Sheriff is down in Prineville getting the bank to verify the notes at this moment."

"… And he'll come back with a great big grin on his face waving the banknotes, saying they're genuine. I don't know how you did it; but you've fooled him." Harriet sighed.

"That ain't nothing to brag about, mind," she continued. "It don't take a lot to fool Rufus where money's concerned. Especially when he thinks some is coming his way."

"Harriet, I would hate you to think that I …"

"… Rufus is a stubborn man, Sir Wynter. Once he's made his mind up about something he'll see it through. And he's made up his mind about this money box."

"I'm sure he talked it over with you."

"D'you think anything I say would stop him?" Harriet looked away and sighed. "He's never listened to me where money's concerned."

She looked up at Wynter, who noticed a stiffening of her jaw.

"The only reason I don't call the FBI over your money box, Sir Wynter, is that I'm afraid Rufus would end up in prison with you."

***

Hellman stared out of his office window and across the roofs at the distant north tower of the Golden Gate. Perched on the Marin County side of the bay, its peculiar orange color appeared to glow as it reached up into the clouds. The weather also cast its gloom over Hellman as he reflected that building another bridge across the bay, with all its engineering challenges, would be easier than finding a few of acres in San Francisco.

Relaxing into his high-backed executive chair, he let his mind run loose down hitherto unexplored avenues. What if he'd been looking through the wrong end of the telescope?

Simply because Kauffman was the head of the city's Planning Department didn't mean he was the man who could make things happen. Planners said no to everything as a reflex action, in Hellman's experience. Maybe it was time to try a different approach. When playing by the rules didn't work, you could either change the rules … or change the game.

Might it be time to go political and investigate the price of some of the city's more pliable councilors? It could be worth sounding out the State Government too. The support of a few members of the Assembly and State Senate wouldn't go amiss. It would hardly be the first time the well trodden path of corruption had led to the State Capitol.

Hellman pressed the intercom button on the speakerphone. His secretary's disembodied voice answered.

"Yes, Mister Hellman."

"Get me Senator Reece, and I mean the Senator. Not his PA, not his public relations man … the Senator."

"Yes, Mister Hellman."

Hellman released the button with a satisfied smile. He'd found Hogan Reece to be very reasonable in past dealings. An approachable man, Hogan was a good listener and sympathetic to voters' problems. Pass him an envelope stuffed full with hundred dollar bills and he could even become accommodating.

***

As the sheriff got out of the pick-up and walked over to his office, that nagging thought came back to him: perhaps he should have left the cell open; perhaps he should have given

131

Wynter the opportunity to leave town. It might have been the better option: it would have saved fifteen thousand dollars. But then the drive home had made up his mind; it didn't really matter because he wasn't about to hand over that kind of money anyway. Not to an Englishman.

The sheriff pushed the door open and walked into his office. Taking his keys from his pocket, he unlocked the deep, bottom drawer of his desk. Taking out the box, he put it on the desktop and gave it a little parental stroke: wasn't every day a man got to make his own money. Pouring himself the dregs from the flask of coffee Harriet had made for his trip, he grasped the door handle, and went through to see Wynter.

"Behave yourself while I was away?" said the sheriff, grinning.

"What else was I going to do?" said Wynter, sitting up.

"That's what I like to hear, acceptance of the inevitable." The sheriff produced the two, hundred dollar bills. "The banks say they're good."

"They would."

"Went over them with a magnifying glass."

"I told you, can't tell them from the real thing. To all intents and purposes, they are the real thing."

"That's one hell of a machine, Sir Wynter. Sort of thing the Government would give a lot to hear about." Wynter felt his heart rate increase. This isn't what he had been expected at all. He gave a fleeting frown - had the sheriff just being playing him along? Was he going to hand him in for counterfeiting? The sheriff had noticed the slight change that hurried across Wynter's face. "Oh, don't worry yourself; I ain't going to tell the Government." Wynter relaxed a little. "Mind you, being a sworn law officer ... I ought to tell someone."

"Like who?"

"I believe there are people who deal with this sort of thing ... specialists."

Wynter's stomach tensed up again. This wasn't going well. "Specialists" could only mean the Secret Service. The Service had only two missions in life; to protect the President; and to safeguard the currency. They didn't like counterfeiters. Not even people pretending to be counterfeiters. They were tough, and relentless. People the Service prosecuted ended up serving a long stretch in prison. Wynter's mouth was getting dry. This wasn't what he had intended at all.

"You see, Sir Wynter, you got a problem. Actually you've got a few problems, but let's roll them all into one big one. The *box* ... is out here." The sheriff pulled the fifteen thousand dollars out of his pocket. "The *money* ... is out here." He put the roll of banknotes on the chessboard where Wynter could see it and paused to let the situation sink in. "The big problem you've got ... is *you're* in there. And it seems to me that jail ain't the best of places to be if I was to say something ... and my conscience is beginning to worry me real bad."

Wynter began to think that there might be something in the town's water supply that triggered people's consciences. He swallowed hard and found his voice. "But if you did say something, you'd lose the box and a lifetime's supply of money … and you've got to think about Harriet."

"Ahh, Harriet," sighed the sheriff, taking his gun out of its holster and laying it next to the money on the chessboard before he sat down in his old wooden chair. "Harriet," he sighed again. "There you got me. She's *my* little problem. She's why you and I are going to do a little re-negotiating."

"Re-negotiating?"

"Yeah," said the sheriff. "I'm going to make some proposals, and you're going to agree to them."

"Do I have a choice?"

"Well 'course you got a choice, Sir Wynter; it's a free country. General George Washington fought the War of Independence against you English to give us a choice," grinned the sheriff. "You can either agree … or you can stay in jail."

"You can't keep me in jail for ever."

"No, but there's an unsolved murder in Redmond that happened last Fall. Sheriff Lovell down there is still looking for a suspect … reckons it was a drifter. Bet he'd like to get that squared away."

"But I've never been to Redmond," said Wynter, getting alarmed.

"Don't get there much myself these days. Not as quaint as us up here in Alyson. They got a new sheriff's office, and a modern jail with flush toilets; not to mention a fancy new Court House. You'd like it."

Wynter closed his eyes and took a deep breath. "So, what are these proposals?"

The sheriff grinned. "Number one; we forget all about the fifteen thousand dollars." He picked up the money and stuffed it back in his pocket. "That always was just wishful thinking on your part." Wynter watched the notes disappear and gave a quiet sigh. "Two; your Uncle Andrew's box becomes my property, you make it over to me as a gift. You always had it in the back of your mind to do that - didn't you?"

"Then you'll let me out of jail?"

"Three; I'll make another hundred dollar bill. Just to see that I'm doing it right. You can give me the instructions from in there: wouldn't want you disappearing with me not being able to work the box properly. When I got a new hundred dollar bill in my hand, *that's* when I let you out of jail."

"I've told you how to work the machine, Sheriff."

"Let's just say I need to practice."

Wynter's stomach began to tie itself into a knot. This was beginning to turn into a gigantic nightmare. Without secreting a genuine hundred dollar bill in the machine before operating it, all it would produce would be a soggy piece of blank paper, and a very suspicious sheriff. He could probably bluff it out once with the excuse that you didn't follow the instructions properly, but that wouldn't work twice. Twice meant trouble; and trouble meant a choice between Redmond and the Secret Service, neither of which he relished. He decided it was worth an appeal to the sheriff's conscience.

"It's not very Christian, Sheriff, promising a man one thing, then doing another - not very hospitable."

"And it ain't very neighbourly pitching up in a strange

town and trying to walk away with six thousand dollars."

"It was a straight game."

"No such thing as a straight game up here, Sir Wynter. If you weren't cheating, you were the only one at that table who wasn't."

"Nothing was proved … and I ended up in jail. Now, you're going back on an honest deal, and I'm still in jail. Hardly Christian, Sheriff.

"The Lord helps those who help themselves. You might not like it, but I'm just following His teachings."

"You sure? I don't recall reading that in the Bible."

"You might not be familiar with the plain, old Oregon version of the Good Book, Sir Wynter; you being English and an aristocrat. It ain't quite as fancy as your King James version."

It slowly dawned on Wynter that the sheriff's conscience was that of the old frontier; the survival of the fittest; grab what you can, when you can. If you can hold on to it long enough, it becomes yours. Wynter closed his eyes: he felt sick. This was not looking good.

"We're wasting time," said the sheriff. "You want to get out of jail, and I want to try the box. You accept the deal … or shall I ring Sheriff Lovell in Redmond County?"

Faced with the choice between a hard place or a *very* hard place, albeit with flush toilets, Wynter bowed to the inevitable.

"I accept," said Wynter.

He had little choice. At least it bought him a few hours to come up with a plausible reason why the box didn't work.

He didn't want to think of the other option.

The sheriff didn't hear the car draw up. His attention was concentrated on making sure all the dials were set correctly, before he wound the blank paper into the box. Wynter heard it, but he was too busy wrestling with what he hoped would turn out to be a plan to pay it too much mind.

He knew the box wasn't going to work the first time, and he reckoned his best hope was to make the sheriff release him so that he could give the box a thorough checking over before trying again. Once he was out of the cell, then he'd have to take whatever chance came up; grab the sheriff's gun; hit him over the head with the stove's poker; or just make a run for his pick-up and pray that the sheriff would let him go rather than have the hassle of shooting him. After all, he'd got what he wanted and saved himself fifteen thousand dollars - surely enough for one day.

Wynter thought that he might even get a chance to secrete another hundred dollar bill in the machine. That would be the ideal solution, the answer to all his problems. He began to feel slightly better and had even managed to get his stomach under control.

The sheriff was bent over the box, fiddling with one of the dials, when the door to the office opened.

"I thought I put a notice on the door, *Do Not Disturb – County Business*. Can't you folks read? Now go away," said the sheriff, not looking around, his attention still on the box. The visitors didn't move.

In the cell, Wynter froze. Through the open door to the office he could see what the sheriff couldn't. Two people had walked in, two official looking people: regulation black with crisp white shirts. If they weren't government agents, thought Wynter, they were the nearest thing to them this side of Hell. Wynter felt his knees wobble and he sat down on the bed. His stomach was busy churning concrete and he wanted to be sick. The increasing hopes of freedom a couple of minutes before, now turned into the despairing depths of twenty years without parole.

"I thought I told you to go …" the sheriff's voice tailed off as he turned to be confronted by two strangers.

"Sheriff Richards?" asked Meredith.

The sheriff nodded. They looked very official, and until he knew what he was up against, he wasn't about to give any more information than was absolutely necessary.

"Sheriff Rufus Richards, of Alyson County?"

"Yeah."

Meredith held out a folded piece of paper.

"I have a warrant for the arrest of Gerald Wynter."

***

The sheriff studied the warrant. He couldn't recall seeing one quite like it. Federal warrants rarely made it as far as Alyson, and this was the first he'd seen from the Secret Service. As far as he could make out, there was nothing to quibble over; it was all duly sworn and countersigned by a Federal Judge in San Francisco. What *had* surprised him were the agents they'd sent. On reflection he guessed it was only to be expected. They employed women to do just about anything these days; some women even insisted on it.

As Meredith dealt with the sheriff, Lance was looking around the room in disbelief. The old wooden desk, the antiquated stove, the gun rack - the place couldn't have changed in over a hundred years. And what on earth was that wooden box with all the dials on the desk? It might be the nineteen-eighties in the rest of the country, but in this forgotten outpost of Oregon, it was still the eighteen-eighties. He peered through the open door to the cell, half-expecting to see Butch Cassidy sitting there. The sound of the sheriff's voice dragged him back into the present.

"Seems in order," he said, handing the warrant back to Meredith. "You want me to put the cuffs on him for you?"

"I think my colleague can manage that, thank you," said Meredith.

The sheriff nodded. "You aiming to head straight back, or do you want some coffee before you leave? Fresh made last night."

"No thanks," said Lance, in a business-like manner. "We're not here on a day out."

"Has Wynter got any effects?" asked Meredith.

"Effects?"

"Possessions, personal items," said Meredith. The sheriff looked confused. "You know; things you took off him when you arrested him?"

The sheriff shook his head, "Didn't have nothing."

Wynter lifted his head and stared through the open door at the sheriff. Nothing? What about the five thousand dollars he'd won at poker? What about his pick up? What about the box?

The sheriff ran his hand up and down the side of his face a couple of times. "There's a suitcase over at the hotel, I think."

"We'll swing by and pick that up," said Meredith, "anything else?" The sheriff shrugged and shook his head.

"How did he get up here?" asked Lance.

"What d'you mean, up here?"

"Well, I didn't see an airport or bus station, and I don't suppose he walked."

Meredith and Lance waited for the reply in silence. The sheriff sucked breath through clenched teeth as he wrestled with his thoughts.

"Should be a red, Toyota pick-up parked out there," said an English voice from the cell, breaking the silence.

Lance turned and walked over to the window and looked out. "Yeah, still there. You got the keys, sheriff?"

The sheriff gave a snort as he turned and stomped off to a row of keys hanging on nails behind his desk. The pick-up was only three years old; his worn out Ford was coming up twelve.

"Don't see why you need all this fuss. It's safe enough until he comes back."

"That might be a very long time, sheriff. Besides, forensics need to see it. It could be concealing evidence."

Not anymore, thought Wynter. The only evidence was sitting on the sheriff's desk. A thought began to materialize in Wynter's mind.

"Anything else of his you've overlooked?" said Meredith.

The sheriff shook his head. "Nothing comes to mind …"

"What about my fifteen thousand dollars?" said Wynter.

"You didn't have no fifteen thousand dollars when I arrested you," said the sheriff, glaring in the direction of the cell as his face started to turn crimson. Meredith and Lance looked at each other, then they looked at the sheriff. "That's God's honest truth. He didn't have no fifteen thousand," he protested.

"You got any paperwork to back that up?"

"Ain't no paperwork 'cause I didn't take nothing off him."

They all stared at the sheriff in silence. The impasse was solved by Wynter.

"Ask him to turn out his pockets. He was about to release me and give it back just before you showed up."

Wynter was gambling on the fact that the sheriff wasn't going to own up to buying a counterfeiting machine – not to the Secret Service. Besides, Wynter reckoned the sheriff wanted to use it. If the sheriff gave up the money and said nothing about the box, then Wynter reckoned the main evidence against him would stay safely up here in Alyson. No box meant no evidence; no evidence meant no trial; no trial meant no jail sentence. That line of thought helped settle his stomach.

"Well, sheriff?" said Meredith.

"Well what!?" said the sheriff, his face now purple.

"You're getting real wound up for someone telling the truth," said Lance.

"So!?" said the sheriff, almost shouting, "you going to believe him?"

"He called it right about the pick-up," said Meredith.

The sheriff turned and glared at her.

"We'd like to see proof," said Meredith, smiling. "No arguing with proof."

The sheriff didn't move, just stood there, breathing heavily and looking like he was working up to a heart attack.

"Wouldn't do for a County Sheriff to obstruct the United States Secret Service, now, would it?" said Lance.

The sheriff ground his teeth.

"Not a career move I'd make," said Meredith.

This was new territory for the sheriff. Until now, he'd always done the threatening; being on the receiving end wasn't something he enjoyed. Puffing and squirming, he finally thrust his hand into a pocket, pulled out the wad of notes and threw it down on the desk.

"Well … well …" said Meredith. "Anything else he didn't have?"

In the cell, Wynter smiled. He now knew that Uncle Andrew's box was going to stay safely in Alyson.

"No … that's all," said Wynter.

The sheriff opened the desk drawer, took out the old rusty key ring and headed towards the cell.

"I think it's time you took your prisoner and headed on out of town."

He spat the words rather than spoke them as he turned the key and the bars clanged open. He stood at the cell door and glared. If hate had been a weapon, Meredith, Lance and Wynter would have dropped dead on the spot. Lance produced a pair of handcuffs and indicated that Wynter should stand up and hold out his hands. The cuffs locked and Wynter walked out of the cell.

As she gathered up the wad of notes, Meredith looked at the wooden box on the desk. "What *is* that?"

"Nothing for you to worry about," snarled the sheriff.

"It's one of those old fashioned radios," said Wynter as he gave the sheriff a sly grin.

"Surprised this town's even heard of radio," said Lance as he led the way out of the office and onto the square.

The sheriff stood on the boardwalk in front of his office and watched as they escorted Wynter to the car and put him in the back. Meredith stood with her hand on her pistol as Lance looped a thin, steel chain around the cuffs and locked it to a ring in the floor. Then Lance walked to the Toyota pickup, unlocked it, got in and started the engine. Meredith opened the door of the Chevrolet Caprice, looked over at the sheriff and smiled.

"I'd like to thank you for your co-operation, Sheriff."

The sheriff spat into the dust of the town square as the car and pick up pulled away and gathered speed.

Chapter 11

In the middle of the high brick wall a solid wooden gate slowly slid back to reveal the Chevrolet Caprice with Meredith at the wheel. Wynter was sitting in the back seat with his hands folded on his lap, the handcuffs still securing his wrists. The car slowly nosed its way into the service area at the rear of the hotel, and parked by the door that led to the kitchen. The red pick-up followed, and stopped by the refuse bins. Lance got out and joined Meredith, and they got Wynter out of the car. As they led him through the kitchen door the high wooden gate began to slide back, and the service area was isolated from the rest of San Francisco once more.

They walked down a wide corridor and through another door leading to the service lift. The lift stopped at the third floor, and the little procession filed out. Meredith turned left and walked towards a door marked 'Housekeeping'. She removed a card from her pocket, swiped open the door and entered the room. Lance brought up the rear and the door closed behind them.

The room served as an office. The walls were painted a

neutral white, and the furnishings were straight out of a catalogue. A desk with a high-backed swivel chair was behind the desk, with two smaller chairs in front. A cabinet with a coffee machine and two cups on a tray made up the rest of the furniture. There was a second door to the left of the desk that led to another room. A couple of non-descript landscapes relieved the white paint of the walls, and a rug threw a splash of color on the floor. Meredith walked over to the desk and picked up the telephone while Lance removed the handcuffs from Wynter's wrists.

"We're here, Leo … yeah … could you send up some coffee please … three… Thanks." said Meredith, and replaced the receiver.

Lance opened the door to the other room to check it was empty. Wynter flexed his wrists and arms: it had been a long journey. His eyes darted around the room taking in the doors and windows - evaluating possible means of escape.

Meredith saw him surveying the room. "How far do you think you'd get?" she asked.

They stared at each other for a few seconds. This woman paid attention, thought Wynter. Lance closed the connecting door and Wynter carried on rubbing his wrists.

"You've got no money, no ID, and every cop in Frisco would be looking for you within three minutes," continued Meredith. Turning her attention to her attaché case, she put it on the desk and opened it. "You'd be back here within the hour, trust me." She removed a thick file from the case and laid it on the desk.

"Sit down, Mister Wynter; make yourself comfortable."

Lance moved one of the chairs to a position in front of the desk, and with a gesture, she invited him to sit. Wynter hesitated. He'd been arrested a few times before and thrown in a cell. This was the first time he'd been thrown into a hotel. Something wasn't right. He took two paces to the chair and sat down. What did these people want?

Meredith sat down behind the desk while Lance sat on the chair between Wynter and the door.

"Well, Mister Wynter ... you've had quite a career," said Meredith.

Wynter gazed blankly at her, determined not to give anything away.

"To make things easier, we'll drop all your aliases and just use Wynter - less confusing."

She put on a pair of stylish, black framed spectacles and glanced down at a piece of paper that lay on the top of the open file.

"Right, let's start in Trenton. That's where you first appeared on our radar: something to do with an oil delivery, or lack of delivery ... then there was the Becker Organization in Baltimore. We're still not sure how you did that ..."

She reeled off names, places and stings, interspersed with phrases like ... 'that was you, wasn't it?' or 'it had your fingerprints all over it'. A lot of it was guesswork, but it was good, informed guesswork and not far from the truth. Wynter sat and listened, hoping his rising state of shock was not visible. Whoever she was, this woman had done her homework. There were gaps. Some names were missing, as were places, but she'd had him on the radar for a long time.

The police hadn't got even half this much on him - but *she* knew … or guessed. The list finally came up to date.

"… that took care of the Kontakis brothers in Chicago; and then, from what we could see, you were pulling the Romanian Box scam on Sheriff Richards up in Alyson."

She eased back into her supple leather chair, crossed her legs and removed her glasses.

"Congratulations, Mister Wynter. You're good … really, you are."

It was only shock that prevented him from agreeing with her.

There was a knock at the door and Lance got up and answered it. A waiter entered with a tray and placed a coffee pot, three cups and saucers, milk and sugar on the side table.

"Thank you," said Meredith as the waiter put the tray down and moved to the door. He turned as he opened the door and inclined his head in a small bow then disappeared, closing the door behind him. Lance went to the side table.

"How do you take your coffee?" he said to Wynter.

Wynter maintained his silence. Lance put a cup of black coffee on the desk in front of Wynter then followed it with a jug of milk and a few sachets of sugar. He then poured two more for himself and Meredith.

Wynter stared at the coffee, then at Meredith. Say nothing. Let this woman do the talking. So far, she'd come up with a lot of guesswork and a few facts, but those facts were enough to put him away for thirty to forty years: that's if he survived. Prison wasn't a healthy place, and there were a few people on that list who could arrange an accident, even in a high security jail. He stared impassively across the desk.

"I don't expect you to admit to any of it. Why would you?" said Meredith. "It wouldn't make any difference to me if you did. I don't spend my life agonizing over greedy people who part with their money in scams that most intelligent ten year olds could see through." She leaned forward, picked up her cup and took a sip of coffee, then continued. "How you make a living doesn't really concern me. Of course, it might concern some Police Departments … or the FBI …" She paused and searched Wynter's face for a reaction - nothing. She replaced the cup, leaned back into her chair and relaxed, "… but we don't talk to them."

Still say nothing, thought Wynter. Admit to nothing. She's lying; softening you up. He didn't believe that the Secret Service didn't talk to the FBI. He tried to fix his gaze on a piece of wall behind her head while he wondered where the hell all this was leading. "The FBI don't talk to us …" she said, "… so why should we talk to them?"

She smiled; her eyes sparkled and her face took on a glow. Wynter couldn't help but notice that she was a very attractive woman. She must have got a lot of attention when she was younger … probably still did. Hell, if the situation were different, *he'd* like to give her some attention.

"I guess you're wondering how I know so much about you."

Wynter thought it, but didn't say it.

"We've kept an eye on you because all our experience points to the fact that con artists like you eventually can't resist the lure of counterfeit money. It's the ultimate sting.

Not only do you take the mark - but you also con the Government."

She stretched out and picked up the cup and saucer. "Must be quite a high while it lasts." She took a sip of coffee.

"You guys might not produce the notes, but you're very good at distributing them; getting them out there on the street. Takes a lot of nerve to do that, but then you've got that haven't you … all you guys have." She raised her cup in a toast. "To chutzpah."

Wynter almost smiled. He hadn't been tempted to pass fake money, but he knew people who had - paperhangers in the trade. He also knew that they had a limited shelf-life. The Government didn't like funny money because it struck directly at the financial system, and they moved very quickly to suppress it. Taking on a greedy fool was one thing: taking on the Government sounded like suicide.

"You seem to have had more sense than most, Mister Wynter. Stick to what you're good at: always sound advice."

Who was this woman, and what did she want? Surely she hadn't picked him up and driven him the best part of eight hundred miles to discuss the methods and aesthetics of con-artistry. On the other hand, she didn't seem in a hurry to charge him with anything, or to pass him on to the police. Wynter wondered if he should ask for an attorney. California allowed anyone to be held up to forty-eight hours without charge; then you entered Habeas Corpus territory. Problem was, who exactly was holding him … and where? Silence was still the best option, Wynter reckoned, at least until he'd found out what this woman wanted.

Even when accepting the coffee, he'd said nothing. In one respect Meredith thought this was encouraging - he knew when to keep his mouth shut. On the other hand, it made broaching the subject difficult. His face betrayed nothing; didn't give a clue as to what he might say.

She had thought long and hard about the best way of approaching the subject. Experience had taught her there were three ways, and three ways only, of making someone do something. You pay them; you frighten them; or you persuade them it's the right thing to do. There were many variants, but all of them boiled down to one of these three ways. She had finally decided to use all three - the stick of retribution; the carrot of financial reward; and the moral glow of having done something good for society.

"Of course, I could have you on a plane back to England within two hours," she said.

Wynter blinked, this wasn't what he wanted to hear. Returning to England could have very unpleasant consequences.

"I believe there are two warrants out for you under your real name. I could extradite you and let Scotland Yard know you're on your way."

Meredith paused to let this sink in. For the first time she saw a reaction; a small bead of sweat had formed at his hairline and was about to roll down the side of Wynter's face. He took a couple of deep, silent breaths; his brain needed oxygen.

"It would be useless trying to resist," she continued, pushing home her advantage, "or trying for a writ of Habeas

Corpus. No-one knows you're here, and by the time they do - you would have left."

He swallowed. His mouth was getting dry and he felt sick. Keeping his mouth closed, he took another deep breath through his nose. He had to hang on. All this ground work was leading up to a proposition.

Reeling off his track record demonstrated that she knew what he'd been doing, but then she was seemingly in no hurry to do anything about it. Wynter knew it was meant to unsettle him, as was complimenting him on having the good sense to steer clear of counterfeit money. It also kept him off-balance. It was a technique of the game; she'd read the manual - all interrogators had. He knew the object of this conversation was to point out that all avenues of escape were closed, apart from the one she would eventually offer him. It was standard practice. This threat of sending him back to London was part of that process; to get him to the stage where he'd be grateful to do what whatever she wanted.

Taking a couple of deep breaths, he fought back his rising nausea. Pride was making him hang on; at least until he'd heard what she was offering.

"Be a shame to see you off to London; wave goodbye to all that talent. But I'd do it … if I had to."

The steely tone of her voice reinforced her threat and left him in no doubt that he would be on a plane if he didn't co-operate. She relaxed back into her chair and looked him straight in the eye. It was time for him to talk: time for him to ask what she wanted. The silence was only broken by the beat of the quartz wall clock as it measured the passing seconds. She held all the cards. She could afford to wait.

Going back to London was not an option as far as Wynter was concerned. Apart from the inevitable lengthy spell in jail, it could prove far from healthy. There were outstanding scores people would want to settle. He looked back over the desk. Could he trust her? She didn't seem to be in a hurry to hand him over to the FBI or any of the US Police Departments; but she could be lying.

She obviously wanted him to do something, thought Wynter, but what? He studied her face, but found no clues; she just sat there … impassively. He ran over the possibilities in his head and came to the conclusion that he'd run out of choices; he'd have to trust her.

Taking a deep breath, he cleared his throat.

"What do you want?"

They were the first words Wynter had spoken since leaving Alyson.

"Thank you," said Meredith, her face breaking into a smile. "I thought you'd eventually see things my way."

Wynter nodded. "So … what do you want?"

She leaned forward. "You and I, Mister Wynter … are going to pull a con."

Chapter 12

The hundred acres clinging to the coastline that made up Lincoln Park was far enough from San Francisco's city centre to be missed by most tourists. Used mainly by local residents, its woodland paths and walkways were never over-crowded, and the well manicured greens and fairways of the golf course just added to the impression that the land was off limits. The neighborhood was especially loath to admit that one of the best views of the Golden Gate was to be had from the park. That's when the bridge wasn't shrouded in mist.

As Hellman swung the Jaguar into El Camino Del Mar and headed towards Land's End parking lot, golf and the distant prospect of the giant suspension bridge couldn't have been further from his thoughts. If Kauffman and the Planning Department wouldn't see sense in regard to Van Buren's project, there were other ways of approaching the problem. Parking the car, he got out and walked towards the ocean.

In the trees on the opposite side of the parking lot, an elderly jogger in a grey tracksuit stopped to get his breath while he watched Hellman's progress. Hellman stopped leaned against a rail and lit a cigarette. The jogger started to do a few leisurely exercises: like any other older man hoping to extend his life by getting a little fitter. Hellman finished the cigarette, and ground it into asphalt with his shoe. He looked at his watch. As the jogger continued his stretching routine he cast the occasional glance in Hellman's direction, but he seemed more intent on looking around the parking lot and the trees surrounding it.

His attention was fixed for a few seconds as a car drew up and parked a few spaces from the Jaguar. Gently twisting from side to side loosening his back muscles, he watched closely two young women and two small children got out. They walked to the edge of the parking lot, and he seemed to relax as they disappeared over the edge and started on the downward path to join the coastal trail.

Hellman had smoked half his second cigarette when the jogger pulled the hood of his jacket over his head and jogged slowly across the parking lot towards him. He was looking out over the ocean and sheltering from the wind behind a solid railing when the hooded jogger came to a stop and leaned against the rail a couple of yards from him. After a cough and little throat clearing, the jogger spoke.

"You know what you're leaning against?"

Hellman glanced to his right and saw the jogger looking out to sea, his head obscured by the hood. Glancing down at the railings, he waited for the jogger's explanation.

"Part of the bridge from a warship: still got the shell holes from the Battle of Guadalcanal."

Hellman hadn't taken much notice of the railings until

now. They weren't railings, as such; they were higher than normal and solid from handrail to ground. Closer inspection confirmed that they did seem to be part of a ship's superstructure, with a number of jagged holes and twisted metal where shells had passed through. Most of the holes were inches wide, but two of them were feet across.

"To be precise," continued the jogger, "the bridge wings of a New Orleans class cruiser – the *USS San Francisco*. The grey paint gives you a clue."

"Yeah, guess it does. Anyone get killed by these shells?"

The jogger turned his head to the left and Hellman recognized Senator Reece.

"An admiral, the ship's captain and seventy five sailors - a hundred odd wounded too. You're standing in the middle of their Memorial … names are on that plaque over there, bottom of the flagpole." The senator turned and gazed back out to sea. "Keep your voice down and don't look over at me. Make out you're waiting for someone."

Hellman looked towards the flagpole where he saw a large cast metal plate recording the names of the sailors and marines who lost their lives on board the *San Francisco*.

"I should have been on it by rights," continued the senator, "but luckily I contracted a severe case of amoebic dysentery. I went out as replacement crew when Admiral Callaghan took command; that was October '42. But by the time I arrived on the island of Espiritu Santo, I couldn't fight my own shadow, let alone the enemy, and got taken back home by the supply ships. When I eventually pitched up at the service hospital complications had set in, thank God."

"Thank God?"

"Sure," said the senator. "Kept me out of the rest of the war: took it as a sign. Been lucky at getting out of things ever since."

State Senator Hogan Reece had ridden the political switchback for over thirty years. Always available for an interview or TV appearance when he was in the ascendant and riding high, when his star turned and hurtled down towards the skids, reporters were hard pressed to find him. A slick survivor, Reece knew that it was only the media and a small group of committed activists that were interested in the day to day scandals of political office; to the vast majority of the electorate the local sports results were far more important. Reece reckoned that as long as he said what people wanted to hear and always had a smile, he could get away with almost anything. So far, he'd been right.

Thirty yards down the coastal path, the young woman was crouching, hidden in the undergrowth, and pointing a parabolic microphone back up the hill to where the senator and Hellman could be seen against the skyline. She was listening on a small pair of headphones while she recorded Senator Reece discussing his war record. The children were skipping down the path, walking with their mother's colleague in search of ice-creams.

Up at the memorial to the USS San Francisco, the senator did some stretching exercises and looked out over the ocean.

"I hear you're looking for a site," he said.

"Yeah, up to four acres."

The senator laughed. "That isn't a site; that's a district."

Hellman shrugged. "It's what Van Buren wants."

"And Kauffman isn't playing ball?"

Hellman shook his head. "Says there's nothing available."

"There's always something," grinned the senator. "I guess he just doesn't like you."

"I get the feeling he's freezing me out."

"Yeah, well," said the senator, as he did a couple of bending exercises. "Four acres is a big chunk of land: it'll come expensive."

Hellman turned towards the senator and was about to speak, but was cut short. "Told you not to look over here: turn around and lean back on the rail," said the senator. "Check your watch; make out she's late."

Hellman did as he was told while the senator held onto the Memorial and started to do some light ham-string stretches on his left leg.

"That's a big site. Getting that round the City Planning Department alone would cost more than last time," said the senator.

"How much did I give you last time?"

"Not enough," said the senator, smiling as he started to stretch his right leg. "Still, Van Buren can afford it. Time he spread it around a bit more."

"Reckon you could find something?"

The senator gave a slight shrug. "There's always something; whether it fits the bill or not is another thing. Look at your watch again … act a little annoyed, like she's real late."

Hellman glanced at his watch, grimaced, then lit a cigarette and exhaled a plume of smoke. "How do we play it from here?"

"You get twenty to me in the usual way, and I'll see if I can find some answers."

"Twenty? Thousand?" said Hellman, "That's a lot of money."

The senator smiled to himself and nodded, "They're difficult questions."

Hellman paused: he wasn't going to commit himself straight away. "I'll speak to Van Buren."

"Sure." The senator started some very gentle jogging on the spot, "That all?" Hellman gave a slight nod and the senator continued, "Okay look at your watch, give her another ten minutes and when she doesn't show, you leave - understand?"

Hellman nodded again and ran his hand along the Memorial's top rail. "Shame about the ship."

"She was luckier than the *Juneau*."

Hellman looked puzzled, "Yeah?"

"The *Juneau* took a direct hit in her magazine from a torpedo that caused a massive explosion. She broke in two and went down in twenty seconds." The senator glanced over towards Hellman. "Close to six hundred men dead, and one hundred in the water."

"Jesus! They all get picked up?"

The senator gave a slight shake of his head. "Sharks got all but ten."

Reece jogged slowly northwards, in the direction of the

distant Golden Gate Bridge, leaving Hellman contemplating the shell holes in the Memorial, and, beyond them, an ocean full of sharks.

Thirty yards down the slope, the woman switched off the small tape recorder and began to fold up the parabolic cone.

***

This time it was going to work. He'd checked and re-checked everything at least three times. He was even using a stop-watch to be absolutely sure about the timing. It had to work.

He held the machine's brass and mahogany handle with his right hand, and had his eyes fixed on the moving hand as it counted down the seconds. Sheriff Richards was sweating: his concentration total. When the hand reached the top, he turned the handle and wound out the drawer. As he did so, he screwed his eyes tight shut and mumbled a prayer. After a couple of seconds, he took a deep breath, slowly opened his eyes and stared down - at a soggy piece of blank paper.

He blinked twice … three times. How? He stepped back, shaking his head in disbelief. He'd done everything right - been real careful to make sure. Why didn't it work?

He was still standing there when Harriet walked in with his lunch on a tray. She put the tray on the desk next to the box, and removed the inverted plate she had used to keep the food hot during her walk over.

"I guessed you might be getting hungry."

The sheriff continued gazing at the box in disbelief. "I

done it right this time, Harriet, I swear. Exactly how he told me …" The sheriff's voice tailed off in disappointment, and he shook his head again.

"Eat your lunch, Rufus," said Harriet, giving a sigh. "It's been over an hour since I called you, so I reckon the steak is past its best."

The sheriff stood gazing at the machine. "I was about to come over."

"Sure," she nodded, not believing him. "Now sit down and eat; you've got to get some food inside you."

The sheriff sat down at the desk, picked up the knife and fork, then stared at the mahogany box. "I don't see why it ain't working. It did for him, and I've done everything he told me."

Harriet put a sympathetic hand on his shoulder. "Perhaps he didn't tell you everything."

"You mean he kept something back?"

Harriet had decided that now was not the time to tell Rufus about her doubts about the machine and Sir Wynter: it was too soon. She knew that given time he would come to the same conclusion.

Harriet sighed. "It might not have been his fault."

The sheriff jerked his head up to look at her. "Eh?"

"Those agents grabbed him pretty quick. Hardly gave him time to say anything."

"He was pretty quick to talk about the money … and the pick-up."

"It *was* his truck, Rufus."

"Yeah, well …" said the sheriff. '… Didn't have no call

to say anything about the money though. Fifteen thousand dollars, Harriet: fifteen thousand dollars!"

"Which you had no intention of paying him, Rufus," said Harriet, which silenced the sheriff temporarily. "Anyway, he could hardly give you instructions on making counterfeit money in front of two Secret Service agents now could he?"

"No, but ..." said the sheriff. His voice faltered, and he calmed down a little as he grasped the logic of her statement, "... But ... but I paid for a machine that worked! Hell, Harriet, it ain't right!"

"Making counterfeit money ain't right either, Rufus."

"It ain't counterfeiting, it's duplicating - there's a difference."

"You believe that?"

"It's what Sir Wynter said."

"That don't make it true," said Harriet, "and I doubt if the Secret Service would see it that way." Harriet took a breath and decided to voice her doubts ... just to see how Rufus took it. "Could be the machine never worked in the first place."

The sheriff thought for a few seconds. "No, Harriet, you're wrong.

I saw it working ... and I've got a hundred dollar bill to prove it."

Harriet sighed. Rufus wasn't ready to face up to the fact that the box had never been going to work from the beginning.

Chapter 13

It was a source of pride to Meredith that the Service's arrangement with the hotel had been kept quiet. It was known to very few and Meredith intended to keep it that way. The hotel's bill was submitted by a company using a lawyer's address for 'services supplied', as and when required. If any staff queried it Meredith referred them to Bill Bradshaw, the Director of the Service. That had kept prying eyes at a distance for the last few years. As for the hotel, the manager was Swiss, very discreet, and used to keeping secrets. The few employees who were let in on the arrangement had all worked at the hotel for a minimum of ten years and were all highly trusted. Because of this discretion, and the fine service it offered, it was a favorite haunt of the rich and minor European royalty, who appreciated the hotel's style and wanted no intrusions or disturbances.

Nothing but a discreet, well polished brass plaque next to the door, engraved with a name, suggested that it was anything other than a large town house. No neon advertised its presence; no concierge hailed taxis; no flags enticed tourists. Most of the neighborhood's residents lived and died without realizing that it even was a hotel.

In one of its rooms on the second floor, Meredith stirred the fizzing contents of a glass then handed it to Wynter.

"You had stomach problems long?" she asked.

Wynter took the glass and drank it. As the soothing liquid made its way down, he began to have hopes of relief. He could almost believe that she was concerned.

"I always get an acid reaction when I hear that name. You should have warned me."

"I wasn't sure you'd know who he was," said Meredith.

"Oh, I know who he is," Wynter grimaced. "I first heard about him when I was in New Jersey; and what I heard I didn't like. Nothing's happened since to change my mind."

"I just wanted you to get used to the idea before …"

"Look, I don't get violent with them, and they don't try and con me. It's a promise I made years ago … never get involved with the Mob."

"He's not in the Mob."

Wynter's raised his eyebrows in disbelief, "Sure about that?"

"At best he's an associate," said Meredith, trying to sound convincing. "A peripheral character."

"The Mob doesn't have peripheral characters," said Wynter, rubbing his stomach. "You're either in or you're out."

Meredith tried another tack.

"You won't be involved. Just set him up and leave the rest to me."

"Like it's that easy? What does the Secret Service want with Van Buren anyway? He's FBI territory, surely?"

Meredith hesitated, unsure of how much she should say. Then she relaxed a little and gave a sigh.

"OK. We're ninety-nine per cent sure that he's the American end of a counterfeiting ring. It operates, we believe, out of Central America. The notes are extremely high quality: even the Treasury had difficulty in spotting them to start with. They're brought in via a number of routes, private plane, yacht, road freight. We pick up some, but not all by any means."

"How much gets through?"

Meredith shook her head. "We don't know. We do know that Van Buren arranges for the notes to be laundered through casinos in Las Vegas, New Jersey, Miami …"

Wynter's eyes looked skywards. "Casinos run by the Mob."

"… Alright, Mob casinos," sighed Meredith, conceding the point.

Wynter shook his head.

"Gamblers buy chips with real dollars," continued Meredith, "and if they win they get paid out with counterfeit, mainly twenties and fifties. Not usually the high rollers but the small guys on holiday, mainly playing with a few hundred or a thousand dollars. That way the notes get distributed all around the country and are harder to trace back to the casino. A few of the tables are rigged so the house loses more often, which attracts more gamblers, which means they get to unload even more of the stuff."

It was the first time Wynter had heard of a game being rigged to lose. But then, they were taking in real money and paying phony money out. Wynter knew enough about casinos to be able to imagine the figures. He also knew that counterfeit money, even the highest quality, cost only fifteen cents on the dollar. Even less if you were buying the amounts that the Secret Service thought Van Buren was bringing into the country. Take in one dollar and pay out fifteen cents, and you show a very healthy profit, all in cash and all tax free. This was all on top of the casino's legal edge.

"We think the casino takes a skim off the top equal to the counterfeit notes," continued Meredith. "Out of this they deduct expenses - the cost of buying from the counterfeiter, getting the notes into the country and distribution and the usual payoffs - what's left is then split between the Mafia bosses who run the casinos and Van Buren. We reckon they're clearing close to seventy per cent of face value."

Wynter took a slight breath and nodded; even he was impressed. "You could bribe most of Washington with that."

"Who says they haven't?"

They looked at each other in silence. Neither wanted to go down that road.

"So if you know all this stuff, why don't you hit the casinos with warrants?" asked Wynter.

"Because we'd just get the small fry; I need a line leading back to Van Buren."

"And you think that's where I come in."

"Well, if you don't, you're on a plane back to London: your choice."

He hadn't expected sympathy, but he had hoped for a little more understanding. Wynter took a couple of deep breaths.

"You realize I get one shot at this man, and one shot only. After that they fish what's left of me out of San Francisco Bay."

She nodded.

"And you still want me to go ahead with this?"

She nodded again.

Wynter closed his eyes in resignation and breathed deeply.

Meredith began to explain what the Secret Service knew about the counterfeiting operation and the people involved. She briefed him on Van Buren, his interests, financial and otherwise. She then set out the ground rules. She was in charge of the operation: Wynter needed to know that. She conceded his expertise in the method of operation and field work, but final decisions were hers. This wasn't necessarily how Wynter saw it. If he was out there putting himself on the line, he reckoned he should at least have as much say as her, but he kept his thoughts to himself. He was in no position to argue.

When she'd finished, Wynter turned to face her. "For the past quarter of an hour you've been telling me about a man I could never get near … even if I wanted to."

"You'll find a way."

Wynter shook his head. "I haven't seen one so far."

"Then look a little harder." The edge had crept back into Meredith's voice.

***

The guy sitting in the basement of the house staring at a bank of monitors had been aware of the Jaguar's progress since Hellman took a left at a fork in the track three hundred yards back. He pushed a button on the console and the heavy gates began to swing open. He watched the car slow so that they would be fully open by the time it reached them. Hellman always had a feeling of foreboding every time he drove in those gates, never knowing if they would let him out. He parked the Jaguar in the graveled forecourt and made his way to the front door.

The butler led him through the large entrance hall, through the vestibule and out onto the large terrace that ran the length of the south-western aspect of the house. Past the terrace, the land fell away and there were paths that led down through shrubs and glades with haphazard clumps of wild flowers. Large ceramic pots were dotted about the terrace containing more flowers. There was a dining area with a large table and a dozen chairs, and then a few smaller tables, more comfortable chairs, and some recliners spread about the paved area. At one of these smaller tables sat Jago, surrounded by cloths and a couple of small brushes, cleaning a pistol.

Van Buren was standing near the edge of the terrace. Seventy years old and a little under six foot, he wore, as only the very rich can, a torn pair of trousers, a rumpled blue shirt and a yellow sweater tied around his shoulders displaying a large hole at its left elbow. He had a battered pair of deck shoes on his feet but no socks.

"Mister Hellman," said the butler, announcing him.

"Steven," boomed Van Buren as Hellman approached, and they shook hands. "Bring me some coffee,' said Van Buren, turning his head to the butler.

"Very good, Sir," said the butler. 'Should I bring two cups, sir?"

"That depends on whether Mister Hellman has brought good news," said Van Buren, looking at Hellman.

"Kaufman at City Hall is pretty confident," lied Hellman, trying to sound relaxed.

Van Buren gave his guest a questioning stare, unsure if he was being told the truth. Hellman looked uncomfortable and began to breathe deeply. The silence continued. Jago stopped polishing and looked up. Then Van Buren's face broke into a smile.

"Two cups, Barker."

"Sir," said the butler with a nod of his head, and disappeared back into the house. Hellman breathed a sigh of relief and relaxed noticeably. Jago returned his attention to cleaning.

"Do you shoot?" asked Van Buren as picked up the shotgun and raised it to his shoulder with startling speed - as if he were going for a high flying bird.

"No," said Hellman, apprehension colored his voice.

"You should, you know; it teaches you to study your opponent." He brought the gun down. "So, Kaufman is confident."

"I think so," said Hellman, hoping he sounded more confident than he felt.

Van Buren stared at his guest. "I hope so." His attitude

softened: he smiled and threw the gun to Hellman. "What d'you think? I've been offered a pair of them. Are they any good?"

Hellman caught the gun rather clumsily and started to take a look at it, without knowing what he was looking for. It was highly engraved on the side-plates and the figuring on the stock was shown perfectly by the highly polished finish. He noticed the name of the maker: *J. Purdey and Sons*.

"It looks … okay."

"It looks … okay. That's your considered opinion?"

"I know nothing about guns," said a hesitant Hellman.

Van Buren sighed and shook his head in disappointment. "What did Kaufman say?"

"He was worried about the funding … he didn't think that I could fund such a large development."

Van Buren smiled. "I can see his point; what else did he say?"

Hellman shrugged. 'Sites that size don't come on the market every day …"

He shifted uncomfortably and Jago, sensing his unease, put the pistol down on the table and looked over at Hellman. He enjoyed seeing the developer twist in the wind.

"… and have you thought about going inland, away from the Bay? It'll save you money," said Hellman.

"Save me money," repeated Van Buren, laughing. He looked over at Jago. "Do you hear that … Kaufman wants to save me money."

Jago gave a twisted grin.

"Not everyone is as short of money as Mister Kaufman,"

continued Van Buren. His eyes narrowed and he turned to face Hellman. "It has to be on the Bay." He spoke softly but a hard edge had crept into his voice, a warning that Hellman didn't miss. "I want people to see the building ... to remember who built it."

Hellman nodded and Van Buren's face broke into a smile. "You can assure Mister Kaufman that there is more than enough money."

"That's what I told him."

Van Buren took the gun back from Hellman's sweating hands. "What news from the Senator?"

Hellman closed his eyes and took a deep breath. "He wants twenty thousand."

Van Buren gave him a blank stare.

Hellman hated these meetings. Never knowing how Van Buren would react played havoc with his blood pressure. The developer felt his heart begin to thump again.

"Twenty thousand," said Van Buren, a distorted grin spreading over his face. "I could have bought someone *really* useful for that." He turned to Jago. "Go and get five thousand for the Senator." He turned back to Hellman as Jago disappeared. "Tell the Senator he can have another five when I get my site."

"Yeah," a relieved Hellman nodded. "Yeah, I will."

"What about Washington?" Van Buren cocked his head to one side. "You or the Senator heard anything from DC?"

"No, no ... should I?"

Van Buren shrugged. "Always something going on up there. You've got to be listening in if you want to stay ahead."

Hellman was left with the feeling that he was on the outside; he was missing something. Something he should know about. What was going down in Washington? Van Buren turned to the table and broke open the action of the shotgun and reached for the box of cartridges.

"Who the hell is Kaufman to question if I've got enough money?" he muttered. Snapping the gun shut he shouted, "Miguel!"

"Sir," replied a muffled voice from down the slope.

"Loose!" Van Buren shouted as he put the gun to his shoulder.

The pigeon fluttered up, got its bearings and began flying towards the ocean. It never made it. It was hit by a dozen lead pellets propelled by a nitro charge from a fully choked Purdey shotgun forty five yards away. A puff of feathers spiraled down in the wake of the dead bird. Van Buren smiled in satisfaction and lowered the gun.

Chapter 14

In her office, Meredith listened to the tape recording for the umpteenth time. The sound was muffled, uneven, and the background wind made it difficult to hear, but after listening, and reading a partial transcript, she had managed to make something coherent of the tape.

"... get twenty to me ... usual way, and I'll see if I can find some answers."

Meredith switched off the small recorder on her desk as Lance walked in.

"What do we know about this guy Hellman, and what's this site that Van Buren wants?" asked Meredith.

"Hellman's a real estate developer. Started small but has grown quickly: too quickly to be totally legit, some think. He's got no qualms about crossing the line when he thinks it necessary, and it's thought he's got some unsavory connections. This confirms it."

"They don't come any more unsavory than Van Buren," Meredith nodded. "Think he's connected to the counterfeiting scam?"

"Hellman?"

Meredith nodded.

Lance shrugged, "He hasn't shown up so far."

"But we don't *know* that he's not involved?"

Lance shook his head. "No."

"What about this site that Van Buren wants?"

"You know as much as I do," shrugged Lance, "but four acres points to something big. Could be he's investing his share of the casino profits from the counterfeiting scam in property."

"Mmm, run a check with the city's Planning Department. Hellman must have contacts there; they might have heard something. I'll check with people I know," said Meredith. "Hellman must have come to someone's attention."

She took the mini-cassette from the recorder.

"This is evidence of Senator Reece soliciting a bribe," she said, "and both he and Hellman admit to a previous bribe. It also ties them to Van Buren. Quite a cozy little arrangement they all have going."

"Shall I bring Hellman in?"

Meredith shook her head. "Not our jurisdiction: corruption is the FBI's problem."

"What about the Senator? He did turn up at the hotel in Vegas the night Petersen was murdered, remember."

Meredith thought for a moment. "Mmm … leave him be, for the time being, but let's take a close look at him and Hellman … see if we can apply some pressure."

***

Wynter was lying on the bed when Meredith unlocked the door to his hotel room. He sat up and swung his legs to the floor, as she walked to the table, joining her as she took a couple of files from her attaché case and snapped the case closed.

"You wanted a way of getting to Van Buren. I think I might have found it."

She handed Wynter a file with a name on it.

"Hellman? Who is he and what's he got to do with Van Buren?"

"He's into real estate, and we think Van Buren looking to develop a site."

Wynter started to flick through the file.

"A site? A site for what, exactly?"

"To put up a building, some kind of memorial. Whatever it is, it's going to be big - Hellman's looking for four acres."

"Got plenty to choose from here, right out into the desert."

"Out of town isn't in the brief. According to Phil Kauffman, he wants four acres on the bay."

"Who's Phil Kauffman?"

"Director of Planning at the city council."

"Well, he'd know if anyone would. I would have thought Hellman's going to have trouble finding a site that big on the bay."

"That's what Kauffman said."

"Has he found anywhere?"

Meredith shook her head. "Not yet."

Wynter flipped over a few more pages of the file.

"And how do you know that this …" Wynter flipped to the front of the file and read the name … "Hellman … is working for Van Buren?"

"Kauffman said that Hellman had let slip Van Buren's name," continued Meredith. "Almost threatened him with it."

"It's a good name to use if you want to scare someone."

"Then there's Senator Reece. Not as violent as Van Buren, but just as unpleasant in his way. We've got him on tape soliciting a bribe from Hellman to ask questions on Van Buren's behalf."

"About this prospective site?"

Meredith nodded. "Yeah."

"Why Hellman? There are plenty of real estate developers."

"Van Buren's worked with him before, mainly on smaller stuff. I guess Hellman is a trusted pair of hands."

Wynter nodded at Meredith's point. "And you think this is our way in?"

"Only you can answer that, but I'd start looking at maps if I were you. You wanted to get closer to Van Buren … this is the only way we've found."

Meredith swept her attaché case from the table and turned for the door.

"I'll be sending you some more files."

"And what do I do with them?" said Wynter.

"Read, inwardly digest, and find the way we're going to con Van Buren," said Meredith as she pulled open the door.

"Just as easy as that?"

"There's always a plane to London, remember," said Meredith as she disappeared through the door. Wynter heard the click of the lock behind her. He looked down at the files on the table and sighed. He might as well sit down and start reading … there was precious little else to do.

***

The police file on Hellman listed the usual information and as Wynter read it he took in the basics: full name, address, date of birth and occupation. On the face of it, Hellman wasn't a major offender. There were a couple of minor vehicular offences, eight contraventions of the building regulations, and a complaint for noise lodged by a neighbor.

The three paragraphs on the penultimate page were more interesting. There had been whispers and allegations that Hellman had been involved in bribery and intimidation regarding three building projects. Intriguing, but hardly unexpected, thought Wynter. Most property developers were far from being saints, and there were quite a few stories about swimming pools miraculously appearing in city planning officials' gardens. Although no-one would speak on the record and nothing could be proven, there were suggestions that Hellman had connections to the Mob. Wynter felt a grumbling ache in his stomach which confirmed those suspicions.

In the second file was an explanation of what they'd uncovered so far about how the property deals were financed. How the money was channeled from a bank in the Bahamas, through a shell company in Panama, only to re-surface in an investment corporation in Delaware where it sat until needed. They were still working on the link between Van Buren and the bank in the Bahamas. All these movements were designed to keep the owner of the money well insulated, and keep him out of view of the authorities. Needless to say, any profits found their way back to the Panamanian shell company which transferred them into an impenetrable fog of off-shore beneficial trusts. These trusts Meredith now suspected were designed to benefit only one person … Van Buren.

Wynter looked up as he heard the door being unlocked. Schmidt, a member of the hotel's security staff, entered carrying a large cardboard box which he put down on the table. He glanced over at Wynter and smiled, then turned and walked out of the room, re-locking the door behind him.

Wynter opened the box - more files, more papers. He began to realize how much influence the Secret Service could exert. Apart from official channels, Meredith must be pulling in God knows how many years of favors.

He looked at the building permits, land transfers, leases, income tax, insurance, credit agencies - a request must have gone to every Department in the State - and not just California. There were school and college reports, and a record of an admission to hospital for appendicitis. The fax machines must be red hot. He was starting to put together a picture, but as yet it was a picture without much personality. He needed clues to what drove Hellman and why. Did he simply want money, or was he looking for professional acceptance? Could it be that he yearned for a social position?

Wynter sat back from the files and relaxed. Having all this information about a target dumped in front of him was a new experience. Normally he would meet someone in a social setting and let them take the lead in conversation. Bars and parties were good. Alcohol loosened the tongue and encouraged people to talk, especially about themselves. Experience had taught him that if you let someone talk long enough they'd tell you all you needed to know to take them for every last penny. The more you listened and agreed, the more people liked and trusted you. Over time you'd learn their hopes, dreams, weaknesses, strengths and aspirations - if you had patience. And Wynter had patience, unlimited amounts of it. It went with the territory.

He turned back to the paperwork. He flicked over the pages as he gave them a cursory glance, then one short paragraph made him sit up. He read it again, this time giving it his undivided attention. A germ of an idea began to take shape in his mind.

**

Senator Reece cussed and swore as Hellman described Van Buren's reaction to his demand for twenty thousand, but he knew better than to push too hard. Eventually Reece accepted the five thousand up front, with the promise of the rest if he came up with the site. Realistically, he knew he'd be lucky if he ever saw another cent. Still, five thousand dollars was better than a plate of rotting fish … and Reece had never intended doing too much for it anyway.

Hellman wondered if it was worth ringing Phil Kauffman, then he thought again. Their last meeting had been less than successful, and it was unlikely that Kauffman would be quick to do him any favors. His deputy, Joey Battista, would be a better bet. For a good lunch and a couple of tickets to the up-coming Billy Joel concert, Joey could be persuaded to bring him up to date with the city's rumor mill.

***

Wynter rocked back in his chair and smiled to himself. Now he knew. He couldn't have told you how, but instinctively he just knew he'd found the bomb that was going to blow Hellman's world apart.

A lot of work still needed to be done. It would have to be primed and given the long fuse of a convincing story to allay suspicion, and, of course, they'd have to insulate themselves against any fall-out from the blast, but that was normal in any con-trick. Wynter allowed his smile to broaden into a grin. He was confident that he now knew the direction in which they were headed.

He studied the map and wondered why it had taken him so long. The answer was there, right in front of his eyes. So simple and so obvious, he hadn't been able to see it for looking. He'd thought it through a few times, considered all possible angles, and could only see minor problems. Nothing he couldn't solve. He'd even begun to get that warm feeling that always accompanied his good ideas.

Meredith had burst out laughing and told him to be serious when he told her the plan; she couldn't believe he'd even suggested it. But having gone over the idea a few times, and with Wynter having answered all her questions, she was beginning to see the possibilities.

"You sure it's not too big?"

"Big is better, more room," said Wynter, shaking his head. "It's also unique, so no-one will know how to value it - that gives us a lot of scope."

"Perhaps too much. Remember the old saying about enough rope."

"But we're giving out the rope; it's Hellman who'll hang himself."

"I'm still not sure. It's a lot for Hellman to take in … and there's Van Buren, remember. It'll have to convince him."

"Remember Josef Goebbels? '*The bigger the lie, the more people will believe it*' … and he fooled a whole nation."

Meredith didn't look convinced. "He had the Nazis behind him. You're on your own."

Wynter shrugged. "He was still telling lies. And I thought the Secret Service was backing me up."

"They will … for a sensible proposition."

"This is sensible."

"You reckon?"

Meredith settled back in her seat and gave Wynter a long, searching look.

"Look," he said, "in nineteen sixty-six the Coliseum in Rome changed hands. An American tourist leased it for ten years, at twenty million lire a year. He had plans to turn it into a restaurant."

Wynter warmed to his favorite theme.

"The year before that, a man paid two English airline stewards a twenty thousand dollar down payment on the purchase of their Boeing airliner during a three day stop-over in Tokyo."

Wynter paused for emphasis. Was Meredith wavering? Dropping his voice to a reverential tone, he continued "… and in nineteen twenty-five, Victor Lustig invited scrap metal dealers to bid for seven thousand tons of wrought iron, popularly known as the Eiffel Tower. He was so successful that a month later he came back and sold it again."

Wynter's eyes met hers.

"The bigger the lie …"

She twiddled with a pencil, turning it end over end on the desk. He was good, very good, she knew that … but could he do it? Would Hellman go for it? Would Van Buren believe it? It might just appeal to him, in an off the wall sort of way. He had ways of checking, she knew that, and they would have to be covered, but she could cope with that – Van Buren wasn't the only one with good contacts in Washington.

The irony of the situation struck her: she must be feeling exactly how one of Wynter's marks felt before being taken for a load of money. She was probably going through the same mental processes: the evaluations; the questions. Was he telling the truth? How much can I trust this man? Is he conning me? Is the reward worth the risk?

"I'd understand, of course, if you didn't want to do it," continued Wynter. "It would take some skilful setting up, and you'd need the right contacts. You might not feel that you could … well, didn't quite have …"

"I've got everything necessary to set this up, and see it through," she said sharply, stung by his questioning doubt.

"Of course," said Wynter, "of course: then perhaps …?"

He was getting to her, and she knew it. Using his experience and powers, Wynter was easing her, nudge by nudge, in the direction he'd chosen. She had to admit that he could be very persuasive. He also had a great instinct for what would convince, and how to frame a conversation to produce the right reaction. She imagined that when he chose to use it, his charm could be devastating, especially if he used it on women. She had no doubt that he'd left a trail of cold, empty promises as well as empty wallets behind him.

"It's the best site we're going to find given the short notice," said Wynter, interrupting her thoughts. "And I think it's the best shot you'll get at Van Buren."

"Perhaps."

"They'll go for it, I promise you. It'll offer Hellman the recognition he wants, and give Van Buren an ironic memorial."

Meredith sighed. There was only one way to find out how good Wynter really was. "You think you can do it?"

"Yeah," said Wynter, nodding, "I really do."

"Hellman's no pushover … you reckon you'll talk him round?"

"I've just talked you round, haven't I?" said Wynter softly.

Chapter 15

It was one of those mornings when Wynter missed a good cup of tea. He'd always found thinking easier with a pot of tea. The problem was that Americans just didn't grasp the importance of adding *boiling* water to the tea; hot water simply would not do. He'd even resorted to the kitchens of some very superior hotels to make it himself, but then, why pay fancy prices if you have to do all the work?

Americans might not be able to make tea to his liking, but Wynter had to admit that they made good coffee. In that respect they were miles ahead of English hotels, which often resorted to catering-sized tins of brown powder claiming a dubious relationship to coffee.

Meredith had supplied another box of documents, this time all related to the chosen site, and Wynter had been slowly working his way through them as he drank his coffee. Who owned the place; its history; and if there were any current or future plans for re-development. The answers all being positive to his way of thinking, he had started to formulate a plan when he heard the door being unlocked and Meredith walked into the room.

"How are you getting on with the reading?"

"These senators up in Washington, the ones Van Buren has in his pocket, you know any of them?" said Wynter.

"I met a couple of them at a reception once, but I can't say I know them. I wouldn't want to know them," said Meredith, with a certain amount of distaste. "I avoid going to DC as much as I can. I find the atmosphere there ... unhealthy."

"We need someone who's known and accepted there, a part of the machine, someone they'll believe."

"What do you want to do?"

"Plant a rumor."

Meredith rolled her eyes. "When it comes to rumors, they listen to anyone and believe everything."

"Perhaps," smiled Wynter, "but it'll sound more authentic if it comes from a known source."

Meredith thought for a couple of seconds. "I could ask someone," she said, in that deliberate way that let Wynter know that she'd got somebody in mind.

"One of the Secret Service agents in Washington?"

Meredith shook her head. "I wouldn't use one of our agents there."

Wynter raised a questioning eyebrow.

"Just because my West Coast unit doesn't talk to the CIA or FBI doesn't mean that the East Coast boys don't," continued Meredith.

"You don't trust them?" asked Wynter.

"Not entirely."

"Any reason?"

"Let's just say that a lot of drinking gets done in Washington, leading to some loose talk. We wouldn't want the intelligence agencies poking their noses into what we're doing … would we? That's the one way to guarantee that Van Buren will get to hear of it."

It was also the quickest way to alert Tobin and Boles to what she was doing, but Wynter didn't need to know that.

"But…" said Wynter.

"It happened once before," cut in Meredith. "It's not going to happen again."

She spoke with a finality that ended the matter, making Wynter think that behind the words there was a personal involvement, but that he wasn't going to be told about it.

"So, who's your man?" said Wynter.

"An old friend of my family, someone I know I can trust … James McLennan."

"McLennan?" said Wynter, impressed. "Senator James McLennan?"

Meredith nodded.

"Even I'd trust him," admitted Wynter.

Meredith had spoken one of the few names in politics that almost all American politicians would trust. After naval service in the Pacific during the Second World War, for which he was decorated, James Fielding McLennan started out on what would become an illustrious career in the Senate. Looked upon by many as the nation's conscience, he was respected by Republicans and Democrats alike as a statesman in the old mould; putting right above expediency, and country above party. If the New York Times or the

Washington Post printed an article described as being from an '*unimpeachable source*,' they were usually referring to McLennan.

"Well, if you've got McLennan to light the fuse …"

"Oh, he's not going to light it, but if I ask him he'll be ambiguous when asked about the rumor, which will be as good as a confirmation."

"So, who have you got in mind to start the whispers?"

"Senator Grant," said Meredith. "North Carolina. A lawyer before he became a senator; he's fought a battle against organized crime for over twenty-five years."

"Good. Just tell him not to say too much, keep it vague and don't name the site."

"He won't name the site because I won't tell him what it is."

Wynter smiled. Meredith would make one hell of a con artist.

"I'm a little surprised at McLennan, though," said Wynter. "Won't his reputation take a knock?"

"I doubt it. All he'll be doing is saying nothing. It wouldn't be the first time that Washington has interpreted nothing to mean something. He's hardly to blame for that, is he?"

"I guess not," said Wynter, "but what makes you think he'll do it?"

Meredith hesitated, wondering if she should say anything; after all, McLennan's motivation shouldn't make any difference. Finally she relented. Perhaps she did owe Wynter something of an explanation.

"He was a very good friend of my father's. They were in the Navy together."

Wynter opened his mouth, but before he could say anything she waved a hand to silence him.

"We've got work to do," she said.

The way she closed down that avenue of conversation just reinforced his feeling that there was a lot of personal history tied up in this operation that he knew nothing about … and probably never would.

***

Lance Holland had spent a fruitful time at the city clerk's office chasing down the casino and its owners. He'd enlisted the help of a bottle-blonde clerk who was in the middle of a midlife crisis. The fact that her husband hadn't seemed to notice just added to her problems. After listening to her for a couple of hours, Lance eventually put it all down to sex … she wasn't getting any.

Crisis or not, she was a good researcher and knew where to find financial documents that Lance was unaware existed, and suggested people he should phone. Between them they finally nailed the link between Van Buren and the casino to Lance's satisfaction. True, Van Buren's name didn't appear on any documents, but two of the companies that the blonde turned up had been traced back to the Bahamas. They were in turn owned by a company where it was known Van Buren was the main beneficiary. It was as close to proof as they would get.

On his way back to the office he wondered how Meredith

was getting on. She had told him that she would be discussing the next move with Wynter. Lance felt that they were finally getting somewhere with the counterfeit case. Van Buren's connection to the casino had been established, and Lance had hopes that Wynter would come up with something positive. He'd hardly settled behind his desk when Tobin walked in.

"I thought you were in Washington," said Lance.

"You thought wrong. Landed at lunchtime," replied Tobin. "You don't happen to know where your boss is, do you?"

Lance looked as vacant as he could and shrugged. "Eliminating possibilities?"

"Eliminating possibilities," said Tobin, "or running a sideshow to keep me in the dark?"

Lance looked confused. What did Tobin know? Had he heard anything? Lance decided it best to say nothing.

"When you've been doing this job as long as I have," continued Tobin, "you get to sense when you're being led up a dirt track to nowhere. I'm getting that feeling now."

"Well, you must know more than I do, because I haven't a clue what you're saying."

"Did Miss Delaney tell you to check out the casino at the city clerk's office?" asked Tobin.

Lance showed no emotion but the euphoria he had felt after establishing the Man's connection to the casino suddenly began to wear off and he started to feel uncomfortable. How did Tobin know he had been to the city clerk's office?

"Only thing I learned on my trip back to DC," said Tobin, "is that you're hiding something. Something that you and Miss Delaney don't want me to know about."

Tobin gave a menacing smile to Lance, who stared back in silence. Lance felt his mouth getting dry.

"Naval college taught me that when you lay a smokescreen, make sure it's a good thick one so the enemy can't see through it," said Tobin. He turned and made his way to the door then turned back to Lance.

"If I were you, I'd make pretty damn sure I knew where my career was going with this investigation."

Lance swallowed hard.

"Bill Bradshaw's got Delaney's back," said Tobin. "… Who's got yours?"

***

Wynter and Meredith sat opposite each other at the table in Wynter's hotel room. She was reading a letter that Wynter had drafted to be sent to Hellman and five of San Francisco's major real estate developers. He had crafted the prose into a piece of artistry worthy of a Russian novel. It combined a simple invitation with the subtle promise of preferment and success. Wynter was pleased that he had managed to convey so much in two brief paragraphs without referring to anything specific.

"The thing is we have to entice them to come, but not tell them why."

"You sure that's going to work?" asked Meredith.

"If we get it right, it will. By the time they receive the

letter, the rumors from Washington should have filtered down, so they'll already know there's something big lurking in the shadows."

"Do you think they'll all show? These are busy people, remember."

"I reckon so. How often do they get personal invitations from the Secretary of the Interior, and hospitality from the government?"

"Not often," Meredith admitted. "Not this side of prison anyhow. I'd turn up just to see what it was about."

"That's always a pretty good indication."

"What?"

"Ask yourself what you'd do in the same situation."

"Is that how you assess your targets?"

"Sometimes - but then, I'm not a greedy man."

Meredith raised her eyebrows. "And they are?"

"They all want something," nodded Wynter. "The trick is to find out what that thing is. Quite often it isn't about money."

"Sure?"

"Is what you're doing here about money? Do you think Hellman is chasing this site for money?"

Meredith had to admit there was a lot in what he said.

"Van Buren thinks he's putting up his own memorial," continued Wynter. "It's all about power and social ambition; the money is incidental."

"But not to you."

"Hardly," he said smiling. "Play it right and they end up begging you to take their money. The more you say no ...

the more money they offer you." Wynter looked over at Meredith and grinned. "Didn't your mom teach you that? Treat them mean and keep them keen. Bet you've said 'no' a few times."

Meredith smiled, but her expression made it clear that Wynter would have to wait some time for an answer. She picked up the letter and read it through again. She had to admit she was impressed. The wording was precisely nebulous enough to attract, while the fact it purported to come from the government guaranteed its substance.

"*To discuss the placing of a contract*'. I like that," she said. "Leaves it wide open."

"Gives room for maneuver."

Meredith put the letter back on the table.

"There's nothing in there about bidding," she said.

"That comes later. I'll explain the bidding to them all at the meeting."

"Do you think they'll all bid?"

"I think they'll all give it very serious consideration. Chances like this come along once in a lifetime, and I would expect four out of the five to bid. Arnstein's overextended himself and I reckon he'll pass. Johansson will bid, but hope he doesn't get it. That leaves three serious contenders."

Meredith looked down at the letter again. All it lacked was the signature of the Secretary of the Interior, or, to be more precise, the Deputy Secretary … one Gerald Wynter.

"What about Hellman?" she asked.

"What about him?"

"Will he bid?"

"Oh, he'll bid alright. This is his ticket into the major league."

"And Van Buren?"

"He'll back Hellman."

"You sure?"

"How else is he going to get his site?"

Chapter 16

Van Buren was the first to hear the whisper. But then, Van Buren was the first to hear about a lot of things. He'd had a snatched telephone call from a Congressman in Washington, telling him that something was going down. He had then spent the next hour calling his East Coast contacts, trying to find out what was happening. In his world, being one step ahead was what gave him the edge, and the edge was what counted. The final telephone call he made was to Hellman. Bringing the property developer up to date, Van Buren instructed him to talk to his contacts on this side of the country. See if anyone had heard anything. Shake the tree a little. See what falls to the ground. That's was Hellman was about to do.

A waiter led Joey Battista to the table at the back of the restaurant. As Joey sat down, Hellman smiled and pushed the envelope containing two Billy Joel tickets across the freshly starched linen tablecloth.

"*Uptown Girl* is my favorite; always reminds me of my girlfriend, Lee. You got a favorite?" asked Hellman.

Joey smiled and shook his head. "I like them all - but I

guess *Tell Her About It* has got to be up there."

"What about Karen?"

"*Leave a Tender Moment*," said Joey. "… she's romantic," he added apologetically.

"And you're not?"

Joey smiled. "The Planning Department's a pretty hard nosed place: can't say yes just because the building plans looks nice."

"I guess not," said Hellman, taking a sip of wine. "Got to be tough to survive; especially with Phil Kauffman for a boss."

"Ahh, Phil's OK - just likes things done his way."

"But that isn't always *your* way …"

Joey shrugged, but the point hit home. "What can you do?"

"He won't be there forever, Joey," said Hellman sympathetically.

The conversation over lunch started with music, strayed into where the 49ers would finish in the league, and meandered around whether the Giants would ever get off their current losing streak. By the time they'd put San Francisco's sporting efforts back on the right track, Hellman nudged the conversation eastwards.

"You guys in Planning, do you keep an ear to what's going on in Washington?"

"Have to … things keep changing so much."

Hellman leaned back. "You got someone looking out for you in DC? Giving you the heads up?"

"Yeah," nodded Joey, "an old college buddy. Married a

girl from Maryland and moved over there."

"Yeah?"

"Works for the Environment Department. Keeps telling me I should join them. Says how they're always on the look-out for good men."

"He's right: you are a good man; be a shame to lose you."

"Oh, you won't lose me. Karen wouldn't move - not now."

"Glad to hear it. Someone's going to have to sit in Kauffman's chair when he goes."

"That's a way off yet."

"Perhaps, but it wouldn't do you any harm to earn yourself some brownie points while you're waiting."

"How?" asked Joey. A little nervous tension had crept into his voice. "I'm not going to do anything out of line."

"Joey," said Hellman, spreading his open hands in supplication, "have I ever asked you to do something out of line?"

Joey sighed and shook his head. "I guess not."

"That's not the way I do business."

"So ... what are these Brownie points?"

"There's talk in Washington about something happening on the West Coast. Something in the Bay Area, I'm told."

"News to me if there is."

"It might just be gossip; you know how Washington can be. They'd talk about rug weaving if they thought there were votes in it."

"What's supposed to be happening?"

"I don't know, but I'm hearing rumors that it's

something big. That's where your friend in the Environment Department comes in. You think you could give him a call? Get him to check it out?"

Joey took a breath. "Let me think about it."

"Joey, I don't know how much time we've got on this."

"I dunno …" Joey shifted in his chair.

"The right answer would do you a lot of good when Kauffman retires."

"Yeah?"

"I've got good friends in the State Senate that would be pleased to hear you're with them on this."

"Senators …?"

Hellman nodded. "Always helps to have friends in Sacramento."

"Well," said Joey, "I don't see that talking to an old friend can hurt."

"Wouldn't hurt at all," smiled Hellman as he picked up the menu.

"Now … cheesecake or pecan pie?"

***

Wynter was sitting at the table, the remnants of lunch before him. Meredith took a file out of her attaché case and held it out to him.

"That's what we've managed to get together for you."

Wynter took the blue file and opened it.

"Not much, I'm afraid," Meredith continued, "but it's all we could do in the time."

Wynter flicked through pages of his fictitious life -

birthday, school, college, job, marriage, children … a life on paper.

"We keep a number of them running," said Meredith, "never know when one may be needed. We update them to suit the situation."

"But what about the name?" said Wynter in a measured tone. "No-one in the Department will recognize it if Van Buren has me checked out."

"Have you any idea how many people work in Washington?"

Wynter looked blank and shrugged his shoulders.

"DC's a transient place," said Meredith. "Names don't mean much, it's titles that matter. By the time people in the Department get to know your name, you've been moved; or they've been moved; or the Department has been merged."

"But no-one's ever met me."

"True, but they'll all admit to knowing *of* you, it would be rude not to. They'll *know* about ten or so people in their immediate line of work and a few more on the periphery. The rest will be either way above their pay grade or way below. They'll guess that's why they haven't met you."

"But …"

"Wynter, they know the Deputy Secretary of The Interior exists, but none of them have ever met him, or are ever likely to. Staffing is in a constant state of flux. Up, down, hired, fired - but if it makes you feel any better, there's now a Gerald Wynter listed as a Deputy Secretary in the Department of the Interior, with his own office, staff and telephone."

Bill Bradshaw had worked a minor miracle since Meredith's phone call yesterday afternoon.

"And what if they ring the number?"

"They'll be told you're on holiday."

Wynter slowly nodded his approval. "You've pretty much covered everything."

Meredith smiled. "Quite a compliment, coming from a pro."

Wynter closed the file and put it back on the table.

"You're putting a lot of time and effort into this. Above and beyond the call of duty, I'd say."

"Your time, my duty, Mister Wynter," smiled Meredith.

He figured there was more than just taking down a counterfeiting scam involved in this operation. He scanned her face for any clues - none were visible. No tightening of the jaw, no slight glance away. Not even an imperceptible pursing of the lips - nothing. Wynter made a mental note never to play poker with this woman … not even for fun.

"I know why I'm doing this …"

"We both know why you're doing it," interrupted Meredith. "To avoid a long stretch in an English prison. I think you Brits refer to it as being, '*a guest of her Majesty*'."

"Yeah," Wynter smiled, "but …"

He was interrupted by Lance opening the door and clearing his throat rather loudly, while he waited expectantly.

"Yes, Lance?" said Meredith.

"Can I speak to you?"

His voice conveyed an urgency that Meredith felt she

couldn't ignore. She stood up and made her way to the door. Wynter heard the click of the lock as Meredith left the room, leaving him to wonder what Lance wanted to speak to her about.

***

"Tobin knows we're up to something," said Lance.

They were sitting in a drug store around the corner from the hotel.

"He had to pick up on it sooner or later," said Meredith. "I'm surprised it's taken him this long."

"He suspects that we've been laying a smokescreen to hide what we're really doing."

"That comes of winging it. How much do you think he really knows and how much is suspicion?" asked Meredith, as she raised her cup and took a sip of coffee.

"A lot of it is suspicion, I reckon; he's still guessing … but he's not dumb."

Meredith nodded knowingly. "Mmm."

Lance took another mouthful of beer and looked at her. "What d'you think his next move will be?"

"Depends how close he thinks we're getting."

"To what?"

"Whoever it is he's protecting."

"Tobin's protecting someone?"

"Yeah," nodded Meredith. "Bill Bradshaw's almost certain of it. Tobin might not realize it, of course; to him, he's heading up an investigation, but, to some-one in the shadows, it's a game of cat and mouse."

"Van Buren?"

"I doubt it. I'd bet on it being someone closer to home in Washington. Van Buren is expendable; he just runs the distribution."

"Do you think Washington's involved in the counterfeiting operation?"

"Senators, Congressmen, the CIA ..." Meredith shrugged. "Who knows?"

"The CIA? That could mean Carter Devlin's involved."

Meredith nodded and took another sip of coffee. "Drugs were always the CIA's big thing ... they might have diversified into junk money, but I doubt it."

She returned her coffee to the table. "I think their interests overlap. They're using each other. Van Buren can move large quantities of drugs at street level, and I mean large. In exchange, the CIA brings the counterfeit money into the country with their regular drug run."

"And Van Buren would be the cut-out, giving Carter Devlin deniability."

"Wouldn't be the first time the CIA's been caught on the wrong side of the law," said Meredith. "Vietnam corrupted quite a few CIA agents and gave them a taste for drugs and money. When the war finished they got bad withdrawal symptoms: not so much from drugs - they mostly didn't use them - but from the large amounts of money they had been making. So they set about finding new suppliers, and the cartels in Central America obliged."

Lance nodded. "The CIA gives protection ..."

"... And Van Buren's got the organization and the perfect

way to get the drugs and junk paper into circulation …"

"The casinos," said Lance.

They looked at each other in silence.

"How long have you known this?"

"Bill hinted at it last night when I phoned him. He said that Devlin had let slip something in a meeting that only Tobin and his investigation would have known."

"Taking down Van Buren is going to be hard enough" said Lance. "Going after the CIA is plain suicide.

"Let's just stick to Van Buren."

"There may be collateral damage."

Meredith nodded. "How much will be down to how well Mister Wynter plays it."

The hubbub of the drug store began to recede as the stark reality of the situation began to sink in. Both of them realized that with this new information, Wynter's plan began to have a diminishing chance of success. Meredith had been talked into it, against her better judgment, by persuasive words and a cute English accent. All her experience and intuition now told her it was time to adopt plan B. Trouble was, there was no plan B, and besides, plan A was up and running.

Lance sat there looking straight ahead. His eyes glazed over and the interior of the bar went steadily out of focus as his mind turned over Tobin's words: *"If I were you, I'd make pretty damn sure I knew where my career was going with this investigation."*

He lifted his cup and finished his coffee in one gulp.

"Bill Bradshaw's got Delaney's back … who's got yours?"

Lance put the empty cup back on the table.

Chapter 17

Hellman leaned back in his chair and read the letter for the third time. He still wasn't sure what to make of it. Why would the Deputy Secretary of the Department of the Interior ask him to a meeting?

"An opportunity has arisen ..."

An opportunity for what ... and for whom?

Hellman was naturally cautious when it came to dealing with Government Departments. Experience had taught him that politicians either wanted something for nothing, or they were using him to kick a difficult project into the long grass. He remembered spending four years, on and off, working on a development that he was later told never stood a chance, but which had been the price of a political alliance. Who was to say this wasn't another time wasting exercise? He glanced down at the signature - Gerry Wynter? Was this really an *opportunity* for Hellman, or something to advance this guy Wynter's career? Hellman turned his attention to the letter.

"... to discuss the placing of a contract."

Was this guy Wynter looking for advice, or was he offering a deal? Hellman looked up. If Wynter wanted advice it was going to cost him. Lawyers, attorneys, doctors: they all charged for advice; why should property developers be any different.

"In view of your experience, expertise and standing in the San Francisco property market, you are invited to attend a meeting ... "

Hellman smiled. He liked the sound of that. It had a ring to it. At least the Federal Government was beginning to recognize his talents, even if some of the Bay's older residents kept their heads firmly up their asses. But why was the meeting being held in a hotel and not in one of the government's own buildings? He put the letter down on his desk and reached over to the intercom.

"Julie, come in here."

"Yes, Mister Hellman," said Julie's disembodied voice.

Hellman leaned back in his chair, re-read the letter and savored the words. *"Experience ... expertise ... and standing."* He said them out loud, rolling them around his mouth and enjoyed their resonance. He had also noted that the letter said West Coast and not just San Francisco. He was getting to be known as a player - someone they couldn't just ignore.

The door opened and Julie entered with her pad and pen in her hand.

"When did this letter arrive?" said Hellman, waving it.

"About an hour ago," replied Julie, "when you were out."

"In the mail?"

Julie shook her head. "Special courier."

Hellman nodded. "It's an invitation from the government - to a meeting."

"In Washington?" asked Julie, almost impressed that she worked for someone who received government invitations.

"No," said Hellman shaking his head and looking at his secretary as he would an errant child. "Here, in town."

"Just you?"

"That's what I want you to find out."

"How?" asked Julie, a little worried. "You want me to ring Washington?"

"No," said Hellman, giving a dismissive sigh. "But you're friendly with Joe Arnstein's secretary, aren't you? You two got on pretty well over the problems on that Jackson Square site."

"I speak to his PA now and then, yes."

"Go give her a call. Ask her if Arnstein's received one of these letters. Then suggest she calls Johansson's secretary to see if he got one. Check out the other big property guys. Use that secretary network of yours to check out who might be at this meeting."

"OK," said Julie, as she turned and made her way to the door. "But we stopped being secretaries some time ago; we're Personal Assistants, if you hadn't noticed."

"Sure," smiled Hellman as the door closed behind her. "Of course you are."

He sat back and wondered if the rumors coming out of Washington could tie in with this meeting. Galvanized into action, he leaned forward, picked up the telephone and dialed a City Hall number, drumming his fingers on the desk's leather inlay while he waited for an answer. Until he knew something more definite, he decided against saying anything to Van Buren.

"Joey: you enjoyed Billy Joel?"... Good... Sure, love to, just tell me when... Yeah, so did I... Look, Joey, have you had a chance to get in touch with your guy in DC ... you did ... and ..."

Hellman picked up a pen and began to make a couple of notes. Those over-priced concert tickets were turning out to have been a good investment.

"That's interesting, thanks ... get him to check out a guy called Gerry Wynter, that's W-Y-N-T-E-R ... that's it ... he's the Deputy Secretary of the Department of the Interior ... could be following on from these rumors ... that's what I thought too; he's coming out to the West Coast in a couple of days ... OK ... call me when you have."

Hellman put the 'phone down and swiveled gently from side to side in his chair, tapping his pen on the pad as he thought about what Joey had just told him. He reached out and picked up the telephone again: it seemed a good time to see if Senator Reece had heard anything.

***

It was late evening and almost everyone had left the building. Meredith was still in her office, and so deep in her thoughts about tomorrow that she didn't hear her office door open.

"Still working?" asked Tobin.

His voice startled Meredith, and she looked round.

"I never seem to catch up with you these days, and that got me thinking ... is that by accident or design?" continued Tobin. There was no menace in his voice; it was just a gentle enquiry.

Meredith spread her hands and shrugged her shoulders.

"Bad timing, I guess. I've been busy ..." she looked him straight in the eye. "You've been busy ..."

"I guess we've both been busy," agreed Tobin. "Mind if I sit down?"

"No," she gestured to the vacant chair on the other side of her desk. "Of course not."

He settled himself into the chair and crossed his legs. He had taken a hard line with Lance the day before; now it was time for the more measured, conciliatory approach.

"Join me?" asked Meredith, holding up the whisky bottle.

He nodded his head, and she poured a generous measure into the second glass and pushed it towards him. She raised her glass.

"Here's to a successful outcome ... whatever that is."

He raised his glass and they drank a toast to the operation.

"I thought it was time we had a talk."

"I think you're right," she said.

"Where d'you think things are going with your investigation?" said Tobin, settling back in the chair.

"We've come to the conclusion that the counterfeiting gang will stop operations for a while, until things have calmed down."

Tobin nodded. "You caused quite a stir over Petersen's death."

"Shake the tree ... see what falls out."

"Pick up anything interesting?"

"Just a few small twigs, nothing substantial."

"Your assistant ..."

"Lance?"

"Yes. He seems to be pursuing his own separate line of enquiry. Got it into his head there's a drug connection. You know anything about that?"

"Lance thinks there's a drug connection with all crime; it comes of spending three years in Florida's drug squad."

"He thinks it might be a combined operation: drugs and counterfeit money."

"I wouldn't have thought that would be wise."

Tobin looked puzzled. "Why not?"

"Think about it. If the drug cartel got it into their heads they were being paid with counterfeit money, it would result in a lot of dead bodies about the place." Meredith paused and looked directly at Tobin. "Would you take that risk?" She took a sip of whisky.

Tobin nodded his head slowly in agreement as he thought about this.

"You may have a point."

"How's Washington?" asked Meredith, changing the subject.

"As it is always," said Tobin, leaving his thoughts about drugs behind. "Full of rumors."

"DC runs on rumors."

"There's a rumor surfacing about the West Coast at the moment."

"They'll be talking about the East Coast tomorrow," shrugged Meredith. What had Tobin heard?

"Something about a deal out here in California."

"They make thousands of deals a day out here," she said. "Deals aren't exclusive to Washington and New York, you know."

"A real estate deal … something about planning." Her rumor was spreading. "You heard anything about it?" continued Tobin.

"Planning? In California? It's got to be worth a try," said Meredith, aiming to keep the mood frivolous.

"Can't have reached here yet," said Tobin, taking a sip of whisky while he thought of events in Washington.

"Most rumors don't; they get run down trying to cross the Beltway."

"Rumor is this deal's pretty big. That's why they're keeping it quiet.

"Well, there's a thing: a silent rumor. I must tell Lance."

"I don't think Lance is too happy," said Tobin, trying to catch Meredith off balance.

"No?"

Tobin shook his head. "He's not sure where this investigation is headed."

"I'm not too sure myself."

"Of course you've got Bill Bradshaw looking after you … but who's watching his back?"

There was a silence between them. Was Tobin bluffing? A fleeting thought went through Meredith's head … did Tobin know something about Lance that she didn't?

"I spoke to him yesterday," Tobin continued. "He thinks you may be going down the wrong track."

"We're investigating all possible angles." She decided that Tobin was bluffing.

"Lance is worried that this wrong track is going to take his career to a place he doesn't want to be."

Tobin took a mouthful of whisky. The veiled threat to both Lance and Meredith was left hanging in the air between them for a few seconds.

"Well, we'll have to make sure it's not the wrong track."

A hard edge had entered Meredith's voice. She was certain that Tobin was playing games, but just to make sure she'd discuss it with Lance. "I'm not going to be around much in the next few days" - the hard edge softened and she smiled - "Too much to do out there."

Tobin nodded and drained his glass of whisky. Standing up, he looked at Meredith.

"And I've been called back to DC - you aren't the only one with things to do." He walked over to the door, then turned. "If I were you, I'd keep an eye on your assistant."

Meredith nodded as Tobin left the office.

Chapter 18

There was nothing more that Wynter could do.

He looked at his watch: they were due in fifteen minutes. He scanned the room. Was everything in place or had he overlooked something? Walking over to one of the windows, he glanced out. The small cul-de-sac leading to the hotel was quiet. These people would rather turn up late than early: that's if they were going to turn up at all.

Wynter had moved, and was occupying a suite that looked out over the front of the hotel. The staff had followed Meredith's instruction to the letter. In fact the room looked better than Wynter could have hoped. A round table was at one end of the room with plates of canapés - appetizing enough to tempt, but not so extravagant as to be ostentatious. He couldn't be seen to waste money - these people were tax payers. Two coffee machines were on a side table, the final drops of freshly brewed Blue Mountain dripping into the glass jug of one, while the other would be switched on when the guests arrived. Half a dozen fine porcelain cups and saucers stood waiting to one side, with cream and sugar. Two hotel waiters, one by the coffee and one by the canapés, stood ready to serve the guests.

He glanced out of the window again: still quiet. A rising panic gripped him. What if nobody turned up? What if they were all busy? What if they had all figured out it was a con? He looked at his watch: thirteen minutes to zero - then closed his eyes and took a few deep breaths to steady himself. He'd be fine when things got going, he always was, but the waiting played havoc with his stomach. It really wouldn't surprise him if he was starting an ulcer.

The door opened and in walked Meredith, followed by Lance, who carried a small pile of folders. Meredith quickly assessed the room in one sweeping glance then turned to Wynter.

"Got everything you need?"

Wynter nodded as Lance went to the other end of the room, where a Regency dining table took up most of the space. There were seven matching mahogany chairs: three on each side and one at the head. On the polished surface of the table in front of each chair, Lance placed a folder.

Meredith moved towards Wynter and, for a split second, all the Englishman's poise and confidence was stripped away and she caught a glimpse of vulnerability behind his ice-cool facade.

"You sure you're going to …" she said, quietly. "You look a little …"

He managed a nervous smile. "Always do … just before …"

She smiled back. "I can imagine."

"One roll of the dice … no second chance."

She moved her head closer to his and whispered, "Separates the *real* men …"

For a couple of seconds, there was a charge of electricity in the air between them. Wynter thought that she was going to kiss him. He'd like that … he'd like that a lot. A nervous voice from the other end of the room intruded and shattered the moment.

"Anything else you want me to do?" asked Lance.

Meredith gave Wynter smile of encouragement. "Good luck," she whispered, then turned to Lance at the other end of the room.

She looked at her watch, then glanced at him. "No, Lance, I think we've done everything."

She took a last quick look around the room, then turned her head to Wynter. "I guess this is where we find out how good you *really* are."

"I guess you're right," said Wynter. He took a deep breath; his stomach had started to churn again.

**

Hellman had wondered whether he should drive himself to the meeting, or whether he should get a driver. Parking was a bitch in that part of town and he didn't want the embarrassment of having everyone at the meeting seeing his Jaguar being towed away. Better to have someone drive him and take care of the car.

"I'll send Jago to drive you," had been Van Buren's reaction when he had told him about the meeting. "Can't be seen to drive yourself; creates the wrong impression." Hellman tried arguing but Van Buren cut him short. Jago would do the driving. Hellman could hardly explain that he wanted to keep as much of the meeting as possible to himself; with Jago around, information would inevitably leak back.

As far as Hellman was concerned, the less Van Buren knew about the meeting, the better. He needed control of this deal, whatever it was. He had no intention of being sidelined, or worse, cut out. He'd seen that happen before when greed took over, and Van Buren was known to be greedy.

As Jago turned the Jaguar into the cul-de-sac, Hellman saw that he wasn't the first to arrive. Peter Johansson's five liter Mercedes straddled the double yellow lines, and in front of it was Joe Arnstein's Rolls Royce. A Lamborghini Miura was parked to one side of the hotel's front door, with Arnstein's and Johansson's drivers standing around smoking and admiring the Italian supercar. Hellman's Jaguar might well turn heads downtown, but it couldn't compete in either style or expense in this company. Hellman began to feel nervous, his sense of inferiority never far away. He would have to put on a show; let these people know he was as good as them. The Jaguar pulled up behind the Mercedes, and Hellman waited as Jago got out and opened the back door for him.

Joe Arnstein munched a canapé as he looked out of the window. What was Hellman doing here? This was a little out of his league, surely? He watched as Hellman disappeared into the hotel's front door beneath him, while Jago sauntered over and joined the two men looking at the Lamborghini. Joe smiled: the chauffeurs' union. He'd get to hear all about it later, during the drive back to the office. Peter Johansson joined him at the window.

"The British for aristocratic style; the Germans for boring reliability; but if you really want to turn peoples' heads, it has to be Italian," said Johansson.

"Totally impractical …"

"Of course … but absolutely stunning."

"Hellman's arrived."

"Hellman?" said Johansson, raising his eyebrows. "Really?"

One of the hotel's waiters walked over with a cup of coffee on a small tray.

"Thank you," said Johansson as he took the cup.

"Any idea what this contract's about?" asked Arnstein.

"Not a clue," said Johansson, shaking his head.

Just then the door opened and Hellman and Alex Perez, the owner of the Lamborghini, were ushered into the room by the middle-aged bell boy.

"Just been admiring your new toy, Alex; does she drive as beautifully as she looks?" asked Johansson.

"She's Italian …" shrugged Perez, as he helped himself to a canapé from the plate offered by the waiter.

"Needs a firm hand then," said Johansson. As an afterthought he turned to Hellman and gave a rather reserved nod: "Hellman."

Hellman nodded back, but said nothing as he waited for his coffee. He looked around the room; Arnstein and Johansson he knew would be there; Perez he'd heard about, but never met. He took the cup from the tray held out by the waiter while he wondered who else would show.

"I take her out two, three times a month; just to keep her up to it," said Perez.

"Rather like a mistress," said Arnstein.

"But not as expensive," smiled Perez. "She's a collector's piece. They only made one hundred and fifty of that model … twenty years and she'll be worth ten times what I paid for her … a mistress only deteriorates."

Perez walked over to the side table. While the waiter was pouring his coffee he turned to Hellman.

"You still selling industrial units?"

"Why?" said Hellman. "You want one?"

Perez gave a dismissive smile, and turned his back.

"Here's Stapleton …" said Arnstein, who was still at the window as another Mercedes turned into the cul-de-sac, followed by a green Bentley, "… and O'Brien."

Arnstein glanced over at the table and counted the chairs: seven. He went through the names in his mind: Johansson; Perez; Stapleton; O'Brien; adding himself, and allowing for one place at the head of the table for this guy Wynter, made six … Hellman made seven. They had all arrived. Arnstein looked over at Hellman; he'd always thought of him as someone on the edge; a little too sharp for his own good, especially with the company he kept. Had he rounded off some of his rough corners and started putting deals together big enough to put him in this company? He sipped his coffee. Was Hellman shaping up to be someone he should start to worry about?

Hellman kept his distance from the others. He could feel

their condescension as it oozed across the floor towards him. God, how he hated these people. Whatever this contract was, Hellman wanted it. He wanted it badly.

The door opened and in walked Wynter. Gone were the nervousness and nausea - Wynter was every inch the Deputy Secretary of the Department of the Interior. Dropping his distinctly English accent, Wynter spoke from somewhere in the mid-Atlantic, tinged with a slight southern drawl.

"Good morning, gentlemen, I'm so glad to see you all here," he said. "I trust you have all been looked after?"

There were murmurs of morning; hello and a couple of nods from the guests. One of the waiters picked up the full jug of fresh coffee and offered re-fills.

"Good. My name is Gerald Wynter … Gerry." Wynter smiled benignly. "I would like to extend the government's thanks to you all for giving up your valuable time to be here. We appreciate that you are all extremely busy men. May I apologize also for the mysterious lack of specifics in your letters of invitation: you'll understand why when the meeting begins."

There was an expectant silence in the room. The waiter finished giving everyone re-fills, and the other waiter put the plate with the remaining canapés on the dining table.

"Thank you," said Wynter, dismissing them with a beaming smile. "If we need any more we can help ourselves."

The two hotel staff bowed slightly, turned and left the room.

Wynter made his way over to the head of the dining table, followed slowly by his guests.

"Gentlemen … please sit down."

They sat down each side of the table, except for Hellman, who took hold of a chair and moved it to the end, opposite Wynter, making a point of sitting on his own.

"I must impress upon you the need for absolute secrecy in the matter we are about to discuss," said Wynter. "If any word of it leaks out to the press or media, I can assure you there will be consequences." He paused to let the warning sink in then he broke into a beaming smile again.

"I am about to share a secret that is only known to me; to my superior, the Secretary of the Interior; and, of course, to the President."

By now everyone sat in rapt silence around the table, waiting for him to share the secret.

"When the information becomes public knowledge, as eventually it must, there will be an outcry from parts of the population … but by then it will be too late. We shall have closed the deal."

Wynter paused, and looked around the table. All eyes were on him.

"Gentlemen, I am here to invite your bids … for Alcatraz."

Chapter 19

Apart from one or two quiet intakes of breath, there was a stunned silence around the table. Even the languid Perez had looked surprised, while Johansson raised his eyebrows in astonishment. For his part, Hellman blinked rather faster than normal. No wonder they'd kept this quiet.

"No doubt you've seen and read reports in the media about the problems regarding the future of Alcatraz," said Wynter.

There were nods and murmurs around the table.

"I thought that was just talk …" said Arnstein.

"It comes up every few years and nothing ever gets done," said O'Brien.

"I can assure you, Mister O'Brien, this time something *is* going to be done. That's why you're all here."

There was an expectant silence which Wynter spun out to the full, looking at each of them in turn, then continued.

"Due to further cutbacks in public spending, we have to find another role for Alcatraz. After discussing the problem at length, and at the highest level, we have concluded that the private sector is best placed to take Alcatraz into the future."

"Are we talking about just the prison, or the whole island?" said Arnstein.

"Everything: the whole island, and all the buildings on it."

"Would there be any restrictions on what we could do with the buildings?"

"The cell block would have to stay pretty much as it is, and the lighthouse; but the rest ... no."

"So a hotel would be okay?"

"A theme park?"

"What about a casino?"

"I don't think there would be a problem with any of those," said Wynter, nodding.

"Would it be an outright sale, or are you offering a lease?"

"The government is offering a nine hundred and ninety nine year lease ... effectively the freehold."

There was a lull as the group came to terms with what they'd just heard. It was a lot to take in. Big property deals usually took years, decades, to put together; and here they were being offered a whole island in one go. Arnstein took off his glasses and started to polish them, Perez shifted in his seat, and Johansson looked at the chandelier as if seeking guidance from above.

"As you all realize, it is very rarely that such an opportunity presents itself," said Wynter. "You have all been selected because you are the biggest players in the Bay real estate market, and because you are all in a position to close the deal quickly."

"Why quickly?" asked O'Brien.

"I'm sure I don't have to remind you of the occupation in 1969 …"

There were muted murmurs and nods as memories were dredged and forgotten facts coaxed back to mind.

"I was on the East Coast in 1969," said Hellman. "Remind me."

"I'm sorry, Mister Hellman. A group of Native Americans calling themselves the United Indians of All Tribes occupied the island in protest against government policy. They were mainly college students from San Francisco, but, as word spread, they attracted activists from across the country. They claimed that they had a right to the island under the provisions of the 1868 Treaty of Laramie. When that failed, they claimed that as indigenous peoples knew the island before any Europeans had come to North America, they had a claim by 'Right of Discovery'. They hadn't; but it took a lot of effort to persuade them of that and it dragged on for years. A very difficult situation and one we have no desire to repeat."

"Why did they call it off?"

"President Nixon changed government policy."

"So they won."

Wynter shrugged, "Gentlemen, we aren't here to discuss government policy towards Native Americans. If you have any misgivings on a cultural basis you can always withdraw."

Wynter looked slowly around the table. He calculated that no-one gave a damn about indigenous cultures. He was right … no-one moved.

"To get back to your point, Mister O'Brien, this project

requires speed and secrecy in order to avoid a repeat of the events of 1969. I need hardly remind you that since then other protest groups have sprung up to protect the planet; the environment; marine life; animals; birds …" Wynter smiled. "You name it, someone will protect it. When the deal's done, and you've got your security team safely on the island, that's the time we'll make the announcement. Until then, speed and secrecy are paramount."

"How do you intend to sell this lease?"

"At auction, with you as the preferred bidders: in fact, you will be the only bidders. Those of you who wish to take part will submit sealed bids to me here at the hotel. You'll find all the terms and conditions in the folders in front of you."

Everyone except Hellman opened their folders and started to rifle through them.

"You will also find all the relevant facts you need to make those bids – plus plans; descriptions; valuations; photographs. You can, of course, visit the island to verify anything for yourselves, but the contract will be based on the information in the file."

Hellman's mind was working overtime: Alcatraz … a whole island. This was the deal he had been waiting for, hoping for, looking for - the one that would make him. It would also get him out of the hole he was in with Van Buren. Hellman smiled: ironic for someone with Van Buren's background to have the chance of buying Alcatraz.

"Do we get to see a copy of the lease?" asked Perez.

"There's one in each of the files, but as you will see, it's a fairly basic document." All except Hellman started to flick through the file, looking for the lease. "There are two restrictive covenants," Wynter continued. "One covers the cell block and the other the lighthouse; but most of the other clauses are open to negotiation prior to signature."

"How long have we got?" asked Arnstein.

"How long …?" asked Wynter.

"How long before you want the sealed bids?"

"Seven days, gentlemen. Your bids must be in by twelve noon, one week from today, and whoever wins the auction must lodge a banker's draft with me for fifteen per cent of the agreed price within five days after that."

"Ten per cent is the usual deposit," said Johansson.

"How many islands have you bought, Mister Johansson?" asked Wynter, speaking with the assurance of a government official not used to being questioned. Johansson looked down at the table.

"As I said before," continued Wynter, "this is an unusual sale." He looked around the faces, inviting any other objections regarding the deposit: there were none.

"I'll run through the main points and answer any questions that you may have in a moment," said Wynter, "but before I do, I must make one thing clear. As I have already told you, only myself, and two other people in the country knew about this sale before today: now, you also know. It is classified information. If it becomes public knowledge, it will be because of someone in this room."

Wynter paused and slowly looked at each of the potential bidders.

"If word does get out," he continued, "the government will deny all knowledge, and we *will* find out who leaked it. Following a spell in prison, the guilty party may as well kiss goodbye to any future in the property business. He will find it virtually impossible to get consent for any building project, and lines of credit and finance would very quickly dry up. *He wouldn't be allowed to build so much as a dog kennel.*" Wynter paused for effect. "Those were the President's exact words."

For a few seconds Wynter held the stern silence, then his face broke into a great beaming smile.

"But enough of dog kennels. Let's go through the main points of the offer, and I'll be glad to answer any questions that you may have."

There was an audible sigh around the table as they got down to the business of the sale. Wynter smiled: it was working … so far.

***

Jago had no interest in cars, Italian or otherwise. To him they were just a means of getting around: faster than walking, but you didn't get to see so much. Jago liked to see things. Before working for Van Buren, he had been a soldier. He'd been trained to take notice of where he was: to scope out the territory. He liked to know what he was getting into, and wanted to find the quickest way out. He slipped away from the group of other drivers disputing the relative merits of the Lamborghini, and headed into the hotel. He knew that reconnaissance was never wasted. Besides, Van Buren had given him instructions to find out all he could about this meeting. Stepping into the hotel, he heard a voice to his right.

"Good morning, sir," said the doorman, wafting irony in Jago's direction.

"Morning," replied Jago. "Look, I gotta go to the restroom, you got somewhere I could …"

The doorman's voice softened a little. "Oh, yeah …" He pointed to a door in the far corner. "Go through that door and the staff restroom is second on the left."

"Thanks." Jago paused: most doormen were from the military … it was worth a shot. "You ex-service?"

"I'm not ex anything, sir - once a marine, always a marine."

"No kidding. Which unit were you in?"

"The Eleventh."

Jago smiled. "Out at Pendleton."

"Yeah … and you?" said the doorman, relaxing.

"I was in the Fifth."

"Semper Fi."

Jago smiled: "Semper Fi." A bond was forged. He put his hand to his stomach and started across the floor towards the door. "Sorry, got to go, I'll catch you later."

"The kitchen is at the end of the corridor, they'll give you some coffee," the doorman called after him.

Once through the door, Jago took his hand from his stomach, headed past the staff restrooms and down the corridor. The kitchens were usually pretty close to the back door for the sake of deliveries. He came to a junction and turned right and then left; the corridor got wider and he saw large double doors at the far end.

As Jago walked towards the doors, he passed storerooms on his right with shelves full of large cans and catering size bags of flour. One room was marked, "*Cold room - Keep door closed*". From the clatter of pans and muffled orders, Jago reckoned that the kitchen was on his left. This was confirmed when a large door swung open and a white coated man in checkered trousers crossed the corridor and disappeared into one of the store rooms. At the end of the corridor, Jago pushed one of the doors open and walked out into the service area behind the hotel.

He was confronted with a rectangular yard the width of the hotel, bounded by buildings on either side. Casting a military eye over it he quickly saw that three quarters of the yard served as a car park for guests, while at the far end was a high wall with an electronically operated gate which rolled to one side, allowing access to the street. The gate was smooth metal and difficult to climb: anyone wanting to get over that would need rope and a hook. He counted five security cameras that were visible. Jago looked around the kitchen door area. As service areas go, it was quite tidy. There was a pile of flattened cardboard boxes in a tall container on wheels, and various other wheeled bins waiting for the garbage collection.

He walked a few paces into the yard, turned and looked up at the back of the hotel. He was particularly interested in the metal steps of the fire escape which zigzagged down the wall. There was a metal gallery which ran the width of each floor under the windows, connecting with the steps.

Turning to have a look closer look at the security gate at the far end of the yard, he stopped. Two young women leaning against a car were watching him with obvious interest.

Wearing white blouses and black skirts, Jago guessed they were hotel employees, probably maids or waitresses. Jago wondered whether he should just carry on, but then again, this place has the sort of clientele that made hotel security nervous. Someone nosing around on the wrong side of the fence would likely get reported, and make the management suspicious. He walked over to them, better let them know everything's OK.

"Hi," said Jago. "Tom Finn, independent security ... I give the place a look over every now and then. Just checking that everything's as it should be."

"Sure," said the blonde, as both girls nodded.

"You two work here?"

"Yeah," said the brunette, grinding the stub of her cigarette under her shoe.

There was an awkward silence. The girls didn't appear eager to say anything further, and Jago reckoned he'd seen all that was worth seeing.

"Well," said Jago, "I'd better get back to it; got to keep everyone safe. I expect I'll see you again."

The blonde smiled back. Jago turned and made his way back towards the service door of the hotel. The brunette turned to her companion.

"Lehman?"

"I think so," nodded the blonde.

It was an hotel rule that all strangers in the service yard should be reported to the manager, Mister Lehman.

Chapter 20

Meredith switched the Revox tape recorder to re-wind, and the spools hummed as the tape sped between them. She was in the office next to Wynter's hotel room where she was discussing the meeting with him.

"I'm impressed," said Meredith, "you were good ... very good."

"I didn't know you were recording the meeting," said Wynter. He hoped his annoyance didn't show in his voice.

"You didn't need to know. Besides, it would have been a distraction."

"I've had to work with distractions before."

"I wasn't taking the chance," said Meredith as she switched off the tape recorder. "D'you think they believed you?"

"We'll only know the answer to that if they bid. Johansson didn't seem particularly interested, but then we didn't think he would be."

Meredith nodded. "He's stretched financially."

"Perez is a bit of an unknown quantity - unpredictable. O'Brien and Stapleton are both looking for new projects. It depends if they can see a commercial future for the island."

"O'Brien asked about a casino."

"Yeah, that's promising," said Wynter, nodding. "He really believed me: I could see that in his face."

"What about Hellman?"

"Oh, he believed …"

"Yeah?"

"Sure of it."

"But will he bid?"

Wynter nodded. "Yeah, he'll bid. He's got something to prove."

"He didn't seem to care much for the rest of them."

"He hates them. They treated him as if he shouldn't be there. Not a member of their club."

"There were some pretty snide comments."

"He made them think," nodded Wynter. "Now they've all gone away wondering if Hellman's pulled off a few big deals on the East Coast they didn't know about."

"Not my concern. Let them wonder."

Wynter went over to a side table and poured himself another cup of coffee. "Where was the bug?"

"Bugs," said Meredith, emphasizing the plural. "One in each chandelier, above the tables. Why?"

"Guess I just like to know." It irritated him that she hadn't told him, but not enough to be worth making it an issue.

"There's something else you ought to know."

Wynter looked up. The hint of reluctance in her voice made him think that he might not like what he ought to know. "What?"

"Hellman's driver was seen in the service area at the back of the hotel. He was giving the place a pretty thorough once over, checking the exits, the fire escape and the back gate."

"Why do you think he was doing that?"

"We don't know yet," shrugged Meredith.

"Then why mention it?"

"Because he's not Hellman's driver," said Meredith. "He works for Van Buren."

"Doing what?" said Wynter

"His chauffeur, also his bodyguard. An ex-Marine by the name of Jago."

Wynter sighed, "How long's he been out?"

"Not long enough to have forgotten anything."

Wynter nodded. "Got any more surprises?"

Meredith shook her head. "I thought you ought to know about Jago."

"Thanks," said Wynter, taking a sip of coffee. "You got a photograph of the guy?"

Meredith nodded. "We're getting you one."

"Anything else I should know?"

Meredith shook her head. She had decided that Wynter didn't need to know that Jago killed people.

Not yet, anyway.

***

As Hellman stepped into the house and followed the butler, Jago peeled off and went to the kitchen for a sandwich. When they had left the hotel, Hellman initially wanted to go back to his office, but Jago had thought differently. His instructions from Van Buren were to bring Hellman straight back to see him after the meeting at the hotel, and Jago wasn't one to ignore instructions.

The butler announced him, and Hellman strode across the terrace. For once, he wasn't nervous - a calm feeling, almost of triumph, accompanied him. He'd found the site Van Buren had been searching for. A genuine smile broke out across his face for the first time on that terrace. Van Buren watched him approach but didn't get up from his chair.

"Well?" said Van Buren, avoiding a greeting.

"I've found your site."

"Yeah?" A smile hovered around Van Buren's face. "Where?"

"Six acres, private, quiet, and it's got great views. Not so much 'on' the Bay, as 'in' the Bay."

Van Buren's hovering smile turned into a grin, then a perplexed frown. "Where?"

"Alcatraz," said Hellman, with the flourish of a magician pulling a rabbit from a hat.

Van Buren moved his head as if he hadn't heard properly and the frown intensified.

"The Government's decided to sell it; the whole island," said Hellman. He stood still, like a dog that had performed a trick and was waiting for its reward.

"Alcatraz? You sure you were at the right meeting?"

"Oh yes. They're selling a lease on the place."

"You gotta be kidding me," said Van Buren, in a distant voice. His eyes started to narrow and his jaw to take on the appearance of granite.

"It's been kept quiet because they don't want it occupied again … the Native Americans … like in nineteen sixty nine …"

Hellman's voice trailed off. He got the feeling that he might as well have said they were selling the White House.

"You turn up here," said Van Buren, getting out of his chair, "and try and sell me Alcatraz?"

Hellman took a couple of steps backwards.

"Jesus Christ! I had friends in there!" shouted Van Buren. The veins in his temples began to throb. "Are you trying to set me up?"

"No … no … I swear," said Hellman as he backed away, his euphoria evaporating. He broke into a sweat as the adrenaline began to pump around his body, and suddenly the danger of his situation became all too apparent.

"You got some nerve," snarled Van Buren.

"No … it's … not like that," he stammered. Hellman felt the situation drifting away from him. "The biggest real estate developers on the West Coast were there … Arnstein, O'Brien, Johansson … and the Deputy Secretary of the Interior …"

"George Washington there too? How about Abe Lincoln?"

Hellman desperately played his last card. His hands were shaking as he laid his briefcase on the table and pulled out the file that detailed all the sale particulars.

"This is the file that the Deputy Secretary gave me … the details of the island … plus the terms and conditions of the sale," said Hellman, trying to explain. He held out the file to Van Buren. "It fits in with the rumors that have been coming out of Washington. We know there's a big property deal going down." By now Hellman was pleading. "Everyone's talking about it."

Van Buren stared at him and snatched the file.

"It explains the secrecy as well," continued Hellman. His voice had risen an octave and was thin and reedy. "The Government doesn't want another occupation … Everything fits …" He was falling over his words, his voice tailed off and he stood in petrified silence.

Van Buren flicked through the file, then looked at Hellman.

"I don't know how much truth you've just told me; or how much this man …" he glanced at the file, "… Wynter … has told you a pack of lies. Either way I aim to find out."

Van Buren put the file down on the table.

"Send Jago to me on your way out."

Hellman breathed a big sigh of relief at being dismissed, and his fingers fumbled over snapping the briefcase closed. He had done what he could. It was up to Van Buren now.

***

It was nearing three o'clock when Meredith headed around the Bay to Oakland, where Senator Reece had his office. He liked to be among the people he represented, or so he told them at election time - not that many of his electorate could have afforded to rent an office in the opulent building. From the fifth floor, Reece had a stunning view over the Bay, past Angel Island and Alcatraz to the Golden Gate. It was almost worth the exorbitant rent the building's owners charged. Not that the senator himself paid. The bill was picked up, indirectly of course, by a refuse company. The same refuse company that collected most of Oakland's trash, and had done for the last fourteen years.

The view, however, wasn't the first thing on Meredith's mind as she flashed her Secret Service badge at the two assistants in the outer office and strode purposefully past. One of them followed her in to Reece's office to protest.

"I'm sorry, Senator," said the assistant, glaring at Meredith. "She didn't give me her name."

"If your PA stays in the room, Senator Reece, my visit becomes official," said Meredith, putting her leather attaché case on Reece's desk.

Reece looked at the case, then Meredith's steely gaze. "It's OK, Helen," said Reece, "I know who she is. I'll hear what Ms. Delaney has to say ... you can go."

The PA turned and walked towards the door, as Meredith's voice followed her. "No interruptions, and no phone calls."

The door closed defiantly, and Meredith opened her attaché case.

"When I started out in the Service, Senator, my boss told me a story." Meredith took a large envelope from the case. "I guess all new recruits got the same thing. I think you'd benefit from hearing it."

She took a ten by eight print from the envelope and laid it on the desk. Reece ignored it.

"There was once an agent who thought the Secret Service meant just that: everything was secret ..."

She laid another photograph of the senator's meeting

with Hellman at Lincoln Park next to the first. In the foreground, two children were reading the plaque on which were written the names of the dead from USS San Francisco. His curiosity was building, but Reece still managed to avoid taking a look.

"An agent who thought that his badge and position protected him, so he could play, not just both ends, but *all* ends against the middle - taking a rake-off from everyone ..."

She laid a series of bank statements from a Panamanian Bank next to the photographs. That's when Reece cracked and took his first look.

"... And he thought that because he was in the Secret Service he could keep it quiet."

Meredith took out a transparent plastic sleeve containing four of Van Buren's very good counterfeit hundred dollar bills. Reece frowned. His heart rate had increased and his breathing got heavier.

"Problem was, this agent didn't count on making any enemies while he was playing everyone off against each other; he didn't think they'd know ..."

Two more photographs of the meetings with Hellman were produced and laid next to the counterfeit bills. One of the photographs showed the same two children posing in front of the schooner A.J. Thayer on Hyde Street Pier. Hellman and Reece were clearly visible in the background.

"... And boy, did he pile up enemies."

Meredith pulled out a sheet of paper detailing an inventory that the Secret Service had taken of the security box held by a well known bank in the name of A. Lincoln.

"Well, one day his enemies got together and decided to call the agent out on his crooked schemes …"

Finally she produced a letter from the well known bank with a photograph identifying Mister A. Lincoln as Senator Reece. By now all color had drained from the senator's face.

"The agent ended up in jail."

"You had no right … no *legal* right to open that box," said Reece in a hoarse whisper.

"You want to take it to court, Senator? Go right ahead." There was a pause as Meredith picked up the sleeve with the forged banknotes. "These four bills were taken from an envelope containing five thousand counterfeit dollars found in your box. Your fee, I believe, from Mister Van Buren in Marin County for asking a few 'difficult' questions."

"You had no right," repeated Reece, visibly shaken by the fact that his private security box had been opened, and the revelation that Van Buren had bribed him with junk bills.

Meredith replaced the forged notes and placed her hands flat on the desk, leaned towards Reece and spoke very deliberately.

"I have a legal right to go anywhere. Anywhere that I believe someone is producing, passing, or dealing in counterfeit money."

A brief look of shock passed across the senator's face.

"You still want to challenge me in the courts, Reece? I'm sure the IRS would love to hear about the other two hundred and ten thousand dollars that we left in your box. And that's just for starters."

By now, Reece's mouth was dry. He remembered what

Meredith had said when she walked in; so far this wasn't official … so she must want to cut a deal. "What do you want?" he managed to croak out.

Meredith took her hands off the desk and straightened up. "What do we all want, Senator?" she asked, smiling and enjoying the moment. "A long life and happiness."

"Don't play games."

"I want to see that five thousand declared on your tax return."

"But you said it's worthless," said Reece.

"So? Give it back to Van Buren and demand some real money." Reece winced; that wasn't an option he was going to pursue. "No?" said Meredith. She started to smile. "Well I guess you're just going to have to swallow hard and take the loss."

"What if I don't?"

"Then I would have to arrest you and charge you with being in possession of, and dealing in, counterfeit money …" She leaned over the desk. "… And believe me, with your links to organized crime, I'd make sure you wouldn't make bail. Then I'd give the IRS a call."

Meredith stood up and smiled as she walked slowly towards the large window.

"You wouldn't get out this side of doomsday, Senator." She looked out over the Bay. "Tough places Federal prisons … you might even run into some of your old friends … well, they *were* friends, until you turned them in. Still, I'm sure they'd be real pleased to see *you* again … might even organize some kind of a welcoming party."

She turned and gave him a sweet smile. "How long do you think you'd last?"

Reece was sweating. He knew the chances of him surviving a week without a lengthy stay in the prison infirmary were so remote as to be non-existent … and even that depended on the prison guards getting to him fast. He shuddered at the thought if they didn't.

"So," he said, "I declare the money."

"Good … and remember, I'll be checking with the IRS The next thing you're going to do is make a phone call to Van Buren."

"Why?" said Reece, visibly worried.

"To tell him that Wynter takes bribes."

"Who's Wynter?' asked Reece, by now so scared that he had abandoned all rational thought about anything except his own survival.

"No-one you need worry about. All you've got to do is pass it on as a rumor you've heard coming out of Washington: something to do with this mysterious West Coast real estate deal. It would be nice if you could mention Senator Grant's name."

"Why?"

"Because that's what Van Buren is paying you to do."

For a moment Meredith thought he was going to refuse, but the nightmare of prison loomed too big and black in the senator's mind for anything but acceptance.

"What do I say?"

"You've had a lifetime's practice at lying, Senator - you'll think of something."

She put a couple of the photographs back into the envelope and started to collect the rest of the evidence and put it back in her briefcase.

"Best make it believable, though … I'll be right here listening."

Reece's fingers trembled as he started to dial Van Buren's number.

Chapter 21

The morning had brought glorious sunshine. Gone were the dismal wet sidewalks and fog of the previous night. Wynter enjoyed the sun. It made him feel relaxed. Finishing his cup of coffee, he folded his newspaper, picked up the phone and reached for the number that Meredith had left on the notepad. Once he heard the ringing tone, he leaned back in the chair - time to apply a little more pressure to Hellman.

So far, not one of the real estate developers had called him out over Alcatraz. None had expressed any serious doubts. They hadn't even questioned it. His pitch had been swallowed whole. Just as he hoped it would. But then, experience had taught him that greed could always overcome doubts when the returns were big enough. It all came down to what bait was on the hook and how the fish were played.

Wynter sat forward in his chair as he heard the call being answered and within a couple of minutes a meeting had been arranged. An hour later Wynter was strolling across the grass of Washington Square making his way towards the Church of Saints Peter and Paul. Just before he'd left the hotel, he glanced at the photograph that Meredith had given him. If

Jago was that good, then Wynter had better keep his eyes open for him. Memorizing the face, he'd stuffed the photograph in his pocket and headed out of the hotel, followed at a reasonable distance by one of the hotel's security guys.

Meredith was keeping tabs on the Englishman.

Hellman was sitting on one of the benches outside the church, and stood up as Wynter approached.

"Deputy Secretary," said Hellman, holding out his hand. "Good to see you again."

Wynter smiled as he shook hands. "Good to see you too, Steve."

"Should I call you Mister Wynter ... or Deputy Secretary ... or ...? I'm a little lost on ..."

"Gerry. Just call me Gerry," said Wynter, smiling as he scanned the area for any sign of Jago. He only saw the hotel security guy sitting on a bench forty yards away opening a newspaper.

"Sure," said Hellman.

There didn't seem to be any sign of Hellman's minder, but Wynter took his time sitting down on the bench, casting his eyes over the church façade and the square.

"I'm glad you came to the meeting. You're a breath of fresh air blowing through the rather predictable fog of the Bay's real estate business."

"It was good to be there, and thanks ... thanks for inviting me, Gerry."

Wynter smiled. "We felt it was time that someone else got a look in. Those other guys have been carving it up their way for too long. West Coast real estate needs some new blood." Wynter paused and looked directly at Hellman. "The President's very keen on giving younger men a chance."

"That's all I ask, Gerry, just give me a shot at the big contracts."

Wynter nodded, smiled and looked over at the church. "That's a pretty church, good proportions. Well built too, by the look of it."

Hellman smiled, "The Italian Cathedral of the West. They brought craftsmen over from Europe to work on it. It's where they held Joe DiMaggio's funeral. He's not buried here, but this is where they held it. He got married here too … but not to Marilyn," said Hellman, suddenly full of enthusiasm.

"Marilyn?"

"Monroe … Marilyn Monroe."

"Ah, yes," said Wynter.

"They took the photographs in front of the church, but they couldn't get married here because he hadn't got an annulment."

"He was a Catholic?"

"Yes, he was. They had to have a civil ceremony … but this is where Marilyn wanted their wedding photographs taken …" said Hellman, his voice tailing off.

"Nice," nodded Wynter, enjoying the sunshine and a little silence before he spoke again.

"You realize Johansson hasn't got the money and Arnstein's not interested." He turned and looked at

Hellman. "Perez is flaky. He may bid, he may not, but if he does, it will be low. He doesn't want it. He has two shopping malls which are giving him more than enough trouble at the moment."

"I heard that … about the malls."

"That leaves O'Brien, Stapleton … and you."

"I'm planning on bidding, Gerry, you bet … just working on it now," said Hellman, like an enthusiastic spaniel.

"Washington will be pleased to hear that. The President would like you to get out ahead." He leaned towards Hellman. "You're our preferred bidder. Of course, it would be a great help if you knew what you were up against." Wynter paused, allowing the moment to build. "Alcatraz is a problem we want rid of, but we won't be giving it away. I should think that O'Brien and Stapleton would each come in between eighteen and twenty million."

"Yeah, that's about what I reckon."

"I could be more exact … if you want."

Hellman looked perplexed, "More exact?"

"I *could* let you know what they've bid."

"But that …"

"… Would be between you and me, Steve. No-one else would ever have to know. That way you get what you want … and I would get what I want."

Hellman hesitated. "What would you want?"

Wynter sat back and spread his arms along the top of the back of the bench. "I am appointed by the President. There is an election at the end of the year, and there's no guarantee that the present incumbent will be re-elected. If he isn't, then I shall be out of a job. Contrary to what people think, government pensions aren't over generous. These are uncertain times, Steve. A small commission would help tide me over any difficulties I may encounter." Wynter turned and looked Hellman straight in the face. "It would also guarantee you get that lease."

Hellman lit a cigarette and thought fast. He'd been asked for bribes before. They were a firmly established part of the real estate business. But those guys had been architects, planners, landlords and city hall people. This was the Deputy Secretary of the Interior, for Christ's sake! He knew the President!

"How much of a small commission?" said Hellman, feeling his mouth go dry.

Wynter shrugged, "Shall we say five per cent of the deposit? A trifling sum to you, but to me ..."

"A trifling sum?"

"I estimate about a hundred and fifty thousand dollars. Seeing what you stand to gain in return, I feel embarrassed to ask."

"Yeah ... sure," said Hellman, more amazed than anything. A hundred and fifty thousand dollars! How was he going to get *that* past Van Buren?

"You agree to my little proposal?" said Wynter.

"What?"

"One hundred and fifty thousand ... you agree?"

Hellman shook his head, "Hell, I got to see someone about that ... but ... yes, I agree." Hellman reckoned it didn't make any difference what he said now, as long as he kept the ball in play. He could raise the money himself if need be.

Wynter smiled. "Good, bring it to the hotel. I foresee a bright future ahead of you." He smiled. "For both of us." He turned back to the Church. "Is Marilyn buried here, in San Francisco?"

Hellman's mind was still on one hundred and fifty thousand dollars. "Marilyn? No … no, she's buried down in L.A."

"Pity, I'd have gone to see her grave … such a troubled girl. She's buried with Joe?"

What if he just paid it himself and didn't tell Van Buren. "… Joe?"

"DiMaggio."

"Oh, no … she isn't buried with Joe."

Wynter sighed. "No-one seems to stay together these days." He stood up and looked at his watch. "Well, I've got an appointment I've got to make. I'll be in touch, Steve." He sauntered over to have a closer look at the church, and was struck by the street number, 666 - hardly appropriate for the Italian Cathedral of the West.

He wondered if Hellman was superstitious.

The hotel security guy folded his newspaper and stood up.

***

With Wynter temporarily out of the way, Meredith felt able to concentrate on a matter a little closer to home. She poured herself another cup of coffee and looked over at Lance.

"You okay?"

She didn't know why, but she had a nagging worry in the back of her mind. She had been so busy during the last couple of days that she had neglected Lance and something in his recent behavior didn't ring quite true.

"Yeah," said Lance.

"Sure?" said Meredith, not believing him. "You've been acting like you've got something on your mind."

"I'm okay," said Lance, but there was an echo in his voice that he couldn't disguise.

"We've been so tied up with this operation that we haven't had a chance to talk." She took her coffee and sat down on one of the sofas. "I couldn't have done it without your help. We wouldn't have got this far."

Help to do what thought Lance? Con some property developers into buying an island you don't even own? Tobin's warnings were gnawing away at his mind.

"Are you sure this is where you want to be?" said Lance.

"Yes," said Meredith, and looked straight at him. "Where would you rather be?"

"We're not going to get whoever's behind all this. Washington won't allow it, it's too political."

So that was it, thought Meredith. Tobin had been spreading poison.

"I'm aware of that, Lance, but we will be able to nail Van Buren."

"They might not allow even that. He might threaten to bring everyone down with him."

"Will he?"

"He'll try."

"He's going to have enough trouble staying alive in jail. Naming names would make it a certainty that he dies in prison. God knows he's arranged enough 'suicides' to realize that."

"Sure?"

"Don't you think I've thought of that, gone over that, time and time again?

They looked at each other in apprehensive silence. Meredith could see from Lance's expression that he wasn't convinced.

"It's not Van Buren that worries you, is it Lance? Tobin has been whispering in your ear about me." Lance looked away as Meredith continued, "the same way he's been whispering in my ear about you."

"You've let this become personal between you and Van Buren. At least you'd have the satisfaction of putting him away before you start a ten year stretch in FCI Dublin. I won't even have that."

"Neither of us is going to prison," said Meredith quietly.

"You sure of that?"

"Sure as I can be."

"Yeah, with Bill Bradshaw watching your back, I suppose you're safe. Who's looking out for me?"

"I am," said Meredith softly, "and so is Bill."

There was a tense silence then Lance's demeanor crumpled a little. He sighed, dropped his shoulders and his voice reverted to its usual softer tone.

"Tobin knows we're pulling something," he shook his head, "and his instructions are to not let it happen."

"If we stick to the plan he can't stop us," said Meredith.

Lance looked her in the eye.

"He's out for blood, Meredith … I don't want it to be mine."

***

Hellman hadn't expected the call from Van Buren so soon. *'Get over here,'* had been the instruction. It was not the sort of invitation Hellman could ignore. The forty minute drive to Marin County had been full of nervous tension. What had Van Buren's contacts turned up in Washington? What if he wasn't going to back the deal? What if he had decided that there was no deal? Hellman agonized about the hundred and fifty thousand Wynter wanted as a kickback. Should he even mention it?

The leather steering wheel of the Jaguar was wet with perspiration when he finally turned the engine off, and it was a very apprehensive Hellman that walked over the freshly raked gravel to the front door. As he emerged onto the terrace he saw Van Buren sitting at the table eating a chicken salad.

A few yards away at a smaller table sat Jago wearing dark glasses, watching the real estate developer's every move. When Hellman reached the large table there was no invitation to sit down. He just stood waiting. Hellman felt his palms starting to sweat. Finally Van Buren spoke.

"How come you didn't tell me this guy Wynter took bribes?"

For a few agonizing seconds Hellman didn't know what to say.

"I ... uh ... he, he only just asked me this morning. I didn't know whether you ..."

Van Buren took another mouthful of chicken.

"How much did he want?"

Hellman took a gulp of air. "Five per cent," stammered Hellman, "five per cent of the deposit ... about a hundred and fifty thousand dollars ..."

Van Buren dabbed his mouth with his napkin and nodded to Jago, who stood up and disappeared into the house. Van Buren sat back in his chair.

"He came straight out and asked you?"

Hellman nodded. "Well ... he said he wasn't sure about this president being re-elected ... and then went on to say that government pensions weren't over generous ..."

Van Buren nodded and reached for a toothpick.

"... Said that it would tide him over," continued Hellman, "... help smooth any difficulties ..."

Jago re-appeared carrying a briefcase which he laid on the table in front of Hellman before retiring to the smaller table again.

"You give him that," said Van Buren, "then we've got a hold on him."

It was the first time Van Buren had used "we" in any transaction with Hellman. He smiled and gestured for the real estate developer to sit.

"You've got to get yourself a lever in these big deals, and we just found ours."

Hellman sat down and gave a nervous smile. "I'm glad you think so."

Van Buren nodded and leaned over to him. "I'll bet you are. Scared you a little, did I?" He gave a twisted smile, then relaxed and patted Hellman's arm. "You did well, Steve."

Hellman gave a weak smile. Meetings with Van Buren were like swimming with sharks … unpredictable.

"My people in Washington also picked up a little background. It seems the government really mean it; they've wanted to get rid of the place for some time," said Van Buren, giving a little laugh. "Just think, me opening a hotel and casino on Alcatraz … can you imagine?" He laughed again. "What would Al Capone have said? Or Carlo Gambino"

Once he'd started, Van Buren couldn't stop. He had become genuinely excited. "Just wait until the New York families get to hear about this."

A look of alarm passed over Hellman's face. Van Buren smiled to re-assure him.

"No, don't worry; I'm not saying anything to anyone until we got this deal all nailed down."

***

Dusk was falling as Hellman hummed to himself and swung the Jaguar into the cul-de-sac. Parking where Perez had left his Lamborghini, Hellman picked up Van Buren's briefcase from the passenger seat and got out. Slipping the uniformed doorman twenty dollars to keep an eye on his car, he started towards the elevators, only to be discreetly intercepted by the voice of Susan, one of the hotel's receptionists.

"Can I help you, sir?"

"I've got a meeting with Mister Wynter."

"Ah, Mister Hellman?"

"Yes."

"Mister Wynter did say he was expecting you. Would you care to go up - you know which suite?"

"I do," nodded Hellman as he turned and made his way to the polished oak doors of the elevators. As he slowly ascended, Hellman had the feeling of missing something. He eventually put it down to the fact that he was probably in the only elevator in San Francisco without music. The doors slid silently apart and Hellman stepped out into the wide, deeply carpeted corridor. Between the doors to the rooms and suites, pier tables with lamps or vases stood against the walls, and large gilt frames containing seascapes alternating with landscapes were hung above them. The head of a very surprised looking moose peered out from above the elevator doors.

"Right on time," said Wynter as he let Hellman into his sitting room.

"My father brought me up to be punctual. Time's money, he always said."

"It certainly is," said Wynter, smiling at Hellman's briefcase.

"He didn't teach me much else, but I'm usually on time."

"Drink?" asked Wynter.

"Southern Comfort … if you've got it."

"This is a hotel, Steve; a telephone call and I've got

everything," said Wynter as he searched through an array of bottles on a side table, finally finding what he was looking for. "No need to make the call. I have it here," as he undid the top and poured a generous measure into a tumbler. "Anything with it?"

Hellman shook his head. "Why spoil a good drink?"

"Why indeed? Do please sit down." Wynter indicated two white sofas facing each other with a low table between them. Hellman put the briefcase on the table and sat down: Wynter handed him the tumbler and sat opposite. "I'm beginning to get a good feeling about this deal. I think it will work out well … for both of us." He put his hands on the briefcase and looked over at Hellman. "May I?"

"Sure."

Wynter spun the case around, snapped open the locks, and lifted the lid. Laid out neatly before him were crisp bundles of new fifty dollar bills, each held securely together with a wide paper sleeve with a Treasury logo.

"What do you intend to do with the island?" asked Wynter.

"I guess it's going to be a hotel with a casino … and shows. I think we could attract some big names from the entertainment world …" said Hellman.

Wynter picked up a bundle of notes and riffled through it.

"Perhaps we could even open with Sinatra," Hellman continued, "I'm sure he'd get a kick out of playing Alcatraz. Be one up on Johnny Cash at Folsom Prison."

Wynter nodded. "Frank would like that." He picked up

another bundle and riffled through that. If these notes were counterfeit, then they were the best he'd seen, indistinguishable from the real thing. He gave a slight shake of his head; it would be a crying shame to burn these.

"You know him?"

"Know who?" said Wynter, his mind still on the notes.

"Frank Sinatra."

"I met him when he sang at the White House." Wynter replaced the bundle of fifties in the briefcase, snapped it shut and smiled at Hellman. "Frank's a great guy; I'm sure he'd like to help." Wynter leaned back into the white cushions. "Well, two days and the bids will be in. How does it feel to be ahead of the game?"

"Feels real good," smiled Hellman.

"You've got to have an edge in life, something that keeps you ahead of the rest," said Wynter, taking a sip of his Scotch. "How do you think the big money families got started: the Astors; the Rockefellers; the Gettys? They all found an edge."

"I guess it's what we're all looking for," said Hellman.

"And you just found yours: the edge that lifts you out of that pool with all the rest." Wynter stood up and walked slowly towards one of the windows. "I'll give you a call when the other bids are in; then you can get the winning bid couriered round to me."

Hellman took a mouthful of Southern Comfort. "What if the others want to hand them to you personally?" he asked.

"That end of things will be handled by my assistant; I won't even be in town." Wynter looked out of the window and gave a chuckle. "A casino ... I like that ... with a real captive audience." He looked over at Hellman and gave a big grin. "Don't worry, Frank will love it."

Chapter 22

Wynter had protested that he was never very good first thing in the morning, but Meredith had insisted on the breakfast meeting. She had another meeting later that morning, and she felt that she had to get up to date, and then rehearse the next moves with Wynter.

They sat at the table where the developers had discussed the sale of Alcatraz, surrounded by an array of ham, eggs, hash browns, sausages, toast, bagels and two pots of coffee. Meredith made do with bagels and coffee, while Wynter made an assault on the rest.

"Everything go okay at the bank?" said Meredith.

"Well …" said Wynter, hesitating.

"Well what?" Meredith turned to Wynter.

"The manager was sure it must be a mistake," replied Wynter, chewing a forkful of ham. "I explained it was just a coincidence."

"What was a coincidence?"

"They thought that I was a criminal."

"You are, Wynter," said Meredith, in a matter of fact way, "very perspicacious of them. *Why* did they think that?"

"The bank has an 'intelligence' unit."

Meredith nodded. "Just as well we set you up with a new background. You gave him the number to call in Washington?"

"Yeah, everything's sorted," said Wynter. "We now have a bank account." He munched some hash browns. "Can you imagine; some con-man is going around the country separating people from their hard earned cash … and he's using my name."

"Don't get too smart, Wynter, the bids come in tomorrow …"

"Your man Lance is handling that. I don't want to be involved; it could lead to situations that we don't need. Best I'm not around."

"But you'll be here, in the hotel?"

"Oh yes, just not available."

"Then you'll open the bids and ring Hellman, right?"

Wynter nodded. "Then he brings me the winning bid." He sat back and took a gulp of coffee.

"And how long does Hellman have to produce the check?"

"Five days. Why?" asked Wynter, with a mouthful of sausage.

"Certain arrangements have to be made, and the timing's important." Meredith finished her coffee.

"Yeah …?"

"Some long overdue business."

Wynter could see that she was being vague on purpose. "Like what?"

Meredith dabbed her mouth with her napkin. "Nothing

you'd want to know about …"

Wynter opened his mouth to ask.

"… Nothing you're *going* to know about," said Meredith with a finality that warned Wynter against asking further questions. "I'll send someone over to collect the money," continued Meredith.

"Money?"

"The bribe … Van Buren's hundred and fifty thousand."

"Oh, yeah," said Wynter, with an air of disappointment. "It's real good … for counterfeit."

"That's evidence, Wynter … every last note."

"You're not taking it with you?"

Meredith flashed him an ironic smile. "Someone will collect it." she said, and walked to the door. Opening it, she turned back to Wynter. "And I mean *all* of it."

Wynter nodded and finished his sausage in silence.

***

An hour later and room service had cleared breakfast. Wynter put aside yesterday's London Times and settled back into the sofa's cushions. He had that warm feeling that things were going his way. Meredith had left, the sun was shining and Wynter was looking forward to pulling off what was easily the greatest con of his life. Reaching over to the small table at the end of the sofa, he picked up his cup of coffee. Selling Alcatraz would rank alongside Victor Lustig's sale of the Eiffel Tower, or Arnold Rothstein putting the fix in on the 1919 World Series. He took a sip of coffee and had the satisfaction of knowing that he, Gerry Wynter, was up there with the immortals of the con business. He was among the greats. People would talk about this for years … except he knew they wouldn't.

No-one could ever know.

Not if he wanted to stay out of prison.

It was ironic, but the con game was the only one where you never knew the names of the greatest players. You got to hear of the second division guys; the two-bit losers; the loudmouths … the guys who got arrested and ended up in court. The guys at the top always remained a mystery. Wynter reckoned he was at the top, giving a performance that would put Olivier, Brando, or Hoffman, in the shade. And, unlike them, there were no second takes - you had to get your lines right first time, or the consequences could be very painful … even fatal.

Wynter sighed. Best stay in the shadows. There would be no red carpet or golden statuette for him. Not if it meant thirty years in the slammer.

He was contemplating the dilemma of famous anonymity, when there was a knock at the door. Wynter frowned; then he remembered that Meredith had said that she would send someone over to collect the counterfeit money. He got to his feet and walked across the room.

Pulling open the door he was confronted by the barrel of a Smith and Wesson .38 caliber revolver pointing straight at his head. On the other end of the gun was a very angry looking Sheriff Rufus Richards.

They stared at each other in silence for a couple of seconds then the sheriff growled.

"You are a lowdown English liar. You ain't even got the decency of a renegade rattlesnake."

Wynter thought he was going to have a coronary. His heart rate shot up as he fought hard to control his rising panic. An enormous surge of adrenaline flooded his body, but his limbs felt as if they were frozen and he wasn't at all sure that he'd ever move again. Making a huge effort not to betray any emotion, he managed to force out a few words.

"You want to come in and discuss that."

The sheriff turned it over in his mind, looked up and down the corridor then decided that whatever they were going to do was best done in the privacy of Wynter's room.

"Back up," he said, motioning with the revolver.

Wynter slowly backed up, and the sheriff eased his way into the room, closing the door behind him.

"That'll do," he said. Wynter came to a halt. "Keep your hands where I can see them. Now, you give me one good reason why I shouldn't blow your head off."

"Why would you want to do that?" said Wynter, his mouth near dry.

"You got some nerve, Sir Wynter, I'll give you that. You know damn well why."

Wynter shook his head. "No. No I don't." He didn't dare let his pretence slip - not now that he'd started it.

"Just ask yourself what would make me travel a thousand miles to point a gun at your head."

Wynter slowly shrugged his shoulders, "I don't know. You want to play some more chess?" He reckoned that if the sheriff had really wanted to kill him, he would have pulled the trigger back there in the corridor. Wynter's heart rate was subsiding from nearly lethal to merely dangerous.

"Chess! You want to play some chess?" said the sheriff. "It was in my mind to kill you while I rode up in the elevator, Sir Wynter. That notion ain't altogether left my mind."

Wynter looked deep into the sheriff's eyes. Whatever else he may be, the sheriff wasn't a killer. He didn't have the layer of ice that natural born killers had behind the eyes. He'd kill if he had to. Today he didn't have to.

"Then I can only guess that it has something to do with your purchase of my Uncle Andrew's box."

"Too damn right it has something to do with your Uncle Andrew's box. That box ain't worth shit."

"It's been worth a lot of money to me."

"Sure, from fools like me."

"Look, what exactly is the matter?"

"It don't *exactly* work. But you know that."

"Did you operate it correctly?"

"Just the way you told me."

"Did you get the timings right?"

"What timings?"

"Ah, the timings are critical," said Wynter, beginning to relax a little as the feeling of movement returned to his limbs. "You have to get the right sequence of switching with the correct timing between them. I expect nothing happened when you tried. You just got soggy paper. Am I right?"

"Yeah, nothing got printed," said the sheriff, his revolver beginning to drop slowly, aiming now at Wynter's shoulder.

"Well, it wasn't entirely your fault we were interrupted

when I was trying to explain how the machine worked. I was just getting ready to give you the final instructions …" said Wynter.

"… When you got arrested."

"A misunderstanding, I assure you, and soon cleared up. Would I be in this hotel now talking to you if I were guilty of anything?"

The sheriff had to admit that the Englishman had a point. Rufus was wavering. He still wanted to believe the box worked. "Did it have enough chemicals in it?"

"Yes," said Wynter.

"You sure?" said the sheriff, pointing the revolver at Wynter's head.

"Of course … would I make a mistake like that? Didn't it work when I operated it? Didn't I give you two one hundred dollar bills?" The sheriff was forced to nod. "And didn't you get them verified at two banks?"

The sheriff continued to nod as he let the gun's aim slowly drop again. Wynter was right. Rufus knew he was right.

"So, why didn't it work for me?" asked the sheriff.

"I reckon it's the timing. You've got to be real precise about the timing. Get it wrong and nothing happens – as you've sadly found out. Perhaps you need to get yourself a proper clock up there in Alyson, Sheriff, rather than a calendar."

"Don't you get smart with me, Englishman," said the sheriff, raising the revolver again. "I could still drop you where you stand."

Wynter held up his hands in submission. "Okay, okay … looks like I'll have to come back with you and set it all up again. This time I'll write it all down."

"You'll do that? You'll come back?"

"Doesn't look like I've got much choice."

Perhaps he'd been a little harsh, thought the sheriff. If Sir Wynter was prepared to travel back to Oregon with him and run through the set up again, there might be some good in him somewhere. It also meant that Rufus had been right all along … the box really did make money. The Smith and Wesson wavered.

"Unfortunately, I've just got an important deal to finalize here," continued Wynter, "buying some machine tools and organizing shipping, so I won't be able to leave San Francisco for a week or so …"

The sheriff scowled and the Smith and Wesson lined up once again on Wynter's head.

"So, what I propose, Sheriff, is that I give you your money back - fifteen thousand dollars, wasn't it?" The sheriff's jaw dropped a little, as did the Smith and Wesson. "You can pay me back when we've got the box working for you," continued Wynter.

The sheriff stood there, deprived of speech for a few seconds, until he managed to splutter out a few words. "You're going to give me my money, and come back with me?"

"I think that's fair, don't you? Put us back to where we were before I even mentioned Uncle Andrew's box," said Wynter, finally taking control of the situation.

"Well, I …"

"Good. May I?" Wynter indicated that he'd like to walk over to the table where Van Buren's briefcase lay.

"Sure, go ahead," said the sheriff, training the revolver on him, "but slowly."

Flicking open the locks, Wynter kept the open lid between him and the sheriff and quickly took out three bundles, each of five thousand dollars. Snapping the briefcase closed, Wynter held out fifteen thousand dollars. Faced with an offer he really couldn't refuse, the sheriff put his gun back into his shoulder holster, and took the money.

"Well, this is real good of you, Sir Wynter, said the sheriff, his face breaking into a huge grin as he riffled through each bundle. "I must admit that I had you figured as a crook - one of them con artists."

"Sheriff!" said Wynter in mock disbelief. "After all the times we played chess together? You should know me better than that."

The sheriff looked sheepish, "I guess I should."

"You've had a bad time of it, what with not getting the box to work, then having the trouble of finding me, and all. Still, it's all worked out now. You found me, you've got your money back and we'll soon get that box working properly for you. Now, why don't you use some of that money and enjoy yourself in San Francisco for a few days … you deserve it after what you've been through."

"I think I might just do that," grinned the sheriff, stuffing the money into his pockets.

"You come back here in a week's time, and by then I

should have finished my bit of business, and then we'll travel back to Alyson together. I can't say fairer than that, now, can I?" said Wynter as he gently maneuvered the sheriff towards the door.

"I haven't had a good look at San Francisco in over thirty years …"

"Then it's time you did, Sheriff," smiled Wynter as he opened the door, "and you can afford to do it in style."

Rufus smiled as he bent his head closer to Wynter. "I always knew that box worked," he said. "I'll be back in a week."

"A week," said Wynter, nodding as he gently eased the sheriff through the open door, closing it after him.

Wynter managed to make it to the nearest sofa and sit down before his whole body started to shake and his stomach began to churn like an industrial food mixer. Feeling nauseous, he wasn't sure if the pain was real or just a nervous reaction, but when this was all over he really was going to see a specialist - he felt sure that he had an ulcer.

Chapter 23

Meredith settled into the comfortable leather chair and gazed across the large expanse of mahogany and leather-topped desk. The office of the San Francisco Chief of Police was large, well carpeted and comfortable. Framed photographs of past police chiefs and civic notables took up most of the space on two walls, keeping a silent watch on the present incumbent, while the other two walls had windows with blinds. Chief Connor had hung his coat on the back of his chair while he slowly walked around the room watering his collection of house plants. It had become a lunchtime ritual when he was in his office. He saw no reason to alter his routine simply because the Head of the Secret Service, West Coast Section, had dropped by.

He had nothing against Meredith personally, they had worked together on a number of occasions and he'd found her calm, efficient and well-briefed. But it didn't alter the fact that the Secret Service was a parallel organization, with an overlap of jurisdiction. That overlap caused him a problem. He wasn't too keen on the FBI either. In his experience, if a joint operation went wrong, it was always the

Police Department that got the blame.

"You keep plants, Ms. Delaney?" asked Chief Connor.

"A few at home, but they've got to be pretty hardy. I don't always get to keep regular hours."

"Then may I recommend cacti," said the Chief, as he poured enough water to dampen the earth around a potted Ming Aralia. "Nothing comes much tougher, and some of them flower real pretty."

"I'll bear that in mind when I'm next down at the garden store."

"Spines tend to keep animals away too."

"Not a problem I'm faced with, chief," said Meredith. "I don't have any pets."

"That's a shame; animals help with stress."

"I sure get enough of that," said Meredith.

"You and me both," said Chief Connor as he sprayed a mist of water on a split leaf philodendron. "You've got to have a hobby, another life outside the office. It helps keep things in perspective."

He stopped tending the plants, put the pint-sized watering can down on a zinc tray with the miniature spray bottle next to it, and turned back to Meredith. "So, you want a bit of help."

"That's about it," said Meredith.

The Chief sat down behind his desk. "I've heard the name of course, but from what I know of him, it sounds out of character."

"That struck me too. But I hear he's got connections."

"That rumor's been doing the rounds for a while, but I don't give it much credence. We looked at it a couple of years back; nothing to see. It's as straight as you'll get in the real estate business."

"Hellman plays up to it."

"Sure he does: '*look at me, I'm connected*.' That only impresses the bottom feeders and the whack jobs who think the world is run by shape-shifting lizards." Chief Connor leaned forward. "Times have changed. There are ten, maybe twelve, serious gangs out there on the city streets. The Mafia's just one of them, and even they ain't what they used to be."

"My informant tells me there's a political angle."

"Yeah?" said Connor, with a hint of relief. "Then it's Washington's problem."

Meredith shook her head. "Local."

Connor looked at her intently for a couple of seconds. "You sure?"

Meredith nodded. "My informant couldn't point to Canada on a map, let alone Washington."

The Chief sighed. "Shit. We've only just got over the Brooks scandal." He looked over at Meredith. "You know who this local guy is?"

Meredith shrugged and shook her head. "All I know is that he's a politician who is real pissed off at being paid off in junk notes, and he's looking to get even."

"Jesus! You can't trust anyone these days."

Meredith shook her head. "Crime isn't what it used to be, chief."

"Nothing's what it used to be, Ms. Delaney."

***

The sheriff pushed a crisp, new, fifty dollar bill over the bar to pay for the two beers. He pushed one towards his nephew Tony, a detective with the San Francisco Police Department. He picked up the other bottle and raised it in a toast.

"To the San Francisco Police Department," smiled the sheriff.

They both raised their bottles in a toast and drank.

"Wouldn't have even got this far if you hadn't put a trace out on his pickup," said Tony. "Lucky we picked it up running a red light on Columbus."

"Yeah, well, it was always was going to be a long shot," said the sheriff.

"A Secret Service agent was driving it, not Wynter." Tony took a swig of beer. "What you got yourself mixed up in, Rufus?"

"I ain't mixed up in anything."

Tony didn't entirely believe his uncle, but he sighed and let it pass.

"This guy you're after - sounds as if he's a con-man," said Tony, taking another swig of beer. "Who's to say that Wynter's his real name?"

Rufus shrugged his shoulders.

"Probably worked under so many different names I shouldn't think he can remember his real one," continued Tony. "I know the type, Rufus. Seen them working here in the city … cheap hustlers".

"Look, Tony, I'd be grateful if you didn't … you know …"

"Don't worry, Rufus, I'm not going to say anything. Officially you didn't report a crime … not to me anyhow."

"I appreciate that, Tony." The sheriff took a swig of beer. "Turns out he wasn't the right guy anyway."

"Where do you think the right guy is?"

The sheriff sighed. "He could be anywhere, I guess; Boston, St Louis … Chicago."

"The one place you can guarantee he won't be is Oregon," said Tony.

***

"You did what!?"

Meredith's voice echoed around her empty office as she stood up. It was eight o'clock in the evening and she was back at her desk holding the handset of the telephone to her ear. She closed her eyes and took a deep breath.

"… What did I tell you, Wynter? Just before I left you … what did I say?"

She paused, listened, and took another breath.

"… That's evidence! That's what I said!"

She closed her eyes again.

"… I told you that someone would collect it, *all* of it!"

She made an effort to control her breathing as she listened.

"… Perhaps he *should* have blown your head off!"

There was a longer pause, and Meredith began to calm down a little.

"… Alright, I'm sorry, I shouldn't have said that. Part of me still thinks it, but I shouldn't have said it."

The hard edge in her voice was softening a little, and she sat back down behind her desk.

"… That's all very well, but how am I going to explain this? Sorry Your Honor, but some of the evidence disappeared due to one of Mister Wynter's many previous con-tricks going disastrously wrong?"

She leaned back into the soft leather of the high-backed chair.

"… Alright, so you didn't have too much time to think about consequences. That's where thinking on your feet gets you."

Meredith leaned forward, picked up her cup of coffee and took a sip.

"… No, I'm not trying to be funny, believe me."

She put the cup back on its saucer.

"… How many other guys out there are going to come after you waving guns? No, don't answer that, I don't think I want to know."

She gave a sigh and leaned back in the soft leather.

"… Ok, I'll be over first thing in the morning. We'll assess the situation and see where we go from here."

Meredith replaced the handset, settled back in the chair and sighed as she closed her eyes.

***

The waiter topped up both glasses with the house red in the small restaurant that Tony had selected for dinner. Only open for a few months, it had already built a following and was virtually full. Tony was a little apprehensive, but Rufus hadn't balked at the prices, and they had both settled down to enjoy the evening.

"So, it's been thirty years since you were last in 'Frisco," said Tony, cutting up his steak. "A few changes, eh?"

Rufus smiled and nodded. "Everything changes, Tony, you got to accept it. You don't have to like it ... well, not all of it ... but the world moves on, with or without you."

"Don't remember there being much *moving on* up in Alyson?"

"People there aren't so keen on change as city folk."

"Bet you'll be glad to get back up there: the open spaces, away from all this concrete and traffic."

"I won't miss the traffic, that's for sure," smiled Rufus, "but I thought I might stay on for a week or so, have a good look around. Don't often get the chance."

"Sure," said Tony. "You'll have to come over for dinner. Linda would love to see you again."

"That would be nice."

"But we're away 'til Tuesday; taking the kids up the coast, camping for a few days."

Rufus nodded. "Sounds good."

"What about Harriet? Won't she wonder ...?"

"I told her I'd bring her down here for a week in the Fall. If I say I'm looking out some places to take her between police business, then I reckon she won't mind too much."

"I should think a lot of the places you knew all that time ago have gone, or changed so you wouldn't recognize them. Some are still there: Fisherman's Wharf of course ..."

"Forty or fifty boats were fishing out of it then; now you got forty or fifty restaurants."

"Cooking fish is safer than catching fish, Rufus. More money as well."

"The cable cars are the same."

"Yeah … then there's Alcatraz."

"It was still a prison back then."

"Yeah, I guess it would have been. Well, now you can catch the ferry and take a tour of the place … even sit in Capone's cell." Tony chuckled as he skewered another piece of steak with his fork. "Best of all, they let you out again. Why don't you go take a look?"

Rufus leaned back in his chair. "I might just do that."

Chapter 24

The next morning Meredith eased the Ford Crown Victoria forward until the driver's window was level with the keypad, and punched in the code to open the hotel's rear security gate. The invisible machinery noiselessly slid the heavy metal gate to the left, and the car nosed forward. She parked, and entered the hotel through the service door. The problem had been on her mind ever since Wynter's phone call the previous evening, and it kept gnawing at her until she had dropped off to sleep. As she rode the elevator to the second floor and Wynter's suite, she was still undecided.

"I don't know if I should bawl you out, or congratulate you," she said.

Wynter had poured her a cup of coffee, and they were sitting facing each other over the low table between the sofas.

"Nice to see you alive, would be a start," said Wynter.

"You think he was serious?"

Wynter shook his head. "The more people threaten to do something, the less likely they are to do it. Real killers don't tell you; they just do it." Wynter sipped his coffee. "He'd have pulled the trigger when I opened the door if he wanted to kill me."

"What do you think he's going to do when he finds out that fifteen thousand is worse than worthless?"

"That's going to take some time, and I don't aim to be here when he finds out."

Meredith shook her head. "What *were* you thinking?"

"Hoping the gun didn't go off by accident, mainly."

Meredith picked up her cup and took a sip of coffee. "You realize that you've left us no choice but to take him out of the game."

"Hey, whoa," said Wynter, holding up both his hands in alarm. "I'm not making you do anything, and certainly not killing anyone. He's a County Sheriff, for Christ's sake!"

"You've been watching too much television, Wynter," smiled Meredith. "No-one is going to kill anyone … not here, anyway."

"So … what are you going to do?"

Before she could answer there was a knock at the door, and for a fraction Wynter froze and looked at Meredith. Then he smiled.

"That'll be one of the hotel receptionists." Wynter stood up and started moving towards the door. "They've been accepting the sealed bids down in reception."

The knock was repeated.

"Who is it?" asked Wynter as he got to the door.

"Susan … the receptionist," was the muffled reply.

Wynter unlocked and opened the door and took the bulky envelope from Susan's outstretched hand. "Thanks, there's just one more envelope to be delivered."

"I change shifts in twenty minutes," said Susan, looking at her watch.

"Please, it won't take long, I promise. I've just got to make a phone call, and it should be delivered about twenty minutes afterwards. Half an hour and you'll be finished."

"Mmm … I wouldn't normally, but okay, just for you Mister Wynter."

"Thanks," smiled Wynter. Susan lingered a fraction too long, causing Meredith to frown.

"Half an hour at most … I promise," said a smiling Wynter as he closed the door.

Turning the lock, he moved towards the large table at the other end of the room strewn with the other bids that had arrived during the course of the morning. Getting to the table, he ripped open the envelope, pulled the papers out and glanced through them.

"If I didn't know otherwise, I'd say that this was the winning bid."

"Yeah? Who and how much?"

"O'Brien: twenty one million, one hundred and ten thousand dollars."

Meredith raised her eyebrows, "So what's Hellman going to come in at?"

"I'll suggest twenty one and a quarter million. That leaves a believable margin."

"And he's going to have to find a fifteen per cent deposit," said Meredith, producing a pocket calculator from her bag.

"Three million, one hundred and eighty seven thousand, five hundred dollars," said Wynter slowly, as he did some quick mental arithmetic.

"You're pretty good," said Meredith, holding up the calculator showing the same number.

"That's three million plus, by Wednesday. Think he'll do it?"

Wynter nodded. "I reckon he will. It'll be clean too. Van Buren won't want to risk a once in a lifetime deal like this with junk money."

"That's a big bet."

"Perhaps, but he thinks the odds are in his favor," said Wynter, picking up the telephone. "Now, if you'll excuse me, I've got a phone call to make."

***

Having parked her car in the lot under Portsmouth Square, Meredith took the elevator, emerged into the sunlight and made her way towards Robert Louis Stevenson's monument: a tall stone column topped with a copy of the Hispaniola, the ship in *Treasure Island*.

As she walked, her thoughts went over the morning's meeting with Wynter. Sheriff Rufus Richards was a complication they could both do without. Wynter was under enough pressure as it was, without itinerant law officers threatening to blow his head off. He had tried to appear composed and sure of himself, but Meredith had watched him tense up when Susan had knocked at the door, and noticed the way he had asked who it was. The fact that he kept the door locked permanently told her the truth.

Wynter had been badly rattled, and he was fighting his survival instinct, which she guessed was screaming for him to get the hell out of San Francisco. Push him too hard and there was a chance that he might jump ship and disappear. That couldn't be allowed to happen. Not now they were so close. She wasn't about to stand by and see this operation jeopardized by some hick law officer out of no-where.

Detective Pete Ramirez of the city Police Department was sitting on one of the benches close to the monument, wondering what sort of favor Meredith was looking for, when he saw her approaching. He stood up and held out a paper cup of black coffee.

"Hi. It's still hot; I just got here," said Ramirez. "Doesn't matter if you don't want it. I could drink both."

"Thanks, Pete, I'll take it."

She sat down next to him and sipped the coffee; "How are Barbara and the children?"

"All well, thanks" nodded Ramirez, "How's ... ah ...?"

He paused; embarrassed that he couldn't remember the name.

"Fine ... when I saw him last," shrugged Meredith.

"You're not ...?"

Meredith shook her head, "Not anymore."

"Sorry."

"No need to be. It's just the way things go."

Having started down one wrong road, Ramirez was in no hurry to suggest another, and he took a mouthful of coffee as he waited. The next topic of conversation was her choice.

"What have you got on a real estate developer called Hellman?" said Meredith.

"Not too much," said Ramirez, glad to step out of the mire of relationships. "Skates close to the wind, said to bribe half the City Planning Department; got a couple of councilors on his payroll; he pays the Unions off like everyone else, and Senator Reece is supposed to be covering his ass - for his usual fee." Ramirez took a sip of coffee and looked over at Meredith. "He's not the best in the real estate business, but he's not the worst either."

"What about the Mob?"

"The Marin County connection?" smiled Ramirez.

"Yeah," Meredith nodded.

"Van Buren bankrolls a real estate deal now and then. Far as we can see, the finance comes over from Europe, goes twice around the Caribbean, with a stop-over in Panama, and pops up in Delaware. Most of it sure isn't clean, but we can't prove it's dirty either."

"What if I told you some of it was counterfeit?"

Ramirez thought for a few seconds. "You'd need a bank involved to shift those amounts of junk."

"Not necessarily," said Meredith. "Not if the counterfeiting was real high end stuff. Not if it was that good that a couple of treasury experts took some time to be convinced it wasn't real." She looked over at Ramirez. "The cash goes into a shady Central American bank. It looks good to them; remember, they're not Treasury experts. There's a lot of it - too much for the bank to turn down. They wire a credit to a Liechtenstein account, and the money's on its way. The cash is then used by the bank in normal day to day business, and by the time any questions may get asked, it's too late. Anyway, what bank would admit to it? They'd have to take a loss to the value of the junk they're holding, and believe me, the board of directors wouldn't be holding their hands up; they'd be looking to offload it as fast as they could."

"Hellman doesn't strike me as the type to be into counterfeiting."

"I doubt he even knows about it," said Meredith, shaking her head. "He's the clean end of the operation. Van Buren provides him with finance, all legitimate and above board. In return, Hellman delivers an asset in bricks and mortar, which in turn gives Van Buren a legal income … he even pays tax on it. I don't think Hellman is involved in the counterfeiting scam. It's in Van Buren's interests to keep them separate."

"But you're going after Van Buren via Hellman," said Ramirez, taking a mouthful of coffee.

Meredith nodded. "You could say that."

"The Chief know about this?" said Ramirez.

Meredith turned towards him and gave him an ironic smile.

"Didn't think so," continued Ramirez.

"We both know what would happen if I told him."

There was a pause and Ramirez looked down at the ground. "So, what do you want me to do?" he asked.

"About Hellman? Nothing."

"So …?"

"I've got a small problem with a County Sheriff, one Rufus Richards," said Meredith, pulling an envelope from her bag and handing it to Ramirez.

"What sort of problem?"

"He's a loose cannon. I also suspect him of passing counterfeit notes."

"Then arrest him and charge him," said Ramirez as he studied a photograph, and began to look through a couple of sheets of description.

"I'm … sort of working undercover on this, Pete; it's a little bit unofficial," said Meredith.

"And you don't want to make it official."

"No," said Meredith, shaking her head, "not yet. Besides, it wouldn't be fair. The money came into his possession by pure accident. He doesn't even know it's junk."

Ramirez looked undecided.

"Please, Pete …" said Meredith. "I really need this favor."

"And he's got himself stuck between you and Van Buren."

"You could say that. I want you to pick him up."

"And?"

"Hold him. Just until my operation's over," said Meredith.

"Which will be …?"

"About Wednesday."

Ramirez gave a slight intake of breath. "Wednesday? You know I can only hold him for forty eight hours without a charge."

"Well, release him, then re-arrest him." Ramirez didn't

look convinced. "Oh, I don't know, Pete," continued Meredith. "Put the fear of God into him, do anything, but keep hold of him. I *must* know where he is."

Ramirez was still undecided.

"Tell him about Van Buren. Tell him it's for his own safety …"

***

Hellman sat on the terrace, sipped his drink and watched the sun sink into the Pacific. It was the first time that he had ever felt something near safe and at peace in Marin County. He heard the French windows of the house behind him open, and turned to see Van Buren step out and walk towards him.

"It's a great sight, isn't it," said Van Buren.

"Sure is," agreed Hellman.

"Almost as sweet as watching the 49ers lift the Super Bowl." Van Buren gave a little laugh and sat down at the table next to Hellman. "It's a real good feeling when things are going your way."

"Wynter did give us a bit of help."

"He's doing well enough out of it, and as I said, you've got to find that edge."

"We sure found that."

"So, how does it feel to be the man who's going to turn the country's most notorious prison into the State's most luxurious hotel?"

"I wouldn't be doing it without you … your financial backing."

Hellman didn't know it, but he was wrong. Van Buren wasn't putting up any money himself. He was going to use money entrusted to him by the New York crime families. That way he retained control but it didn't cost him a penny: just the sort of deal he liked. When it came to the planning and construction stage, he'd cut New York in for a percentage, like a king distributing largesse, but until then …

"It'll be your name on the project," smiled Van Buren. "You'll be the one the television stations will want to interview."

Hellman smiled. No more social snubs. No more embarrassing silences at parties, no more eyes down noses, and no backs turned. He would have made it.

"Tuesday," said Van Buren. "We'll do it on Tuesday."

Hellman snapped his mind back from the social whirl of city receptions, parties and television interviews. Tuesday? Do what on Tuesday? What was Van Buren talking about?

"The deal … we'll do the deal on Tuesday. Leaving it to the last minute always looks as if you're scratching around trying to raise the money. Tuesday's the right day."

"Sure," said Hellman. "Tuesday. I'll ring Wynter and set it up."

Van Buren nodded. "You OK with that? Got all your ducks in line?"

"Yeah," Hellman nodded, "in line and counted."

"Why don't you take that boat of yours out tomorrow and have a day's fishing?" said Van Buren, relaxing back into his chair. "A sort of celebration. I'd come with you, but I don't sail too well."

"Well, I …"

"Forecast's clear, should be a good day."

"I suppose you …"

"I know it's a Sunday, but you could take a friend along. I hear Senator Reece is a keen sailor, what with his naval career during the war."

The tone of Van Buren's voice made Hellman realize that these were instructions, not suggestions. "If Senator Reece wants …"

"Good place to have a talk, out there on the water. No chance of being overheard."

"Sure, I'll give him a call when I get home."

"No need, I already spoke to him. He just needs re-assurance about this deal going through. I told him you'd cut him in for a percentage."

"If that's what you …"

"Yeah, it is," nodded Van Buren. "I told him to be on the pontoon at nine. Not too early for you?"

Hellman had been looking forward to a morning in bed with his girlfriend, but now he shook his head. "No … not too early."

Chapter 25

Hellman eased the Jaguar through the private parking lot of the St. Francis Yacht Club, and took the first space in the public lot just past the club house. An outsider might believe he was a member, but anyone who knew would immediately dismiss him as an interloper. Membership of the St. Francis was strictly by invitation, and the committee was in no hurry to invite Hellman to fix the drains, let alone join the club.

He took out a cooler containing food and drink, locked the car and set off towards the jetties. Walking past the old lighthouse, he got to the club house of the less prestigious Golden Gate Yacht Club. Hellman had done a deal with the secretary: a permanent mooring in exchange for minor maintenance of the club house. It averaged out at the cost of a day or two's wages for a plumber or carpenter every month, but was worth it considering the cost of berths around the bay.

He stopped just past the club house and looked out over the water. There were quite a few boats out already, their sails billowing in a gentle force three. Looking over towards Alcatraz, a mile away, he saw the sun glint off the glass at the top of the lighthouse, then came the long, low building of the main prison block looming in relief, with the water tower standing guard at the other end. Hellman smiled. Another couple of days and he'd be the king of Alcatraz. Not even Capone had claimed that. He heard a car behind him and turned to see the senator's Cadillac pull up and stop in one of the bays in front of the club house. Reece got out and walked towards him.

"The secretary isn't going to like you parking there," said Hellman.

"I got a State Capitol invalid sticker with 'Senator' written on it in great big letters. That means I can park anywhere I want."

"It's your car," shrugged Hellman, as he stepped onto the gang-plank down to the wooden jetties.

"Yeah," said Reece.

Strictly speaking, a Silicon Valley tech company owned and paid the running costs of the car, but the senator had a habit of blurring over details like ownership when it suited him.

Hellman's boat was hull, cabin and motor, not a sail to be seen. There was an afterdeck for sunbathing, eating and fishing. Ahead of that there was a cabin, roomy, but not over large; then came the head and a small galley. In the bow was a smaller cabin fitted out as sleeping quarters. It was essentially a day boat, certainly not a vessel to cross an ocean.

They passed under the Golden Gate and out into the Pacific Ocean. Heading up the coast, they stayed a mile or so off-shore of Marin County until Hellman found a spot where he was happy to start fishing. Killing the engine, Hellman let the boat slowly drift with the current. He hadn't been sure if it was best to bring the conversation around to the deal or wait for Reece to bring it up. The senator was in a tricky mood. He hadn't been happy all the way out, making snide comments when various names were mentioned. After they'd got the rods out, settled down and started to wait for the fish, Hellman had decided it was up to him.

"I gather there are parts of this new deal you're not happy with."

"There's a lot I'm not happy with," said Reece.

"Well, that's why we're here, to smooth things over. Make you happy again."

"That's what Van Buren told you to do?"

"Yeah," Hellman nodded and smiled. "Keep you onboard, so to speak."

"Well he can start by giving me five grand, in real money … no, let's make it ten - he owes me. And no junk this time."

"Junk?"

"Counterfeit," explained Reece. "I've got the Secret Service up my ass."

"They investigating you?" asked Hellman, suddenly surprised. "Why would they be interested in you?"

Reece wondered whether he should mention that the head of the western section of the Service had called on him, then decided against it.

"Look, I got a tip off that they're doing some digging. Came from a friend of mine, someone I trust."

"So what's it got to do with the deal?"

"I asked the questions and you got the answers. You got what you wanted; I got stiffed with junk."

"I didn't know. I'll speak to Van Buren. Get you your money."

"Good," said Reece. "It's about time someone told that guy where to get off."

"Lots of people have said that."

"Yeah? Well, I'm different. I could make a lot of trouble. I know where too many of the bodies are buried."

That's when Reece heard someone behind him softly call his name. He frowned, and tried to twist around but the chair was too tight so he stood up and turned around. He frowned as the color started to drain from his face.

"What are you doing here? How did you …?"

For a second, the crack of a Browning 9mm pistol being fired filled the air, and a hole in Reece's trousers appeared, turned dark red and the stain slowly began to spread. The senator stood open mouthed, then clutched his leg and slowly crumpled to the deck. Blood trickled onto the teak planks. It had been a carefully aimed shot; no bones broken and no major blood vessel had been damaged. Jago had clearly done this before.

"Don't worry, Senator, you won't bleed to death," said Jago.

"But, why …?"

"You better give me your car keys."

"Car keys?" repeated Reece.

"Well you can't drive like that, can you," said Jago.

The idea that Jago was going to drive him home after shooting him was so bizarre that Reece didn't even question it. He just grimaced as he put his hand into his pocket to retrieve the keys.

"Beginning to hurt isn't it," said Jago, taking the keys. "Nine mil rounds tend to do that ... hurt.

Reece just stared back up at him, "But why ... why?"

"You said yourself ... you know where the bodies are buried."

Hellman had moved to the side and was leaning with his back to the rail. He knew something like this was likely to happen when Van Buren had suggested that Jago came along too. In fact, it was Van Buren who had said it would be best if Jago slept on board. That way Reece wouldn't suspect ... wouldn't even know anyone else was there.

Jago knelt down and inspected the senator's leg with a twist. Reece screamed.

"It didn't go right through," said Jago. "You're lucky."

"Lucky!?" said Reece, grimacing. "You shoot me and say I'm lucky!?"

Jago let the senator's leg fall to the deck, and Reece screamed again.

"Exit wounds are worse than entry wounds; they really hurt. But then, I used a target load ... didn't want to damage Mister Hellman's nice boat."

"Christ, you're a bastard, Jago," screamed Reece.

Jago smiled and nodded. "Got it in one."

Jago put his arms underneath Reece, and the senator started to panic.

"Whoa! What are you doing?"

"Can't leave you here, best get you into the cabin. Get you lying on some comfortable cushions."

Reece relaxed a little, and Jago lifted him. Reece put his arm up to take hold of Jago's shoulder. "Just relax, Senator, I've got you." Reece let his arm drop.

It was over very quickly. Two steps and Jago was next to the rail. One second later Reece was launched through the air and hit the ocean with a scream.

"You got a life jacket or something to throw him?" said Jago. Hellman looked at him for a couple of seconds to see if he was being ironic, then he pointed to a locker and Jago pulled open the hatch and fished out an orange foam inflatable jacket. He threw it towards Reece, who by now was spluttering and bobbing a few yards away from the boat.

"For God's sake! Hellman! Christ! What are you doing?"

Hellman turned from the rail and retreated to the cabin door. He wasn't like Jago. He didn't possess the simple cruelty of the psychopath.

"Hellman, please," pleaded the senator. "You're not going to leave me ... not out here! Hellman!"

Hellman turned away. Listening to Reece's screams was haunting enough without having to look at the agony etched on his face. Jago just stood there with one foot up on the gunwale. He was smiling, watching ... getting a perverse pleasure from the scene.

"Don't worry, Senator, you won't be on your own for long. You'll have company soon enough," said Jago. "Depends if there are any in the immediate vicinity, of course, but count on it, with you losing that much blood … they'll find you."

Reece was flailing around but had managed to get hold of the lifejacket.

"It's a myth that sharks can smell a drop of blood for miles," said Jago. "It's only about five hundred yards. Then it depends if they're hungry."

Hellman took out a packet of cigarettes, and fumbled one into his mouth. His hands shook as he lit it.

"Looks to me like you got three choices, Senator," continued Jago. "You could try swimming to the shore, but it's a long way and I wouldn't really rate your chances of making it."

"Christ, Jago, please!" pleaded the senator.

Jago smiled in reply. "You could try drowning yourself, but it's harder than it sounds. Besides, you aren't in the right frame of mind."

The senator sputtered as Jago's smile widened into a grin.

"Or, you could take up shark wrestling." Jago looked at his watch. "I reckon you've got about five, perhaps ten, minutes to make up your mind … before something takes that decision for you."

Reece bobbed up and down in silent terror as the reality of what was about to happen sank in.

"You can't leave me here … for God's sake!" pleaded Reece.

"You were in the navy, Senator," smiled Jago. "Served in the Pacific during the war … Guadalcanal, wasn't it? Then you'll know the story of the *Juneau*. You'll remember what happened to the men who survived the explosion."

"You're a bastard, Jago!" screamed Reece.

Jago nodded. "That's what my Mom told me too."

"I'll see you in Hell!"

"Yeah," smiled Jago.

"Hellman, for the love of God, you can't leave me out here!" cried the senator.

Hellman closed his eyes and wished he could close his ears.

"Hellman, please ..."

The senator's face momentarily took on a look of surprise. His eyes widened and his mouth opened wide as he looked below the surface at a large shadow. Terror overtook surprise. His frantic scream turned into a gurgle as he was dragged under the surface. Hellman looked away, and went into the cabin to try and rid his mind of the image of the senator's terrified face disappearing below the water.

Jago chuckled as the senator spluttered and bobbed back to the surface and his arms started to flail, making desperate attempts to get to the boat.

"For the love of God!" screamed Reece.

Before the words had left his lungs, he was propelled at speed away from the boat by another dark shape under the water. His face froze in terror and what started as a scream ended as a gurgle of vomiting blood. The dark shape veered away and the movement stopped, and the senator floated on the surface. An outstretched hand silently reached for the boat, fell back onto the surface of the water, and finally disappeared. What was left of the senator slowly sank beneath the water.

Hellman threw up over the side as Jago fired up the engine and the boat began making its way back to port.

***

Jago helped tie the boat up at the jetty, nodded to Hellman, then walked towards the senator's car. Hellman had no desire to be seen with Jago any more than he had to, and he hung back, busying himself on board.

As far as a casual observer was concerned, one man had driven up and parked outside the yacht club. He joined another man, and both had got aboard a boat and gone out fishing. Three hours later the boat returned, the two men disembarked, and one man got back into the car and drove off. You would have had to be paying attention to notice that the car was driven by two different men. Hellman walked the length of the parking lot to the Jaguar, wondering if anyone *was* paying attention, and whether he should be worrying.

Very little ever worried Jago; two tours of Vietnam had cured him of that. Things either happened, or they didn't. Anything in between wasn't worth wasting time over. Having removed the senator's disabled pass from the windshield and shoved it in the glove box, Jago drove out of the parking lot and headed south. The car had an appointment with a chop shop a couple of miles outside of Palo Alto.

Van Buren had been right. Reece was unpredictable, and liable to shoot his mouth off at any time. He had become dangerous. It was a miracle that Chief Connor had picked up on it so quickly. But then, that's one of the reasons Van Buren paid Connor twenty five grand a year.

The grab descended, and steel fingers smashed their way through the windows. Thirty seconds later the car was in the compactor. Hydraulic pressure of over one hundred and fifty tons crushed the car between the heavy steel jaws. By the time Jago settled down in the grubby office portacabin, waiting to be picked up, the senator's car had been reduced to a small cube. Later that afternoon the breaker's furnace would convert that cube into metal ingots, ready to be re-cast into bathroom fittings.

Between them, the ocean's predators and the breaker's yard would have completely removed every trace of the senator and his car from the face of the earth.

Chapter 26

Sheriff Rufus Richards had been sitting in the interview room for ten minutes, thinking about what Detective Ramirez had said. He still couldn't get his head around it. The fifteen thousand dollars that Sir Wynter had given him back were counterfeit? They were less than worthless? Did Wynter realize that the money was junk … had he known? A great canyon of a hole was opening at the Sheriff's feet. If Wynter had paid him back knowing the bills were worthless, then it was odds on that his Uncle Andrew's box didn't work either. Rufus began to feel sick. However much he tried to avoid it, he was going to have to face up to the fact that he had been wrong all along. Sir Wynter was a con artist.

The door opened, and Ramirez came back in with two paper cups of coffee. He put one on the table in front of the sheriff.

"Two sugars, wasn't it?"

The sheriff nodded. "Yeah."

"So," said Ramirez as he settled down in the chair opposite the sheriff, "seems we've got ourselves into a bit of a mess here."

A *bit* of a mess, thought the sheriff; it was a God damn awful big mess. "Look, I didn't know those notes were counterfeit, I had no idea."

"Problem you've got is that what you *thought* doesn't count for anything. Just being in possession is an offence."

"But I didn't *know* they were junk."

Ramirez sucked in a breath through his teeth and shook his head. "That might have worked if it were just one or two notes … but fifteen thousand dollars? To me, that looks like intent to distribute."

"Christ! I was just buying a drink."

"Ever wonder how junk like that gets into circulation?" said Ramirez, taking a sip of coffee. "It's guys like you, *just buying a drink*."

"But …"

"It doesn't help that you're a US County Sheriff," said Ramirez. "Actually, it makes it worse."

Rufus closed his eyes. This was not looking good, not good at all. In fact it was shaping up to be the nightmare from Hell.

"How much did it cost you?" asked Ramirez. "Fifteen cents on the dollar? Got to be somewhere near that, I reckon, for that quality. They're real good."

"I didn't buy them!"

"No? Someone *gave* them to you to get rid of?"

Rufus shook his head, "No!"

"What then?"

Ramirez looked across the table. He knew where the money had come from, but he wasn't about to share that knowledge. It was Meredith's operation, and it was her call what happened to the sheriff. His job was just to keep him out of circulation. Rufus was breathing heavy, but saying nothing. Ramirez pushed his chair back and stood up.

"Well, it seems like you need a night to think about your position, Sheriff. It might help you remember where you got that money."

The sheriff said nothing. Best he didn't say anything just yet; he needed time to think. Ramirez left the room on his way to talk to the custody officer.

***

The telephone call was unexpected. Wynter had assumed that Hellman would leave it until Wednesday afternoon before he delivered the banker's draft for the deposit, but three million dollars had a way of setting its own agenda. If Hellman wanted to bring it round on Tuesday, he wasn't about to stop him.

Wynter didn't want to get the banker's draft to the bank until just before it closed, that way he minimized any time for second thoughts. He guessed that Hellman would get a kick out of doing business with someone who seemed so close to the President, and they settled on meeting at four o'clock in the afternoon.

As he replaced the telephone receiver, Wynter sat back and took stock of the developing situation. The pressure was starting to build. He wouldn't have admitted it, but moving the whole operation forward twenty four hours had thrown him off balance. It was all very well for Meredith to stand on the sidelines shouting orders; she didn't have to carry them out. And if the whole thing fell apart, she wasn't the one who'd have to explain to Van Buren that he'd been conned.

Meredith had the Secret Service as back-up, but who was going to protect him? Wynter knew that the only defenses he had were the smoke and mirrors he could create, and Heaven help him if Van Buren saw through them. Meredith would be of little help then.

The Service would drop him. Deny any knowledge of him. Ultimately it wouldn't matter what Meredith had promised; the decision would be taken out of her hands. Washington would decide. And Wynter knew full well that the primary consideration of the political operators in the capital was not upholding the law, or ridding the world of psychotic murderers - it was covering their own asses.

If Van Buren didn't get him, the system would.

It was time that Wynter made some plans of his own.

***

Meredith watched from her office window as Tobin and Boles walked into the building. She hadn't been expecting them back from Washington so soon. This was bad news. Moving to her desk, she knew the Treasury's chief investigator wouldn't make the three thousand mile trip just to ask how the investigation was going. They had telephones for that. Something must have happened. Could they have picked up a whisper of her Alcatraz deal? Had someone said something? Either way, Meredith guessed that she was in trouble.

Boles didn't bother to knock; he just walked straight in to Meredith's office and closed the door. Where was Tobin?

"Good flight?" asked Meredith, swiveling slightly in her chair.

"We had turbulence over the Rockies," said Boles. He remained standing by the door and seemed in no hurry to sit down.

"Bad?"

"Bad enough."

Meredith nodded. She decided not to let on that she knew that Tobin was here.

"That's why I stay out here as much as I can. I get claustrophobic on a long flight."

"Stopped over in Vegas last night," said Boles.

Meredith nodded, "Good place to stop over."

"The Vegas PD has put the file of the Petersen murder on the back burner. Joins a mass of other drug-related deaths they've got."

"They sure it was drugs?"

Boles nodded. "Be a good idea if you were too, seeing how I reckon your investigation must be about wrapped up by now."

So … she was being warned off.

Meredith realized it would be foolish to force the issue. Tobin was in the building, and he had the power to close her investigation down immediately. Besides, she wanted to speak to her boss Bill. Had Tobin spoken to him? Was Bill aware of Tobin's intention to close her down?

She played for time.

"Just a few loose ends; give me a day or so and they'll be all tidied away," said Meredith, also wondering why Tobin had sent Boles to give her the news.

"Good," nodded Boles, as he opened the door to leave. "If Petersen's murder is put down to a fall-out between drug gangs, it lets you off the hook."

***

Five minutes later Meredith was hurrying out through the doors of the building. Keeping her head down, she turned right along the sidewalk. What had made Tobin appear back here now? Had Van Buren got wind that the deal with Alcatraz was a con? Forty-eight hours, that was all she needed.

She was heading for a small bistro a couple of blocks away, which was a favorite with her colleagues in the office. She had to speak to Bill Bradshaw, and she didn't trust the office phones.

Had Lance said something? She knew he was becoming increasingly worried about his position in the operation. She'd been so tied up over Senator Reece that she hadn't had time to listen to Lance's worries. Meredith was beginning to feel that she had neglected him. She should have given him more reassurance.

She was still thinking when she saw Shapiro come out of the bistro balancing four coffees and a pile of sandwiches on a plastic tray. He seemed surprised to see her.

"Meredith, I thought you were …"

"Thought I was …?"

"Well, what with …"

"What with what?" said Meredith, frowning.

"You haven't heard?"

"For God's sake Shapiro, just tell me."

"Tobin's detained Lance."

***

Hellman stood by the window and gazed out over the bay. The lighthouse on Alcatraz swept its beam into the night with a lazy rhythm, while the Golden Gate Bridge seemed to defy all the laws of physics as it spanned the straits with no visible means of support. The roadway and towers were lit by lights, but the suspension cables remained hidden in the darkness. Hellman raised the cut glass tumbler to his lips and took a mouthful of Southern Comfort. It had been a good idea to get away from his apartment and book into a hotel for a few days.

He needed some time to settle his mind. As far as he was concerned, Senator Reece had landed back with him on the quay and had driven off. That was the last he had seen of him. No one could prove otherwise, and Jago was hardly going to say anything. Hellman took another gulp of Southern Comfort and gazed out at Alcatraz, silhouetted against the Bay.

The gunshot and the splash as Reece hit the water dominated his memory. He kept hearing Reece's final despairing scream as he went under the waves. It had woken him that morning, and his whole body had gone cold just remembering it. Hellman reflected that killing people wasn't as easy as Hollywood would have you believe. He closed his eyes and kept seeing the senator flailing in the water, alternately screaming abuse, then pleading and crying. He lit a cigarette and wondered how Jago managed to sleep at night.

Walking over to a side table, he picked up the bottle of Southern Comfort and topped up his drink, then moved back to the window and told himself that he'd feel better tomorrow … when he'd finalized the Alcatraz deal. Get stuck into a new project; that's what he needed. Drawing up plans, organizing a workforce, getting clearances and permissions …

For a couple of seconds the beam of light from the lighthouse picked out two small boats bobbing in the Bay: they were night fishing. Hellman watched them fade into the darkness as the beam moved on. He took another gulp of whiskey.

It would be a long time before he went out on another fishing trip.

***

Meredith lay on the hotel bed and went back over the day's events. She had stood on the sidewalk in a state of shock as she watched Shapiro continue on his way back to the office. Lance detained, for what? Suddenly a feeling of nausea swept over her. Taking great gulps of air, Meredith managed to get to the wall and lean against it, still breathing deeply. A concerned passer-by stopped to enquire if she needed any help. Meredith smiled weakly and shook her head.

If Lance had told them about Wynter, and what he was planning to do, then the game was lost. Meredith felt duty-bound to ring the hotel and warn Wynter.

He sounded remarkably calm when told of Lance's arrest, and refused to abandon Alcatraz.

"Having put some much effort into it, I'm not about to walk away now."

"Don't be foolish, Wynter, leave it," Meredith almost shouted down the phone.

"Have they arrested you?"

"Not yet."

"Then we can assume Lance hasn't told them anything. He just has to say nothing for twenty-four hours."

"Well, I ..."

"Where are you?"

"In a bistro."

"Okay, don't go back to the office. Go home, pack some clothes and book into a hotel, then call me again from a public phone."

Meredith rolled off the hotel bed and stood up. Her mind was full of what Lance knew, what he didn't know, and what he could tell Tobin. Perhaps Wynter was right, and Lance hadn't told them anything. How much could she trust Lance? How much could she trust Wynter? Most people stuck in his position would have made a run for the hills before now, but then, Wynter wasn't most people.

Since her abrupt disappearance that morning, she hadn't phoned the office, which must have added to Tobin's suspicions. With Lance out of the picture, there was no-one she dared talk to about what had happened. She had rung Bill in Washington, but he was non-committal. He had said he would find out what he could and ring her back.

The only consolation she had was that the sheriff was out of the game. Meredith sighed and wished Bill would call back. She lay back down on the bed and switched off the light. It was going to be a long night.

Chapter 27

The hotel had sent up breakfast, and it was waiting for him on the polished Regency table. Wynter poured a cup of coffee and buttered some toast as he went over the preparations again. Meredith had managed to fake up a really impressive bill of sale that both he and Hellman would need to sign. The hotel manager and his deputy were on call to witness their signatures, and Hellman should then hand over the three million dollar banker's draft.

He reckoned it would take Meredith eight minutes to get to the bank. After allowing a safety margin of two minutes, it meant he must have that draft in his hands by twenty past four. The bank closed at four-thirty. Was twenty minutes enough to get Hellman to hand over the draft?

Wynter munched a slice of toast, then looked at his watch. It was almost time to go and see the bank manager to give him the last minute instructions, but he had just enough time to catch the news. Swallowing the mouthful of toast, he flicked the TV remote. Putting the remote on the table, he poured himself some more coffee then turned back to the screen. He saw the unmistakable sight of Alcatraz seen from across the

Bay. Wynter froze. Why were they showing Alcatraz?

Quickly fumbling for the remote, he pressed the volume control just as the program crossed back to the studio. He heard the newscaster say *"We'll bring you any up-dates on that story as and when they happen. Now, leaving Alcatraz, as I'm sure many would have liked to have done in the past ..."*

Wynter began to breathe heavily, and just stared at the screen.

Up-dates? Up-dates on what?

***

The elevator whispered to a noiseless halt, and Wynter stepped out. Susan was working on reception. She looked up and smiled.

"Good morning Mister Wynter."

"Morning, Susan," said Wynter, as he smiled back, then hesitated long enough for the receptionist to notice.

"Can I help with anything?"

Wynter took the few paces to the desk.

"'Well, it's such a nice day, I was thinking of taking a trip over to Alcatraz. I really couldn't leave San Francisco without seeing it. You wouldn't know where I can catch the ferry, would you?"

"Of course," said Susan as she opened one of the desk's drawers, selected a leaflet, and held it out.

"Thank you," smiled Wynter, taking the leaflet and giving it a quick glance.

"That's the timetable for the ferry; it leaves from pier thirty three, just round from Fisherman's Wharf."

"The ferry's running today?"

"As far as I know."

"It's just there was something on the news this morning, but I didn't quite catch what they were saying."

"I've heard nothing, but I'll check if you like." She picked up one of the two telephones on the desk.

"You didn't see it … the news."

"No," said Susan, shaking her head. "Do you want me to…?"

"If you could, please," said Wynter, looking at his watch. "I've got a meeting I have to make, but I should be back in an hour or so. I'd be interested to know what's happening on Alcatraz, and why it made the news." He smiled at the receptionist. "It would certainly add to my trip to see the old prison."

"I'll have the answer by the time you get back, Mister Wynter."

Wynter stepped out of the hotel. He was late. Normally that would have worried him, but today was different. He reckoned that the promise of three million dollars could be as late as it wanted.

As he turned left at the end of the cul-de-sac, he felt a stabbing pain in his gut and winced. His stomach had started to play up. It always did when something was wrong. Wynter stopped off to get something for it. The pharmacist sold him some soft tablets she assured him would settle the most upset stomach. Popping four into his mouth, Wynter carried on, chewing his way towards the bank.

***

In his hotel room, Hellman had switched on the radio and tuned to a music station. It was preferable to the television with its twenty-four hour news coverage. The last thing he wanted to see was any report of the disappearance of a State Senator.

He lay on the bed and worked out the best time he would have to leave the hotel to set out for the bank. He had just fixed on two-thirty when he caught the word "Alcatraz" on the radio.

It took him a couple of moments to adjust his mind and stop thinking about banker's drafts. Surely word of the deal hadn't leaked out already? Or was it the Government making an official announcement ahead of time? He tilted his head and tried to catch what the news reader was saying.

***

Wynter arrived back from the bank, and approached the hotel's reception desk to be greeted by Susan.

"Mister Wynter, that information you wanted, about Alcatraz."

"You managed to find something out?" said Wynter, trying not to sound too keen.

Susan smiled and nodded. "Yes, it's going to become a wildlife reserve."

"A wildlife reserve?" said Wynter, raising his eyebrows, "Do you know who came up with the idea?"

"A few environmental and wildlife groups got together and managed to persuade the government."

"Washington?"

"Yes," nodded Susan, "the Federal Government."

"Did you manage to find out anything else?"

"That's all the news station had when I rang them."

There was a pause while Wynter stood considering the situation. "Could you ring the State Capitol and a few newspapers, just to get a wider perspective, and let me know?" Wynter looked at his watch. "Then ring me at quarter to four to let me know if there are any up-dates."

"Of course," said Susan, hesitating as she started to make a note on her pad. This was way more information than was needed to catch a ferry boat.

Wynter smiled as he pushed a fifty dollar bill under the large blotting pad. "I know it's a lot to ask, but you've been so helpful."

Susan smiled at him. "A pleasure, Mister Wynter."

Wynter stepped towards the elevator and pushed the call button. The doors opened silently and he stepped in. Pushing the number for his floor, he popped another indigestion tablet in his mouth and closed his eyes.

A wildlife sanctuary.

Couldn't they have waited for just a day?

***

"I don't know what you think you've have been doing," said Lieutenant Tony Schreiber, "but whatever it is, it doesn't look like police work."

He stood at the front desk of the police station holding Sheriff Richards.

"Think we don't know?" said the desk sergeant, still

concentrating on filling in the form he had in front of him.

"Then why did you do it?"

The sergeant wrote a couple of quick answers. "When the chief detective orders you to hold someone, you do it."

He ticked three boxes.

"Didn't you even think it was odd?"

"If I thought about all the odd things I see from this desk, I'd do nothing but think all day."

Four more boxes ticked and a couple of crosses.

"But …"

"Look Lieutenant," said the desk sergeant, putting down his pen and looking up for the first time. "Everything that happened at this desk was above board and legal. It's not for me to read him his Miranda rights, and you know we can hold him for up to forty-eight hours without charge." He looked up at the clock on the wall opposite. "And if we don't charge him in the next thirty five seconds, he's free to walk out."

The sergeant picked up his pen and ticked the last few boxes.

"Look, what d'you think this is all about, Sergeant?" asked Tony, dropping his voice.

"Someone wants him out of the way," said the sergeant, signing his name at the bottom of the form. "Best thing you could do for him right now is send him back to Oregon."

"*Who* wants him out of the way?"

The sergeant shrugged. "All I know is you're looking in the wrong place if you're looking here, Lieutenant."

At that moment Sheriff Rufus Richards came walking

around the corner from the cells, accompanied by another officer. The desk sergeant produced a clear polythene bag with a few personal possessions: car keys; a comb; a packet of chewing gum; a wallet and some loose change.

"Would you inspect the contents of this bag, Sheriff, and verify that they belong to you and nothing is missing, please."

Rufus looked at the bag and nodded.

"Sign here, please," said the Sergeant holding out a clipboard with the form that he'd just finished filling out. Rufus put a squiggle at the bottom of the form and took the bag.

"We are going to have to keep the counterfeit money you were carrying," said the sergeant, looking at Rufus. "It may be produced as evidence in any future trial."

Rufus sighed and nodded. "Sure."

The sergeant looked up at the clock. "You're free to go, Sheriff." Then he looked over at Tony: "You'd do well to remember what I told you, Lieutenant."

***

Hellman lit another Marlboro, and inhaled deeply. Why would they say it was going to be a wildlife reserve? He had been turning that question over in his mind ever since he'd heard it on the radio. He knew there had been talk of it, but nothing had ever happened - so why now? What was going on?

He was due to sign a deal with the Federal Government in less than two hours. Was he buying a development site or a wildlife reserve?

Was he buying anything at all?

Was he being set up?

These thoughts had tumbled around his mind for the last couple of hours. He had thought about calling Van Buren. Then he'd thought again. After the fishing trip it made him sweat just speaking to him, even with good news - how would he react to this? Hellman consoled himself with the thought that Van Buren listened to the radio and watched the TV. He must have heard about this idea of a wildlife reserve. If he had been worried about it, he'd have called.

Hellman took another lung-corroding drag on his cigarette, and watched the ferry making its way from pier 33 towards Alcatraz. He made a note to double the number of ferry crossings when the new hotel and casino were built.

Still silence - there had been no phone call. Van Buren wasn't worried. He knew about it. He'd had this story of a wildlife reserve checked out and there was nothing to it. His people in Washington had told him it was just wishful thinking by some West Coast hippies. Or it could be some do-gooding liberal senator looking for cheap publicity. It could even be the Federal Government laying some smoke to obscure the deal he was about to sign, just to keep the environmentalists quiet.

Whatever the reason, there had been no call. Hellman convinced himself that Van Buren was OK with it. He walked over to the small desk, stubbed out his cigarette among the others in the ashtray, and checked his briefcase for the fourth time that hour. The original file Wynter had given him, the letter of introduction to the bank from Van

Buren, the letter authorizing the banker's draft, and his own passport as identification. It was all there.

Hellman picked up a fresh pack of Marlboro and looked at his watch. Taking a deep breath, he closed the case and clicked the locks.

It was time to go to the bank.

Chapter 28

"What in Hell's name did you think you were doing, Rufus?"

The sheriff and his nephew-in-law were walking towards Tony's car after leaving the police station.

"What possessed you to get mixed up with counterfeit money?"

"The money wasn't mine," said Rufus.

"You were spending it like it was."

"Sir Wynter gave it to me."

"Sir Wynter. You keep coming back to this guy Wynter."

"He owed me fifteen thousand dollars."

"Yeah, and he paid you with phony bills," said Tony, shaking his head as he tried to remain sympathetic. "What did you expect, Rufus? The man's a grifter, a con-artist. I told you that when you first came down here."

Rufus sighed and nodded. "I know, I know," he said, finally having to admit to himself that Tony was right. They had reached the end of the block and both stood waiting for the lights to change.

"So that guy in the hotel, the one I found, the one you

said wasn't the right guy? Turned out he *was* the right guy."

Rufus nodded again. "Yeah, it was Wynter."

The lights changed and they both stepped off the curb.

"So you threaten to take him in, and he gives you your money back."

"Something like that."

"But it's counterfeit, and you get picked up for passing junk."

"Anyone would think I'm the criminal in all this," said Rufus, beginning to feel aggrieved.

"I'm not saying that, Rufus; really I'm not. But it seems you got in the way of the wrong people on this one ... people who want you out of the way. I think it best if you come and stay with us tonight, I'll ring Linda."

Rufus nodded, he wasn't going to argue. It was a good idea and, as it seemed Tony was going to make the arrangements anyway, he thought it best go along with it. Reaching the car, they stopped and Tony got out his keys.

"I've got to get back to work," said Tony, "but I'll drop you at your hotel. You pick up your things and get over to our place. Linda will be expecting you, and I know the kids would like to meet you."

Rufus smiled and nodded again, but his mind kept wandering back to Wynter.

Tony looked hesitant, but decided that he should pass on the sergeant's warning. "Look, the desk sergeant gave me a bit of advice. He said it would be best if you headed back to Oregon ... not to stay around here too long."

Rufus nodded. "I've been down here longer than I

intended anyway, and Harriet will be wondering what I'm doing." He smiled at Tony. "Don't worry; I'll be heading back tomorrow."

***

"Did you know about this wildlife reserve?" said Wynter, looking out of the hotel window.

Meredith shook her head. "No, it's a complete surprise to me."

"A surprise we could have done without," said Wynter, who had now gone past being angry. There was no point in getting upset, and shouting would only aggravate his stomach, which was playing up enough as it was. They were where they were and had to deal with it. He popped another indigestion chew into his mouth and turned to Meredith.

"Didn't any of your friends in Washington tell you this was happening?"

"I have *contacts* in Washington, not friends. Nobody in DC has *friends*, Wynter. If they want a friend, they buy a dog."

"Ok, but didn't they say anything?"

"I asked a couple of them but they didn't mention it," said Meredith. "Anyway, a decision like this would have been taken some time ago, at least a year. Unless they were directly involved, they'd be two or three projects down the line by now."

Wynter shrugged. "I don't suppose it makes any difference who knew what or when. Do you think Hellman knows?"

Meredith hesitated. "I'd like to say no … but I can't. I think we must assume he does."

"What if he doesn't show?" asked Wynter. "What if he's already guessed it's a con?"

"Then we have a stiff drink and think of what to do next."

Wynter had already made up his mind what he was going to do next, whether Hellman turned up or not, and San Francisco didn't figure much in those plans.

"Let's suppose he turns up," continued Meredith. "How are you going to play it?"

Wynter shook his head. "The honest answer is … I don't know."

"I appreciate the honesty, but please tell me you've got something lined up … please."

"It really does depend on Hellman. If he says nothing, then we go ahead as planned."

"And if he says something?"

"Then I'll have to wing it," said Wynter with a shrug. "I've got a couple of ideas, but it really will depend on what he says and how he sees it. You're just going to have to trust me," said Wynter, a nervous smile on his lips.

Meredith closed her eyes and sighed. "Do I have a choice?"

***

Tobin disliked San Francisco. It had been cold, damp and foggy for most of his previous visits. But even he had to admit that the place had a certain attraction. The cable cars; the

Golden Gate Bridge; the Bay; he could see what drew the tourists. However, it was not the sights that drew him this time, as he and Boles approached the Bay crossing at Berkeley.

It was not entirely true to say that Lance had said nothing about Petersen, Las Vegas and the counterfeiting connection. He had let slip that Meredith was running a covert operation. Having given the name of the hotel, Lance tried to avoid further questions by saying that he knew nothing about it; Meredith was playing her cards close to her chest. He tried to deflect their enquiries by saying that from what little he knew, he got the impression that it was going nowhere and had reached the point where Meredith was winding it up. Boles was inclined to accept this - hadn't Meredith told him that she just had loose ends to tie up and her investigation was over?

Tobin knew what Boles didn't. He'd done some digging of his own in Washington. Tobin knew about the rumor that a real estate deal was about to go down on the West Coast. He knew that there had been enquiries from the West Coast asking various senators to check out this rumor. Tobin had started to get suspicious. Suspicions had turned into a bad feeling when he found out that Van Buren had been the one behind the enquiries. He also knew that Meredith had spoken to a prominent senator before the rumor started circulating. The questions were piling up, but so far Tobin had few answers. That's when he had decided to pay a visit to this hotel that Meredith had been hiding.

***

Sheriff Rufus Richards stepped out of his hotel and onto the sidewalk. It was good to feel the afternoon sunshine on his face after being locked in a cell for forty-eight hours. Pulling out his handkerchief, he wiped the back of his neck. Being on the receiving end of the law had been a new experience, and one he was in no hurry to repeat.

Coming from just beyond no-where in Oregon, Rufus had never felt comfortable in towns. Big cities were positively disturbing. He was looking forward to leaving San Francisco in the morning, but he had one last call to make before he left. He looked up and down the street for a cab and saw three, but none of them were moving. The city traffic had slowed to less than walking pace.

It was all very well for Tony to open his mouth with advice, but he hadn't lost fifteen thousand dollars. With time on his hands in the cell, Rufus had gone over the evidence, allowing his anger and resentment to build until he had convinced himself that Sir Wynter was the sole architect of the entire mess.

Who had sold him the box?

Who had paid him in counterfeit money?

Who had got him locked up?

Rufus spat into the gutter and ran his hand over the reassuring bulge of the Smith and Wesson .38 under his left shoulder. The Englishman had some questions to answer.

He wiped his neck again and looked at the stationary traffic, then shook his head and pulled a street map from his pocket. Why pay a fancy price to sit in the back of a cab when you could walk there just as fast? After checking the map for a few moments, Rufus set off in the direction of Wynter's hotel.

***

Meredith walked over to the regency table and started to check through some of the papers laid out on its surface, in an effort to ease tension.

"You got everything you need? Inventory, bill of sale, title deeds?"

"Yeah," said Wynter, who was now taking a few measured deep breaths in an effort to calm his nervousness. Meredith ran her fingers over the old parchment an acquaintance of hers - who just happened to be a forger - had used to fake up the deeds of title to the Island of Alcatraz.

Wynter continued his deep breathing exercises.

"You do breathing exercises before every …?" asked Meredith, looking up.

Wynter exhaled. "Always. It calms me down; gets me relaxed." He took another breath.

"You've always looked relaxed to me."

That was when the phone rang. They looked at each other and froze. Was that Hellman? Was he crying off? Had he heard the news about the wildlife reserve? Wynter took another deep breath, and went over and picked up the receiver.

"Wynter."

It was Susan, the hotel receptionist, ringing as requested to give an up-date on the Alcatraz situation. No change from the original newscast. The wildlife reserve was going ahead.

As he put the phone down, Wynter glanced at his watch: thirteen minutes to four. Thirteen minutes and Hellman would be here … if he was coming.

There was a knock at the door. Meredith went over and opened it. A waiter entered with an ice bucket containing a bottle of champagne.

"To celebrate the signing," said Meredith. "I thought the occasion ought to be marked in style. Celebrate with Hellman: or if he doesn't show, commiserate with me."

The waiter set the ice bucket down on its stand and fiddled with the bottle, pushing it a little further into the ice and twisting it until he heard the rustle of a five dollar bill. Immediately satisfied that the bottle was at the right angle, the waiter accepted the note, gave a slight bow to Wynter and left the room.

Wynter twisted the bottle to look at the label: Krug '64, an excellent year. He gave a nod of approval. Personally he preferred the more nuanced Bollinger, but he'd drink Krug. He didn't suppose the property developer would appreciate the delicacy of either.

They both relapsed into silence. Meredith stood up, walked over to the table and checked the fake title deed again, to cover her growing nervousness, then looked at her watch. "Do you think he's going to show?"

Wynter slowly took a deep breath and nodded. "He'd have rung if he had any doubts, if only to scream at me. I think he'll show."

He picked up one of the thin glasses the waiter had left, held it up to the light and checked for marks.

"If he doesn't ring in the next few minutes, he's not going to get through at all," said Meredith. "I've told the manager to hold all calls that may come for you or Hellman, just as you asked. When he walks through the front door, he'll be cut off from the outside world."

"Good," said Wynter, checking the other wine glass. "Let's hope he'll still want to buy an island when he gets here."

***

The trip to the bank had gone smoothly. Hellman identified himself with his passport and handed the letter of authorization over to the manager. After reading it and satisfying himself that it was genuine, the manager had pressed a button and a teller had arrived with an unsealed envelope containing the draft for three million two hundred and fifty five thousand dollars. After checking the amount, the manager handed the draft to Hellman to make sure of the amount. After exchanging nods and smiles, the manager sealed the envelope and Hellman put it into his attaché case.

The drive to the hotel had been slow but uneventful. When he had got into the Jaguar, Hellman had transferred the envelope with the banker's draft to a secure pocket in his jacket. There had been too many opportunistic bag snatches in the city and he felt precautions were necessary. He drove carefully, not wanting to give the cops any excuse to pull him over, and it was with a sense of relief that he turned into the cul-de-sac that led to the hotel.

Hellman hadn't noticed the black helmeted man sitting

astride the motorbike as he emerged from the bank. Jago watched as Hellman got into the Jaguar, and as the car eased into the traffic had kicked the motorbike into life. Van Buren wanted to make sure his three million arrived safely at the hotel. Jago followed the Jaguar at a discreet distance, and pulled up opposite the cul-de-sac. Having watched Hellman enter the hotel safely, he retired to have a coffee in a restaurant that Van Buren had connections with, a few blocks away.

Chapter 29

Wynter and Meredith watched the Jaguar from the hotel window as it made its way slowly up the cul-de-sac and parked. Hellman had arrived.

"I guess this is it," said Meredith, a nervous smile on her lips.

"I guess it is," said Wynter, taking a deep breath.

Moving closer to him, she put her hand up to Wynter's face.

"Go get him for me," she said softly.

For a couple of seconds there was a hint of electricity between them. Her finger tips brushed Wynter's cheek. He hadn't realized how far he could see into her deep brown eyes, almost into her soul. Those seconds seemed an age, and he was about to incline his head to hers when she put her hand down, pulled back and gave a little smile.

"Good luck," whispered Meredith.

He smiled and nodded as she turned and left the room.

Wynter began to re-focus on Hellman. He was about to close one of the greatest scams in history. He'd be up there alongside Victor Lustig and his sale of the Eiffel Tower, and

Arnold Rothstein with his World Series fix. He closed his eyes and took a deep breath.

***

As the bellboy opened the door, Wynter glanced at his watch, one minute past four. Nineteen minutes to get hold of the banker's draft.

"Steve," said Wynter, taking a couple of paces and holding out his hand and smiling. "Steve, come in, come in. Good to see you again."

"Good to see you too, Gerry."

After shaking hands, Wynter led Hellman over to the two sofas.

"Do sit down. Would you like some tea? It's a habit I picked up in London, when I was over there in the embassy."

"Sure," said Hellman.

Wynter smiled, and was already pouring two cups on a tray set for afternoon tea, then sat opposite Hellman.

"You ever travel to London, Steve?"

"No, not yet."

"If you like history, you've got to go. They've got places over there a thousand years old."

Wynter was picking up a reticence, a chill, in Hellman's tone which was worrying.

Hellman shrugged his shoulders, "I like looking to the future."

"Of course," said Wynter. "It's Earl Grey. Would you like lemon or milk … how about sugar?"

"Just milk. I'm careful about my weight."

Wynter poured a little milk from the porcelain jug and passed Hellman his tea. Putting a slice of lemon into his own tea, Wynter settled back into the sofa.

"The future is what we're all focused on, Steve. It's why we're both here."

"Good, because I've got a few questions about the future: the immediate future."

"I'd be surprised if you hadn't," smiled Wynter, betraying nothing.

Hellman *had* heard the newscast, thought Wynter. He knew about the wildlife reserve. Now he wanted some answers.

"You catch the news this morning?" said Hellman, taking a sip of tea.

Wynter shook his head, "I had a meeting with the Governor then lunch with a few State Senators, followed by a couple more meetings. I only got back here fifteen minutes ago; I haven't have time to catch my breath, let alone the news."

"Then you haven't heard."

"Hear what?"

"The plans for a nature reserve."

"What plans?"

"Don't play dumb with me, Gerry. You got something going on that you're not telling me about."

Hellman had decided he wasn't about to hand over the banker's draft until he knew the truth about the wildlife reserve. He had no intention of ending up on a fishing trip with Jago.

"I'm sorry but …" said Wynter.

'We didn't give you a hundred and fifty grand so you could feel good about some squirrels on a nature reserve. That's not how it works."

"What nature reserve?"

"The one they're going to put on Alcatraz."

"Ah," said Wynter, smiling and feigning comprehension, "they did it."

"Who did what?"

"The wildlife reserve. They put it out after all."

"Yeah, they did, and I'm left wondering how wildlife fits in with our plans for a casino. The gamblers will want to be playing for more than nuts! I'm also wondering how straight you've been?"

Wynter smiled, "Don't worry about it. I can ex …"

"Don't worry about it!" said Hellman standing up. "Perhaps you *should* worry about it, Gerry." A hard, menacing edge had crept into his voice. "Let me tell you something, we've got a deal. You got a commission to make sure everything ran smoothly. Why is everyone talking wildlife all of a sudden?"

Hellman was angry, and experience had taught Wynter that he had to let Hellman blow the steam out of his argument and get rid of some of his anger before he could come back at him with an explanation.

"Look …" said Wynter, biding his time.

"I've been thinking about this a lot since I heard it this morning," interrupted Hellman, as he turned away and started to pace the room, "and let me tell you, we're not

about to lay out three million dollars on welfare for squirrels
… I don't even like wildlife!"

Wynter's other problem was time. He glanced down at
his watch - he had thirteen minutes.

***

Boles pulled the car into the side of the road, and consulted
a city map.

"Where did you say this hotel was?"

"It's just around the corner from Washington Square,"
said Tobin.

Boles located the Square after a little searching, and
turned to Tobin.

"It's right in the middle of town. Parking will be a bitch."

"The hotel should have a car park of some sort."

"I hope you're right," said Boles as he folded the map.

***

"There is no welfare for squirrels," said Wynter.

"That's not what the news said …" said Hellman.

"They said that because we gave them the story. And
that's all it is - a story."

"But …"

"Do you want to hear the truth, Steve, or shall we just
stick with your guesswork?" said Wynter; only too aware
that time was ticking away.

Hellman took a deep breath then sat back down. "OK,
tell me."

"It took years to get the protesters off Alcatraz after the

occupation in the sixties. When we first floated the idea of selling the island, we were acutely aware of the need to avoid giving anybody an excuse for a repeat performance."

Hellman opened his mouth to interrupt, but Wynter held up his hand and continued, pushing Hellman further onto the back foot.

"If we released news of the reserve at the same time as the sale, it would create a smokescreen. We could say we were establishing an island dedicated to wildlife," said Wynter. "How could anyone protest against that?"

Hellman had to agree with Wynter's logic, but there was still a nagging doubt at the back of his mind. Wynter sensed the doubt and pressed on before it had a chance to grow into an interruption.

"We needed a cover story for any rumors about the transfer of the island and the start of any building work." continued Wynter. "All you'd be doing is repairing some of the buildings and carrying out maintenance. By the time the truth leaks out, it will be too late. You'll be firmly in possession, and able to carry out all the work you need. We can always say later that chemicals from the time it was a prison had contaminated the island to such an extent that regrettably it was unfit to be used as a nature reserve."

Hellman was wavering. Wynter knew the signs; he had seen them so many times before. He made one last effort at resistance. "Yeah, I see that, but …"

"We weren't sure when the TV or radio networks would run the story, and any pressure from us would look suspicious," cut in Wynter. "That's why I couldn't say anything about it."

"Yeah, well. It just seems odd that no-one came out with it before."

"You know what they're like in Washington: no-one wants to take responsibility for anything until it's a success. If they can palm it off onto the press in the meantime they will. That's the beauty of the Federal system: it's always someone else's fault."

"That's true enough," nodded Hellman, who had had enough dealings with politicians to know how they operated. Although now much fainter, that warning bell was still tinkling at the back of his mind, and three million dollars was a lot of money. Hellman had to make sure; the specter of a fishing trip with Jago still haunted him. "I can see what you're saying, but I think you could have given me some warning. I just got the feeling that I was … being set up."

"The only thing you're being set up for is the deal of a lifetime. We all get one big chance in life, Steve. Are you going to let yours pass you by?"

"I've just got to be sure," said Hellman.

Wynter gauged Hellman's resistance to be minimal, one last push and it would crumble entirely. He gambled on a final throw.

"Is that what you really thought, Steve, you were being set up? I have to say I'm disappointed. I thought we'd built up an understanding." Wynter toyed with his cup and saucer. "I was really getting to like you."

"No, Gerry that's not ..."

Wynter stood up and waved away his denial. "Well, if you feel that way," said Wynter, sighing and adopting a tone of deep disappointment, "there's nothing to stop you calling it off and leaving. It would be a shame, of course, a great shame."

"Gerry ..." said Hellman, getting to his feet.

"I had hoped to see your name forever linked with the re-birth of Alcatraz, but I guess O'Brien could do just as good a job."

Wynter looked regretfully at Hellman. Hellman sighed.

Whoever spoke first now was in line to lose three million dollars.

***

Jago was sipping his coffee and reading about the crime wave in downtown LA when the owner of the restaurant came over rubbing his ear, saying that Van Buren wanted him on the telephone. Standing up, Jago followed him and picked up the receiver.

"Yeah."

"Jago!" screamed Van Buren.

Jago quickly adjusted the distance between his ear and the receiver to allow for the raging voice on the other end.

"... Get over to the hotel and stop the deal! I've just had a call from Washington. The Alcatraz deal is a scam! It's a set up! Get my money back!"

Following Van Buren's call to Washington to check out the wildlife story, one of the senators on his payroll had put the pieces together, made a couple of calls, and had come up with the same answer as Tobin. The whole deal was a scam.

"And kill this guy Wynter! Kill Hellman too! Just get my money back!!"

Jago replaced the telephone receiver and felt for the reassuring bulge of the Browning stuffed into the back of his waistband.

In Jago's mind Wynter was as good as dead.

***

"Gerry, I didn't mean call the deal off ..."

Hellman certainly didn't relish the prospect of having to explain to Van Buren that he'd let the only possible site for his project slip through his fingers. Wynter smiled to himself. Hellman had just lost three million dollars. Wynter managed a quick glance at his watch, four minutes left. He'd never do it: time to switch to his backup plan.

"... I just had to check out the wildlife story," continued Hellman. "You'd have done the same in my position."

"Well, I guess I might have done." Wynter smiled at Hellman. "Any other thoughts?" Hellman shook his head and Wynter led the way over to the regency table. "Shall we sign the contract?"

He pressed a button on the underside of the table.

"We thought you'd like the original deeds rather than a typed up copy," continued Wynter, as he opened up the carefully faded deeds. "They go right back to the days when the King of Spain owned the island."

The King of Spain, thought Hellman as he gazed at the

parchment with its copper-plate hand and exaggerated, fancy initial letter.

The door opened and Mister Lehman and an assistant waited quietly until required to sign as witnesses.

"We've got a calligrapher who would add your name and details of ownership at the bottom, in the same old fashioned writing."

"Me up there with the King of Spain? That would be something," said Hellman.

"All you've got to do is sign the contract and we'll get it done," said Wynter as he placed a rather dull sheaf of typewritten papers in front of Hellman, who looked and turned over a couple of sheets.

"What about the ferry operator? Where does he fit in?" asked Hellman.

It was a question Wynter hadn't been expecting. "His contract expires with the change of ownership," he said, thinking quickly, "so you'd have to negotiate a new contract with him, but I don't see any problem. I don't suppose it matters to him whether he takes passengers to see the prison or gamblers to play the tables. You could of course provide your own luxury boat for the high rollers - perhaps even a helicopter."

Hellman nodded. "OK, where do I sign?"

Wynter turned to the final few pages, then opened a small wooden box and produced an old fountain pen.

"Just sign the last three pages against the penciled crosses." Wynter unscrewed the top and held out the pen. "I thought it would be fitting if you used Al Capone's pen. The one he used when he was in Alcatraz."

Hellman stood wide-eyed and took the pen from Wynter's hand, holding it with the reverence due to a religious artifact. Wait until Van Buren hears about this!

He signed against the penciled crosses on the final pages of the contract, and offered the pen back to Wynter.

"Keep it," said Wynter, holding out its small box, "as a memento of a great day."

"Thanks, Gerry," said Hellman. He felt a lump in his throat as he screwed the top back on.

Mister Lehman and his assistant moved forward and signed as witnesses, then left the room.

"All you have to do now is give me the banker's draft, and you are the new owner of Alcatraz."

Hellman hesitated, then smiled; all thoughts of being taken for a ride had evaporated. He pulled the draft from his inside pocket and held it out to Wynter.

"Thank you," said Wynter, taking it graciously and quickly casting his eyes over the wording to confirm the bank and the amount. "Alcatraz is officially yours. Now, if you would please excuse me for a moment, I must put this in the safe."

Wynter smiled and disappeared into the bedroom.

Chapter 30

The sight of a man in a beautifully cut dark suit running along the sidewalk wasn't usual in San Francisco, but in the last few years the bizarre had become commonplace, and few gave him a second glance.

Jago weaved in and out of people on the sidewalk. For the most part they got out of his way. He had the look of a man intent on getting where he was going, and trying to hinder him would be worse than foolish, and possibly dangerous.

Breaking into a light sweat, Jago had been pacing himself to arrive in the best possible time and condition. The Marines had taught him there was no point in getting to the battlefield quickly if you couldn't make a difference, and when he reached the hotel, Jago certainly aimed to make a difference.

***

"Frank was superb that night, I remember. And the band was on fire, I mean they were really stoked up," said Wynter. "All the great songs: *I've Got You Under My Skin,* through

Strangers In The Night, and when he sang *One For My Baby,* you could have heard a pin drop. He finished up with *My Way* - three times! They just wouldn't let him go!"

Wynter had been slowly turning the base of the bottle of Krug while he held the cork in his left hand, helping to ease it. As he finished speaking, there was a subdued pop and he started to pour the champagne into the waiting glasses.

"They'd put up a marquee on the west lawn for the five hundred guests," he continued, "and Frank, well, he gave them one hell of a show. The President himself and the First Lady were the first to start dancing in the aisle, great Sinatra fans," Wynter handed Hellman one of the glasses then sighed, as if remembering. "It was quite a night."

"Sounds it," said Hellman. "And you really reckon he'd do the opening week at the new Casino Alcatraz?"

"Don't you worry, Steve," smiled Wynter, "we'll get him for you. If the President gave him a call, it would be almost a command; an offer he couldn't refuse. Of course, I wouldn't say no to a couple of front row seats for my efforts."

"You get me Frank," smiled Hellman, "and you can have the whole damned front row. I'll even throw in dinner as well."

Hellman was about to continue but Wynter held up his hand to silence him.

"It's customary, I believe, on these occasions to propose a toast," said Wynter. "So, before we go any further, I'd like to propose a toast to the new owner of Alcatraz, and to the success of his latest, and greatest project." Wynter raised his glass. "To Steve Hellman - every success."

He nodded to Hellman, and took a sip of champagne.

"I don't think you realize how much we appreciate you buying Alcatraz. It's been a thorn in the Department's side ever since we closed the prison," said Wynter, turning his attention to his own glass. "Never knew quite what to do with it. People have this romantic vision of the place: the prison where no one ever escaped; where Al Capone was locked up; a place for incorrigibles. We've moved on since those days, Steve. Time the place was turned over to something else - something useful."

"As long as people go on vacation, they'll always need hotels. It'll be good for tourism, and good for the city of San Francisco."

"I'm sure it will be good for you, too," smiled Wynter.

"Give people what they want and they'll give you what you want. It's a pretty simple equation, Gerry. And people will always want to gamble."

"That's true enough," said Wynter, managing a quick glance at his watch.

"Of course, there'll always be a suite available for when you or your family come out this way," said Hellman.

"Well, that's very kind of you, Steve, I appreciate that. And I'm sure the President will be very appreciative of what you've just done." Wynter smiled at Hellman, "I said I'd call to let him know."

Wynter poured some more champagne into Hellman's glass and put the bottle back in the ice bucket.

"The President has taken a keen interest in this project right from the word go," said Wynter.

"Well he would, being a Californian an' all," said Hellman.

"He's originally from Illinois," corrected Wynter.

"Yeah? Well I didn't know that."

"He said to give him a call around now, before he goes into dinner."

"You going to call the President?" said Hellman, sounding both surprised and in awe. "You're going to call him now?"

Wynter nodded. "I guess he'll want to have a word with you too."

"Me?!"

"Yes … to pass on his congratulations."

***

Jago had stopped running.

He walked around the corner into the cul-de-sac leading to the hotel. As he did so he took a few large gulps of air to calm his heart-rate. Experience had taught him he needed a few moments to compose himself before any action.

"Semper Fi," said Jago, and smiled as he walked into the hotel.

"Semper Fi," replied the doorman, smiling as he remembered him as a fellow marine.

"Look, I got to use your bathroom again, is that okay?" said Jago.

"Guess so. Your boss is upstairs, so I reckon you as a guest."

"I'll use the staff restroom."

"Sure, you know where it is."

Jago smiled and nodded his thanks, then walked towards the plain door to the left of the elevators. As he did so the doorman nodded to Susan to give Jago a pass. She relaxed and nodded back as Jago disappeared through the door and headed towards the service elevator.

***

Wynter checked his watch, then looked up and smiled at Hellman.

"The White House is three hours ahead of us, so that will make it just after seven thirty. I know the President will want to speak to you, but would you mind staying in here until I call you? It's a matter of telephone security procedures," said Wynter, apologetically. "You know how they are about these things ..."

"Sure," said Hellman, who had no idea how they were, but was quite overcome by the fact that the President would want to speak to him. "Sure, I'll wait in here."

"I'll give you a call when he wants to talk," said Wynter as he headed towards the bedroom. "Help yourself to some more champagne." Wynter disappeared through the door leaving Hellman alone with his newly-acquired title deeds to Alcatraz, and his thoughts about speaking to the President. He put his glass down on the table and ran his fingers over the title deeds.

Alcatraz, the biggest opportunity in California, and it was his. He owned it. Fumbling in his pocket, he pulled out a pack of cigarettes. He needed a smoke, especially now he was going to speak to the President of the United States.

He closed his eyes, inhaled deeply and heard Wynter's muffled voice through the open door to the bedroom, *'Yes, that's right, the White House ... two, zero, two...'* He didn't catch the rest of the number; he didn't suppose he was meant to - security procedures and all. He opened his eyes. He was about to become one of the prime real estate players on the West Coast.

'Mister President, it's Gerry, speaking from San Francisco ...'

'Gerry', thought Hellman.

Hell ... the President calls him Gerry!

There was a knock at the door. Hellman turned and looked. Who the hell could that be? He wondered whether he should go into the bedroom and say something as Gerry obviously hadn't heard it. He quickly decided against that; he'd be interrupting the President of the United States, and for what? It could just be room service, or the bellboy.

'Everything went real smooth Mister President, just as you'd hoped ... yes, the deal is done, dusted and sealed ... we've even got the money ...'

Hellman smiled as he heard Gerry break into a little laugh, prompted no doubt by the President. His smile froze and he frowned as there was a second, louder knock on the door.

'A hotel, Mister President, with gaming rooms and a concert hall ... I believe Mister Hellman is hoping you might use your influence with Mister Sinatra ... yeah? He'll be really glad to hear that ...'

The third knock couldn't be ignored and Hellman strode over and opened the door.

"Look, whoever you …" started Hellman but he was brushed aside as the sheriff pushed his way in and pulled his gun.

"Where is he?" demanded the sheriff looking around the room. "Where's that jive-talking son of a rancid English bitch?"

Hellman stood back. Best not upset this guy, whoever he was. The newspapers papers were full of drug-fuelled gunmen killing innocent people.

A voice came from the bedroom.

'Of course, Mister President, I'll tell him …'

The sheriff's face broke into a big grin.

***

Jago stepped out of the service lift, turned into the main corridor, and headed in the direction of Wynter's suite. The question of a government sting still troubled him. But why would the FBI pull a con? He kept turning it over in his mind, examining it from every possible angle he could think of, but he couldn't come up with a convincing answer. It just didn't seem logical.

He came to a junction in the corridor and slowed. By checking room numbers, he reckoned that if he turned right here, then Wynter's suite should be at the far end. He paused, then reached back and took the Browning out of his waistband. Pulling the slide back, he loaded a round into the chamber.

That's when he heard the shots.

Not so loud as to be from a large caliber magnum, but loud enough - probably a thirty-eight - and they were close.

He turned his head to gauge the direction, until he was sure they were coming from the far end of the corridor. He counted the shots: five. Then there was a crash; probably Wynter falling against some furniture.

Turning, he hurried back to the service elevator; luckily it was still there. As he went back down to the ground floor he began to draw a few conclusions. He'd lay money that the gun had been a revolver, and that the guy knew how to use it. There had been a measured gap between shots, and five usually meant that the hammer was kept on an empty chamber for safety. He put the Browning back in his waistband. As the elevator doors slid open, Jago stepped out and made his way back along the service corridor.

Someone had beaten him to Wynter, but who?

Now was not the time to hang around to find out. A murder scene was not somewhere Jago wanted to be. Luckily for him, no-one had seen him on Wynter's floor, and he hadn't had time to use the Browning. He was sure that there was nothing forensic to tie him to anything, but the San Francisco PD knew him too well to let him just walk away. They'd try and pin a conspiracy charge on him at least.

***

Meredith had been monitoring Wynter's room with the tape and headphones. When she heard the shots, she ripped off the headphones, pulled her room door open and dashed along the corridor. This wasn't how it was supposed to be at all. Wynter wasn't supposed to die. That hadn't been part of their plan.

She was pretty sure it hadn't been Hellman who fired the shots, but there had been another voice, a voice she didn't recognize. Had Van Buren worked out it was a scam and sent one of his men to put an end to it? But Van Buren would send Jago to finish it, and she hadn't heard Jago's voice.

Her hand tightened on her Glock pistol as she swiped her master key through the card lock and kicked the door open.

"Freeze!" yelled Meredith, holding the Glock in front of her with both hands as she took a pace into the room. Her eyes and the Glock quickly swept the bedroom. There was only one other person that she could see. The communicating door to the sitting room was open, but there was no sign of Hellman.

"Get your hands up," ordered Meredith.

The stranger raised his hands. She took a more leisurely look around the room. Where was the body? Where was Wynter?

"You fire those shots?"

"Yeah," nodded the sheriff, with his hands held shoulder high.

"Where's the body?"

"What body?"

"The body of the man you just shot."

"I didn't shoot anyone," snarled the sheriff.

Still keeping the gun trained on the sheriff, Meredith took a few paces into the room so that she could see the floor on the far side of the bed ... nothing.

No blood ...

No body …

She looked back at the sheriff.

"Who are you?"

"Rufus Richards. Sheriff of Alyson County, in the State of Oregon."

Meredith sighed and ground her teeth. This guy was supposed to be in custody.

"When did they let you out?"

"A couple of hours ago," said the sheriff, his face narrowing with a frown. "How did you know I was …?"

Before she could answer, there was a knock on the open door and one of the hotel's security guards appeared.

"Sorry, ma'am," said security as he pushed a handcuffed Hellman into the room. "I found him creeping down the corridor towards the staircase."

"Very sensible, Mister Hellman; I wouldn't want to get caught hanging around a murder scene in your position either."

"There ain't been no murder," said the sheriff.

Meredith was beginning to have to admit that without a body he could be right.

"You had motive enough to kill him, Sheriff. He'd swindled you out of fifteen thousand dollars, and made you look a fool into the bargain. I've known people end up dead for a lot less," said Meredith.

"Perhaps that's true," said the sheriff, now seriously wondering who this woman was, and how she knew Wynter had swindled him. "But I didn't kill him. How could I? I haven't even seen him."

"But he was here," said Hellman, who was, by now, very confused. "I heard him ... talking to the President."

The sheriff shook his head, "Well he wasn't here when I walked in, and he wasn't talking to no President."

"What?" said Hellman.

The sheriff turned to Meredith. "I don't know who you are, lady, but you'll find five bullets in that bed, might even have gone through into the floorboards. And if you look in the corner behind that chest of drawers there's a portable cassette recorder. That's what I 'murdered', just before I threw it against the wall. Might not be in working order any more, but I guess your forensic boys will still be able be able to find enough tape of Wynter talking to 'The President'."

The sheriff turned and stared at Hellman.

"But where ...?" said Hellman, his voice trailing off as he realized that he too had been taken for a fool. He tried to swallow, but his mouth had suddenly become dry and he felt very sick.

Three million dollars worth of alarm bells started to ring in his ears, and he heard the lapping of water against the side of a boat.

"Perhaps somebody would like to tell us what's been going on?" said a voice from the open door. Tobin had just arrived with Boles.

Chapter 31

Meredith never worked out exactly how Wynter had disappeared. She knew the fire-escape figured initially, and perhaps Susan had helped, but things got hazy after that. He could have managed to hitch a ride on the refuse wagon, or in the laundry which was being collected at the time. On the other hand he could have just walked out of the Hotel's front door. However he had managed it, speculation was useless. Fact was he was gone, and she'd probably never know how.

She shouldn't have been surprised. He'd spent a lifetime fooling people, and he'd become very good at it. Now he'd fooled her. She'd always known it was a possibility, but it still hurt. In her quieter moments she had hoped that perhaps he might change - but she knew that was being foolish. Hope was the con-man's most potent weapon. Didn't he offer the hope of making dreams come true? And what was money against a dream?

***

When he had left the hotel, Wynter, banker's draft in his pocket, had stopped off at the side entrance to the bank. The manager, Mister Rodriguez, wasn't the sort of man to keep three million dollars waiting outside. Three minutes later, with business completed, Wynter had disappeared into the crowds on the sidewalk, and Rodriguez had wired one million dollars to an account in the banking equivalent of a black hole - Panama. It re-emerged after a trip around Europe and the Caribbean, in an account in the Caymans where Wynter could use it when it suited him. After all, Wynter reasoned, he had masterminded the con and taken most of the risks; it was only fair that he should reap some of the rewards.

***

Hellman was in a state of shock. As the situation began to sink in, his dreams of the Alcatraz Plaza and Casino complex disintegrated as fast as the ash on the end of his cigarette. He was in total denial for two days before Meredith forced him to confront reality. Faced with a choice between a twenty-five year stretch for distributing counterfeit currency or a fishing trip with Jago, Hellman didn't take long to turn State's Evidence. Proof of Van Buren's involvement in the counterfeiting operation was the lever Meredith needed, and Hellman obliged. He was taken into the witness protection program, and eventually ended up with a new identity selling dry goods in a small New England town. After a year his girlfriend came round to accepting he was dead.

***

Van Buren was going down. It was just a question of the fall. Did he want to take his chance with the New York crime families after they'd been told he'd lost over three million dollars of their money - or would he let the courts decide? He elected to go to trial. Meredith finally had the satisfaction of knowing Van Buren was going to die in Federal prison, either of natural, or most probably, of painfully unnatural causes. In the last thirty years he had made a lot of enemies, and bars had never posed much of a defense against a mafia contract.

***

After a lot of bluster and a few threats, Tobin and Boles eventually had to accept the situation. All of Washington's political reputations remained intact, and the pair managed to catch some of the reflected glory of being part of the operation that took down the West Coast's most notorious mobster and netted the government over two million dollars. Meredith's unorthodox methods were overlooked, and Lance was accepted back into the fold with an unblemished record.

***

Sometimes, before she went to sleep, Meredith still thought about Wynter. They had worked well together, even if the job had been a little unconventional. She couldn't help but admire his style, and could hardly begrudge him his 'fee' for pulling off the con, even if the government might. She smiled as she pictured him with that bit of hair always flopping over his eyes that she had longed to push back off his face ... the way his nose wrinkled when he smiled, and his cute English accent. His eyes ... those eyes were...

She sighed, turned off the light and tried to concentrate on next morning's paperwork.

***

Harriet had been worrying about paying the electricity bill for the last two months. The hotel had been quiet, and there was little money in her account. She daren't ask Rufus for help. He had been moody and withdrawn these last two weeks since he'd been back. A word out of place and he'd snap at her. She knew it was tough on him, and time was the only thing that would help - but that didn't make her life any easier.

Sitting at the kitchen table, she was nursing a cup of coffee. The mailman had just been, and there was a brown envelope from the Power Company - looked like they were finally going to cut her off. She turned over the other letter. It was handwritten, but she didn't recognize the writing. Reaching for her spectacles, she tried to read the postmark, but it was smudged. She slit open the envelope with the butter knife.

"Dear Harriet,

By the time you receive this you'll know the truth: no doubt Rufus will have told you. I was going to send this to him, but I reckoned that you could find a better use for it. I would say that I was sorry, but we both know that would be hypocritical.

Look after Rufus: somewhere in there is a good man struggling to get out.

Yours,

Gerry Wynter"

Harriet picked up the check. Drawn on a San Francisco bank, it was for fifteen thousand dollars. She could pay the power company.

***

Jago left San Francisco, and is still out there … somewhere.

Thank you for reading
Wynter's Discontent.

It is the first book in a series of thrillers that will follow Wynter's adventures as he makes his way around America.

If you enjoyed this book, you can make a big difference. Reviews are extremely effective in gaining attention, and an honest review would help bring this book to the notice of other readers. It would also help my career as an author, so if you could just spend a few minutes leaving a review, however brief, on the book's Amazon page I'd be very grateful.

Remember

Sign up for my newsletter and get a free short story,
'Wynter's Cruise'
www.nigeldraper.com

Acknowledgements

Books are never written alone, and many friends have helped me with their comments, suggestions and knowledge. I'd like to thank Martin Dow, Jenny Scruton, Denise Newport, Iain McMath and Joan Nash. Special thanks must go to Elizabeth Manners, who patiently read innumerable drafts, corrected my punctuation and always gave encouragement; and to Edmund Pickett for suggesting how I could edit a muddle of ideas and words into a book that people might want to read. Any remaining mistakes are entirely mine.

About the Author

Born in Devon, in the UK, Nigel Draper comes from a long line of engineers and artists. Educated at Chipping Sodbury Grammar School, he later went to Cambridge University as a mature student, where he read History.

There has been no discernible pattern to his career, if a jumble of jobs can be described as career. His experience includes being a hospital theatre porter, working in the City, project managing multi-million pound construction sites, and part-time stage-door keeping. For many years now he has made picture frames and restored furniture.

Nigel enjoys travelling and has lived on the island of Corfu and worked in Germany. Interests include music, cricket, architecture, and wasting time. He has also played drums in various bands.

During the 1970's and 1980's he wrote a number of speculative scripts for television and came close to getting one or two accepted.

He now lives in the Wiltshire countryside with a cat called Wussit and a very old Atco lawnmower.

Wynter's Gold

The next in the series!

A small town in Colorado is divided into two camps over a dispute about the ownership of a gold mine.

The rightful owner is facing an impossible struggle to claim ownership of the mine. A lazy Judge made a slip in conveying the title of the mine and the head of the town's most powerful family is aiming to capitalize on that mistake.

In the background, a trans-national mining conglomerate is stalking the hills, just waiting for one of the claimants to stumble.

Wynter arrives in town and is mistaken for a mining surveyor. But who is he working for? In the middle of a situation which rapidly escalates and becomes dangerous, Wynter decides to go to work for himself.

Printed in Great Britain
by Amazon